THE BLUE TANGO

by the same author

LOVE IN HISTORY
THE LAST OF DEEDS
RESURRECTION MAN

The Blue Tango

EOIN MCNAMEE

faber and faber

First published in 2001
by Faber and Faber Limited
3 Queen Square London WC1N 3AU

This text design © Faber and Faber Limited, 2000
Printed in England by Clays Ltd, St Ives plc

The right of Eoin McNamee to be identified as author of this work
has been asserted in accordance with Section 77 of the Copyright, Designs
and Patents Act 1988

A CIP record for this book
is available from the British Library

ISBN 0–571–20765–0

2 4 6 8 10 9 7 5 3

At 2.20 in the morning of 13 November 1952, the body of nineteen-year-old Patricia Curran was carried into the surgery belonging to the family doctor. Following a preliminary examination Dr Kenneth Wilson concluded that she had been the victim of an accidental shooting because of the pattern of the wounds. In fact a subsequent post-mortem revealed that she had been stabbed thirty-seven times. While waiting for RUC detectives to travel to his surgery in the village of Whiteabbey, five miles from Belfast, Dr Wilson estimated that Patricia Curran had been dead for not less than four hours.

Two men had carried Patricia's body into the surgery: her brother, Desmond Curran, and the family solicitor, a man called Malcolm Davidson. Malcolm Davidson's wife stayed in the car. Desmond led the cortège with dismal authority, like a man who supposed he held rightful office to the carriage of corpses by night.

Patricia's father, Mr Justice Lance Curran, and her brother had apparently been alarmed by her late arrival home and had started to telephone her friends. Her boyfriend at the time, John Steel, said that he had left her to an early evening bus from Belfast, which would have dropped her close to the gates of the Curran house, The Glen, in Whiteabbey at 5.30 p.m. Judge Curran had alerted the authorities at around 1.45 a.m. and had also telephoned Malcolm Davidson. Constable Rutherford from Whiteabbey barracks had arrived at two o'clock. Desmond and his father had gone to the gates to await the arrival of Malcolm Davidson. Shortly before the solicitor's car turned into the driveway, Judge Curran heard a cry from his son. Desmond had apparently stumbled upon the body of his sister on the grass verge of the drive. Desmond told the police that he had lifted Patricia from the ground and had heard her breathing. Constable Rutherford did not think that she had been breathing. Desmond told the other men that she was still alive. Many years later Desmond surmised that the lifting of the body expelled air from the lungs, leading him to believe that she was still alive. Rutherford was astonished to observe the lengths that the men went to in order to get the stiff body into the car, eventually laying it diagonally across their laps in the back seat with its legs protruding from the open window. It was Rutherford's plain observation that the girl was dead and had been dead for some time. However, he was reluctant to point this out to a man of the Judge's position and influence. The Judge went back to the house to inform his wife Doris of what had taken place. Rutherford watched as Malcolm Davidson turned the car carefully in the driveway and started towards the village, then he followed the Judge up to the house, leaving them to the conveyance of their strange passenger.

On 2 January 1953, Chief Superintendent John Capstick, who had been appointed to investigate the murder, began his interrogation of a young British RAF conscript, Iain Hay Gordon. Gordon had already been questioned by local detectives but they had failed to connect him to the crime. The Patricia Curran case had been front-page news for almost two months and public pressure for an outcome was intense. Over 20,000 witness statements had been taken. Public suspicion had fallen on several men, then moved restlessly on. Capstick was frequently drafted in to solve high-profile cases outside London. He recognized the shape of a case like this, its classical texture. A drama that must be impelled to its conclusion. The driven fury of the knife rising and falling. The blood. The pity and terror. Capstick knew that the public would demand that this narrative be brought to its proper conclusion. He understood their unyielding will in this matter.

Following three days of interrogation, Iain Hay Gordon signed a statement that set out, in detail, how he had murdered Patricia Curran in the driveway that night. The language of the statement is notable for the use of procedural mannerisms. The text itself is constructed in such a way as to anticipate and deflect legal challenge. There are factual omissions, issues are skirted, obvious lines of questioning are not developed. It is a fake confession, a fiction couched in the mocking language of death; the death penalty was not to be abolished for another four years and the trial was to be carried out in the full knowledge of this. In fact, the murderer McGladdery from Newry was the last man to be hanged in Belfast, for the murder of a factory worker by the name of Pearl Gambol. Few of the words contained in the confession were ever spoken by Iain Hay Gordon but the true profanity of the text is that many of the participants in his trial were aware of this.

Two photographs of Patricia Curran were printed and reprinted at the time of her murder and in subsequent years. Both photographs are professional portraits, showing her head and shoulders. In the first one she is looking away from the camera, turning into profile, and you can see the haughty line of her jaw, a look of dark amusement in her eyes, and her lips are parted as though about to utter a caustic and worldly remark. But she is turning into profile, towards another perspective, and there is little more to be learned from the picture. She reveals nothing of the independent nature. The reputed promiscuity.

In the second photograph she is looking directly at the camera. She is wearing pearls and a formal cowl-neck dress. The photograph is badly lit so that her eyes are underexposed and can barely be seen. Her cheeks are slightly dimpled and the mouth downturned at the corners but it is the eyes that hold you. Her face is dominated by the shadow of them. You are drawn to their mesmeric void.

Desmond Curran is still alive. Two years after his sister's murder he left the bar to become a priest and exercised his vocation in a South African township where he was known as Isibane. In the Xhosa language Isibane means the Lamp.

In the late afternoon of the day following the murder, the press were allowed up the drive to view the scene. It was an hour before dark but cloud had come up from the direction of the sea, and lamps had been erected around the scene and inside the cloth that had been used to cordon off the site and shelter it from rain. They could see movement inside the canvas and the outlines of men visible against its frail, votive light. A photographer stooped to his camera and straightened the tripod. He looked like a surveyor tasked with taking the measurements of her death. He shot another frame. The light was going. The photographer shot off the rest of the film. The camera flashed and flashed again. There was a cold line of sleet coming up the lough. Afterwards, when they thought about the scene before them it seemed excessive, ceremonial. The heavy cloud. Small figures moving beneath the stormbound mass of the mill. The hiss of sleet on water.

John Capstick is dead. Iain Hay Gordon is still alive. He lives alone in a tenement flat in Glasgow. Doris Curran is dead. John Steel is dead. Lance Curran is dead.

The murder of Patricia Curran. The knife rising and falling. Her father and brother standing over her body. Men's voices lowered in clandestine conference. The wounded and naked body of a young woman laid out on a mortician's slab. One man living who might speak out to relate the events of her last night but he will not and her memory remains devoid of hope of retribution or indemnity. The narrator's voice falls away into conjecture. Her slaughter has been told but not the motive for it, and the face of her killer remains hidden. The narrator's voice falls away into hypothesis and surmise.

ONE

Despite his prominence, Lancelot Curran was deeply in debt at the time of Patricia's murder. He had lost heavily at cards and had been borrowing money from a book-maker in Whiteabbey, and had been forced to hand over the deeds to The Glen as security at the beginning of the previous year. The bookmaker Hughes remembered the day that Curran had given him the deeds. He had been watching from the window as the Judge turned down the alley and walked briskly towards Hughes's office.

The top part of the door was opaque glass with TURF ACCOUNTANT written in worn gilt lettering. Curran pushed it open and entered. Hughes was behind his desk. There was wire mesh on the outside of the windows, which looked onto the barber's yard. Cardboard boxes full of betting dockets stood on the floor. In one corner was a grey asbestos-lined filing cabinet. On top of the desk were copies of the *Racing Post* and a plaster replica of Master McGrath, and behind it was a Chubb safe with a brass nameplate. The rest of the furniture was plain, utilitarian. Steel-legged chairs. Judge Curran thought that things in Hughes's life soon took on the patina of evidence.

Hughes got to his feet when he saw Curran at the door. He recognized the rigid form outlined behind the glass, the stark lines of the man. He turned one of the metal-framed chairs towards the Judge, indicating it wordlessly as though obeisance demanded silence. Apart from that he remained immobile, stressing bulk and containment. Hughes's arms rested on the table in front of him. You noticed the bulk of his head. Heavy, veined, obdurate.

Hughes took a bottle of Jameson's from a desk drawer. Curran suspected that Hughes kept a gun in the drawer. Hughes put two glasses on the table and filled them. He lifted his glass first and waited for Judge Curran before drinking. As Curran put the glass to his mouth, Hughes watched him over the rim of the glass. You had to hand it to Curran, he thought. You had to give it to the fucker. He was a man who gave the appearance of not having a single solitary nerve in his body. Curran tilted the glass back. Hughes thought that Curran always drank like that. With an air of terrible sacrifice.

'How's the family, your honour. Anything strange or startling?'

'They are all well, Mr Hughes. The air of Whiteabbey seems to suit them.'

That was good, Hughes thought, that the air of Whiteabbey agreed with them, for he would not have bought that house for a pension. He would not have had it in any shape, manner or form, with that long, dark avenue and them windows looking at you. Afterwards, if anyone had asked him, Leo Hughes would have been the man to predict all manner of sinister developments arising from that house.

'I wish to extend our arrangement,' Judge Curran said.

'Extend away, your honour. Would you have gave any thought to the sum involved?'

'Five hundred would be adequate, I think.'

Hughes sat without moving, staring at a point above the Judge's right shoulder. The Judge, too, sat unmoving, then put his hand into the inside pocket of his overcoat and placed a document on the table without looking at it, as though his hand were engaged in an action that was separate from him. Hughes did not have to look in order to identify the documents as the deeds of The Glen, for what else did the Judge have to bargain with? Moving with the same deliberation, Hughes opened the top drawer

2

of the desk and removed the chequebook. The Judge reached for his glass and finished his drink. An onlooker would have reckoned that the two men were engaged in an icy arbitrage, a settling of accounts.

'I seen Patricia down the street the other day,' Hughes said.

'No doubt in the company of one of her creatures,' Judge Curran said. He read the cheque then placed it in his pocket. As he stood and reached for his Trilby hat, Hughes thought, May God help you for a dry fucker. If that beautiful child was a daughter of mine no one would cast such remarks upon her. There would be no harsh word or slander spoke if Hughes had his way. The wind wouldn't blow on her.

Judge Curran walked towards The Glen. He acknowledged greetings from several people. He stopped at the Glen Bridge and leaned over the parapet and saw that the water ran red from the dye works. Judge Curran's father had worked in the slaughterhouse. When he was a student, Judge Curran would go to the library, where he consulted illustrated geography books and *National Geographic* for the image of a race that resembled his father. The dark elongated face that seemed designed by a hand unfamiliar with faces. The thin lips. The eyes lost in historical dolour. During the day he killed cattle and sheep with a bolt gun. At night he worked on the books while the next day's cattle lowed in the holding pens and he worked as though he might arrive at an infernal calculus that might account for and reconcile their souls to his own.

One evening he had walked home with his father from the Shambles, where his father was employed. A large sow had escaped from the stockyards and had been cornered by a pack of dogs from the town who were brought to the stockyards by the smell of meat. There were thirteen or fourteen mastiffs in the pack and a small

3

mongrel terrier that had attached itself to the sow's udder, where it dangled unheeded, uttering low, choked growls, the sow's dark, vehement blood dripping from its fur. The dogs stood in a circle with their ears laid flat and their lips pulled back from their teeth, growling softly, as though they bore for the sow a tormented and exacting love. A brindled greyhound detached itself from the pack and approached the sow on its left side, its belly touched the ground in an attempt to get the sow to turn her flank to the other dogs. As the sow turned the pack dipped as one and moved forward like smoke creeping until the sow swung again and they retreated. The greyhound had got behind the sow and snapped at her heels so that she turned again, squealing, and as she did so the man's grip tightened around the boy's hand and he began to draw him away, so that the last image the boy saw was of the sow turning towards him, its head a dripping, furious mask from some ancient familial drama of blood and dishonour and guile.

TWO

After her death the papers described Patricia as an out-going, independent girl. They noted that she had spent the previous summer driving a lorry for a building firm. Several weeks after the murder, Inspector Albert McConnell started to receive anonymous letters. He was used to this. He kept a folder of unsigned letters. Most of them concerned the doings of neighbours, men working and claiming social welfare, the names of those guilty of minor crimes, the names of women sleeping with other men's wives, the rancorous undertow of the town. Many of the letters urged him towards God, spoke of the coming that was near, cursed him as a blasphemer. He liked to think that these faces were not among the faces he saw on the street every day. He liked to think of these people alone in darkened rooms, forsaken by others, knowing that the day was near, convinced of it and consumed by rage.

Three of the letters had been written in the same hand. They said that Patricia frequented bars in Amelia Street and other places. They stated that she had been involved with three married men in the previous year. The men were named. The letters stated that Patricia at the time of her death was suffering from the condition of nymphomania, which the letters described in technical terms as a deviant condition of female heat.

An elderly woman in Glenarm said that Patricia would call while delivering building supplies to her son. She said they drank tea from delft cups and talked about fashion, among other things. She said that Patricia never failed to call or to enquire as to her well-being.

McConnell contacted the three men named in the letters.

Two of them denied having ever known Patricia Curran. The third man said that he had met Patricia Curran in a coffee shop on the Whiteabbey Road. The man had an alibi for the night of the murder. He told McConnell he remembered that she had a certain way of doing things. Brushing her hair, smoothing her skirt. Pausing at the end of each gesture to check the result in the mirror. A sense of high observance. The drama of herself. He said that she had consented to meet him that night in the grounds of the technical college. He agreed that she had been wearing her school uniform that night.

The man remembered that it had been cold. She had walked across the playing fields with her breath hanging in the air behind her like the remnants of some icy grace she had fallen from. He remembered how cold it had been. She was wearing a school sweater, her arms folded, her shoulders hunched. He had taken off his jacket and put it over her shoulders. He told her that it was arctic air. That it was a cold front from Siberia crossing the country. She repeated the word Siberia and laughed.

The cold felt alien. There was a sense of snow-covered landmass, the wintry steppe.

After her death he said that he had wondered if there had been anything of the momentous about that night, something to imply the narrative thread, the narrator's intake of breath. He remembered how cold the metal clasp of her bra strap had felt in his hand.

They had gone to a derelict house that stood on a small rise opposite the school gates. During the day, pupils used the house for smoking and the floor was littered with butts. He remembered a rusted, lidless iron stove and a deal table, which seemed carefully placed, as if there was an artifice in these objects that left them apt to ominous foreknowledge.

Her schoolfriend Hillary Douglas, daughter of the Whiteabbey Presbyterian church minister, confirmed this account. When Patricia went back to school the following morning the others had asked her how it felt. She was silent for a while. Then she said it was like young lovers with fate against them in a story. They said they knew it. They pressed around her. Tell us, they said. They asked her if destiny had brought them together. They asked if fate had joined them. They asked was there a feeling that said from that moment on and for ever? Hillary said that there was a terrible need for sentiment.

The man said that he could never forget that night and wished to make his peace. He remembered that she had been silent throughout, her lips pursed, her eyes open, looking over his shoulder, and that she had held him tight as though the unknowable night itself might tear him from her grasp were she to relinquish her desperate hold. He remembered that she broke her silence then and raged at him in the darkened house as though the night itself had been rendered violate.

The Curran murder case was on the front page of the *Belfast Telegraph* for forty-six successive editions. There was something that Patricia alone could provide. There was an image that they required from her: A lone figure standing at the dark entrance to The Glen, the face unseen. They were impelled towards this mystery. They needed to picture the scene. The noise and lights of the departing bus fading into the background. The figure of a woman in stark profile. Back-lit, doomed.

THREE

Iain Gordon appears in a photograph that had been taken before he was posted to Edenmore RAF base, a mile from Whiteabbey. It appeared to be a photograph of a passing-out parade of some kind. They wore khaki uniforms, berets tucked under epaulettes. The boots polished. The haircuts looked old-fashioned even then. The hair parted to the side, the fringe hanging over the eyes. Their poses of casual fortitude, of odds defied.

When Chief Superintendent Capstick joined the investigation he pointed out an apparent difference between Gordon and the other boys in the picture. The weakness of the mouth. The pallid features of the known homosexual. It was part of his strategy to undermine Gordon by reference to homosexual tendencies, which Gordon has always denied. He told the reporters who met him every evening at the bar of the Europa Hotel that there were certain practices associated with the homosexual community that he found himself unable to condone. Grown men in public toilets. Accused teacher in death leap. You can easily detect a homosexual in a photograph, he told them. Their big sorrowful faces looking out at you like they had a right to all the loneliness in the world. Like they had a dividend taken out on misery.

Gordon worked as an accounts clerk in the supply depot. Sometimes he would get a day pass and walk down to the sea front. From the front at Whiteabbey you could see Larne. A new port complex had been built on land reclaimed from the estuary at Larne. Machinery moved in the vast corridors between stacked containers. Warehouse space was discussed in terms of acreage.

On the front at Whiteabbey there was a small park with a wrought-iron bandstand. The park was a remnant of the days when a train ran between Belfast and Whiteabbey, bringing people to the narrow strip of sand and shingle on the front, its salt-scorched trees and sandy flowerbeds. It had the melancholy air of a garden of remembrance. On the other side of the park there was a small row of tin-roofed buildings built on wooden pilings over the water. An amusement arcade, an ice-cream parlour, a souvenir shop. There was diesel oil in the water. It was a place steeped in estuary woe. The fronts of the buildings were unpainted, looked derelict. You had the feeling that this was part of their function. To remind you of the passage of time. To illustrate aspects of the temporary. To be run-down and evocative.

When he was young, Gordon would take the train to the seaside with his parents. He remembered the train and the holidaymakers from the industrial towns in the middle of the country. The children with their white faces and concave chests so that you thought rickets, hollow tubercular coughing.

Gordon often spent the day in the amusements. The owner sat in a glass kiosk with CHANGE written on it. To Gordon he looked like a specimen in a case in a museum. A desiccated oddity brought back from a voyage of exploration, tobacco-coloured, teeth exposed. Gordon would spend the day walking around the amusements, talking to the people playing the slots. Sometimes he asked them to go for a walk with him. He said he was lonely. He said he would buy them chips.

The third time he got a day pass he knew the soldier on gate duty and decided to stay late. He walked down to the dodgem cars at the front. There were children and their fathers going round in the cars, the weighty trundle on the hard, vulcanized matting, a youth moving among them, going from pole to pole with poise. There were flashing

9

lights and music and a sense of worked-at gaiety that drew you in despite yourself. The youth jumped from car to car without ever looking where he was going, his eyes elsewhere as if he were implicated in a further reality. Blue sparks fell from the grid above the cars. There was a foundry smell. There were danger signs with a lightning decal on the ceiling grid. Signs gave details of tremendous voltages. When the cars stopped, Gordon went over to the boy. The boy was wearing a Wrangler jacket with oil ingrained and there were streaks of oil on his face. This was what working in a travelling fairground was all about. He had a spartan, honed look suggesting self-reliance raised to the level of sanctity.

'What's your name?'

'Iain. What's yours?'

'You're not one of them good-living boys?'

'What do you mean?'

'Born again, that sort of thing. You get a whole show of them down here so you do, looking to save the likes of me.'

'I promise I won't try to save you.'

'Most of them look like a good ride wouldn't do them a bit of harm. What do you reckon?'

'I'm not from around here. All I want is to have friends.'

'Can't. I'm working. You sure you got nothing to do with the Camp crowd?'

'What Camp crowd?'

'Bible Camp. They got it here every summer. They got these tent missions they set up in a field.'

'I'm not very religious.'

Gordon offered him a cigarette. Davy took it and put it behind his ear.

'I'm not robbing it,' he said. 'It's just the cars is starting again in a minute.'

The dodgems started with a jolt. The boy slipped off the rail and grabbed the pole of the nearest. As the car moved towards the centre of the rink, he looked back at Gordon, implying that he knew more than he was saying, then he laughed and turned away.

It was Davy who persuaded him to get a No. 1 haircut. He showed Gordon a *Daily Mail* photograph of shaven-headed GIs fighting with English servicemen on the front in Brighton. Frozen in postures of violence they seemed ardent and dreamless. Davy said that Wesley Courtney in Whiteabbey was the man for the job. He said he would get one himself. He pointed out the need for a heroic dimension to their lives. That was how Gordon met Courtney.

He applied for an afternoon pass to go into Whiteabbey and found Courtney's barber's on the Harbour Road. He paused outside the window. The front window made him nervous. The boxes of Red Spot safety razors flecked with rust. The jars of brilliantine on Bakelite shelves. The photographs of Italianate youths with swept-back hair, their lips drawn away from their teeth as if they had been photographed in the act of discussing an unimaginable jeopardy. Following Davy's description of Courtney he imagined him as a folkloric monster, given to acts of deadly whimsy.

When he went in, Courtney was bent over an old man's head, razoring it until the pink scalp showed. He waved a hand without looking and Gordon sat down. He looked at the metal-framed chairs and copies of the *Racing Post*. He looked at the unswept lino and the unused sterilizer. The wall in front of him had at one stage been covered with posters of women; they were illegible now through damp but were still redolent of unremembered pornographies. He watched the old man's scalp emerge, its nude and profane contours.

Gordon began to read a copy of *Titbits*. After a few minutes he heard the door open and looking up he saw a tall man standing in the doorway. Afterwards he described

Desmond as 'a peculiar man'. He also said that he 'never smiled'. But Gordon's heart almost stopped when he saw Desmond standing there. He knew that he was subject to an implacable and haunting beauty. Afterwards, when he tried to tell people what he thought of Desmond, he told them about photographs he had seen of high divers in Berlin in 1936, pre-war Olympians with blond hair and dramatic torsos. Ghostly purists.

Desmond sat down beside him. As he sat he gripped the fabric of his gabardine trousers above the knee and jerked it slightly upwards to avoid stretching the material. Then he place his hands on his knees and sat very still. Gordon thought that he had shapely hands. The nails were well kept. He looked like a man who spent time on his nails, who knew the importance of presentation. Without introduction, Desmond began to speak. Desmond told him of the battle for moral rearmament of the Province. He urged Gordon to promote the four cardinal virtues of honesty, purity, unselfishness and love. He referred to the hunger of the spirit.

'I must leave you now. My father is expecting me. We live in The Glen. Do you know where it is?'

'The big house up the road?'

'That's it. Good man. You have to call up some evening. We could talk more.'

Desmond nodded to him and left. When Gordon turned back from the door, Courtney was watching him with a knowing look on his face.

'Come on up here, son, till we get a look at you.'

Gordon sat down in the chair and Courtney put the cloth round his neck.

'National service boy?' Courtney asked.

'RAF,' Gordon said almost under his breath. People like Courtney with their knowing eyes scared him. He had a legitimate dread of cruel mockery.

'Reckoned so. I seen you met Mr Curran?'

'He gave me things about religion.'

'He's a brave man for the religion, Mr Curran. He'd be a bit too fond of the Roman Catholic for the father's taste I would say. The RC wouldn't go down all that well at The Glen. Mind you, it wouldn't be in the nature of the family to be all that wild religious.'

'Who is he?'

'The da's a big man around here. High Court judge, MP and all. Moved here ten years ago. Never did hear where they come from. I hear tell they never see hide nor head of him up in The Glen. He's stuck in that Reform Club in the city all hours of the day and night.'

'What does Desmond do?'

'You never see much of the mother. She's day and night in that big house on her own. The daughter's not much use. Patricia, they call her. She'd be brave and fond of the men. Desmond went for the law as well as the da. A barrister, so he is.'

'He asked me up to the house.'

'You may mind yourself or he'll have you turned good-living. He goes round the pubs and bookies handing out them things. He's on a class of crusade, that boy.'

'Does he come here to get his hair cut?'

'He does. Come here till I show you a thing he told me.'

Courtney placed his scissors and his comb on the chipped Formica surface of the mirror stand. He levered the chrome and leather chair to eye level then tilted him back. He took Gordon's head between his hands and examined it with infinite care as though he were not there to cut hair at all but was instead tasked with the bloody and painstaking reattachment of each hair to its individual root.

'He told me about this thing by the name of phrenology. He says you can tell the character by the shape of the skull. He done it to me. He says they used criminals from the prisons and you could tell most of the time.'

Gordon felt Courtney's fingers move over his skull. He

was looking straight up at the ceiling. The ceiling was covered with pictures torn from barbers' magazines. The photographs featured predatory men with 1930s haircuts who looked as though they had been interrupted in the commission of an unsavoury sexual act. Suddenly Courtney released his head and straightened the chair. He thrust his face towards Gordon.

'If I was you I wouldn't pay too much mind to the like of Desmond Curran. There'll be no luck with that family. You have the skull of a boy apt for all shape and manner of wrongdoing. Them Currans will pull you down into the gutter they come from, you listen to me, son.'

At his trial for the murder of Patricia Curran, attention was paid to the fact that Gordon had made few friends when he had come to Whiteabbey and the acquaintances that he had acquired were described by the prosecuting counsel as being numbered among the more aberrant or degenerate members of local society. But Gordon told people afterwards that he had found a difficulty in making friends among ordinary people that he had not experienced in his home town of Dollar. He said that people seemed to avoid him, that a silence fell whenever he walked into a shop or a public house, a premonitory hush.

FOUR

The Glen was not a comfortable house. Doris thought that it was cold and difficult to keep. It faced north and Doris always felt that there were parts of the house where the sun had never penetrated. She tried to alter the house with feminine touches but it remained a place of cold parquet floors, unlit corridors.

The housekeeper, Mrs Crangle, told Inspector McConnell that she had often overheard rows between Doris and Patricia. These rows involved the leaving of her room in a state and the keeping of unsuitable company. Mrs Crangle said that when Patricia took a job driving a lorry Doris told the world for shame of derision that she had taken a position as a private chauffeur. Mrs Crangle said that Patricia seemed a nice, well-brought-up girl. She held the opinion that Doris was took bad with her nerves after several years living in The Glen. She said she had never spoke to the Judge but that he came across as distant and strange. She said that Desmond was the same. The apple never falls far from the tree, she said.

Judge Curran paid £3,500 for The Glen in 1943. The Glen stood on a rise at the end of an avenue 600 yards long. Even in the summer the avenue was a dark place. Local schoolchildren said that there was a red woman who lived on the avenue. They said she reached for you with her long, strangling fingers.

The house was close to the dye works and the railway line. There was a marshy area between the avenue and the railway line. The Glen was often hidden in a low evening mist on still evenings when cold air coming up the lough met the warm, brackish waters of the marsh. You could hear eerie bird cries from the seaward side of the town. Local people stayed away from the marsh. It seemed a place for the hooded lantern, the corpse floating in the shallows.

In his later years, John Steel often wondered what Patricia would be like now if she had lived. A woman in her sixties. The faintly lined mouth. The hurriedly applied lipstick. A woman who played bridge. A woman who spoke with a shrill note of dissatisfaction.

At the time he was referred to as Patricia's boyfriend, but Patricia's friend Hillary Douglas described the attraction as being 'all one way – his way, that is'. He used to see Patricia every Sunday at the morning service in Whiteabbey Presbyterian Church. Desmond sat on the outside of the reserved pew. Patricia sat between Desmond and her father. He thought about being married to a girl like Patricia Curran. He imagined himself coming home in the evening, turning into a gravelled driveway. There would be a sense of post-war bounty. The tennis party, the well-tended lawn. There would be a croquet lawn, hidden behind tall hedges. Drinks on a summer's evening, the shadows lengthening.

When he told Patricia about this later she smiled and said nothing. She did not say that The Glen was not like that. That there was another presence in The Glen. Something afoot in the lightless shrubbery.

After the service the family walked back to The Glen. Judge Curran and Doris walked together in front. Desmond and Patricia walked behind. They never spoke to each other on the way home. They seemed bound to silence.

Two years later he met her at the young Unionist dinner dance at the Culloden Hotel. Steel was a keen amateur photographer, and he had been asked to photograph the dance by one of the organizers who would submit the photographs to the *Belfast Telegraph* and the *Ulster Tatler*. She had been seventeen then but he had thought that she was much older. She wore a black dress in crushed silk. She had a habit of making awkward shapes with her hands bent at the wrist as she talked, strange gestures that seemed to imply forewarning. In each of the photographs there seemed to be a man staring intently at her. A man dancing with another girl. A man drinking at the bar with his friends. They were not looks of outright desire. They were the look of a man exposed to a plain truth.

Many of the women turned their backs on her. Beside them Patricia looked almost haggard, an essay in mortality. When he saw her debutante photograph in the paper after she had been killed, he realized that she had always been growing into this demeanour. The widow's dress. The tragedian's gestures.

He remembered her sitting down beside him on the Whiteabbey bus and lighting a cigarette.

'Lancelot,' she said, 'Lancelot. What sort of a name is that? Where does the man think he came from? Lancelot? His daddy worked in the stockyards. Then he goes and calls his son Lancelot.' It was the only time he had heard her criticize her father.

After her murder there had been talk that she had been seeing a married man. When was the last time she had seen him. Did they talk? Did they fuck? Patricia underneath him. A married man. All that weight and outrage.

Steel had always considered Patricia to have sophisticated looks. It was the era of air hostesses standing in front of silver-fuselaged Stratocruiser aircraft. It was the time of men with determined jaws smoking menthol-tipped Consulate. He took photographs of Patricia and Hillary in cafés. He took photographs of them on the front at Portrush. He thought at the time that they looked like something from a magazine. They were sitting against a wall with their legs on the ground in front of them, smiling at the camera. Patricia had her head tilted to one side. They looked artful, versed in resilient teen myths.

The summer before her death he had telephoned Patricia and arranged to meet Patricia and Hillary at the Sorrento café for coffee. Patricia liked the coffees there, made with steamed milk from a machine. Patricia and Hillary had walked down the drive from The Glen together. It was a warm summer's evening just after dusk. When they got to the wooded part Hillary said that it always made her shiver. Patricia laughed. In fact the woods at that point would prove themselves fecund with historic evil and the attack on the two girls that night seemed not to be the work of the two men who tried to pull them under the trees but the act of a sombre and occult will made manifest.

The attack would later prove to be a complicating factor in the investigation into Patricia's murder. It would become clear that any involvement by the two men could be discounted. However it is possible to detect a thematic progression from the incident, a narrative elaboration.

The two men came out of the trees at speed. One was dark and stocky. The other was of medium height and build with pale blue eyes. Hillary thought that they were the eyes of a drifter from a film. The eyes of a solitary killer. The eyes of a man so bent on profane outcomes that he is indifferent to capture or retribution. Hillary said afterwards that a calm descended on her which she attributed to a religious upbringing. She knew when she saw them that they were going to be attacked but she thought that there were protocols to be observed. That the men would speak to the girls first, a rough request for a cigarette, a crude remark or other act of prelude. Instead they put their arms around the girl's necks and started to drag them back towards the trees. Hillary said that she could hear Patricia make choking sounds. She said that she couldn't be sure but that she thought that they were really after Patricia. She said that men like that always drifted towards Patricia. That they could detect her victimhood and were drawn to it.

Hillary didn't know how Patricia managed to break away from the blue-eyed man. But as soon as she did so the small man released Hillary and took no further interest in her. Hillary fell to the ground. When she looked up she saw Patricia standing on the driveway. The blue-eyed man stood on the edge of the trees. They were looking steadily at each other. Patricia's face was white and her lips were pursed but she held the man's gaze with a deathly aplomb while he looked at her with a small smile on his face as though he had wrung a secret from Patricia. Hillary said afterwards that they were almost like lovers from a book with a secret shared by none.

The man turned and walked slowly back into the trees. The other man ran after him. Hillary said that she was shaken but that Patricia was in a state of collapse. The attack was not reported to the proper authorities, a course of action that Hillary was to bitterly regret until it was proved that it could have had no connection with Patricia's death. Neither man has ever been traced.

The autopsy on the body of Patricia Curran was performed by Dr A. L. Wells at the morgue of the Royal Hospital on 14 November 1952. Also present were Staff Nurse Sarah Evans and Inspector McConnell. Professor Wells noted thirty-seven distinct stab wounds on Patricia's neck, torso, abdomen, right upper arm and thigh area. The wounds had been effected by a broad-bladed knife with a triangular aspect. There was extensive bruising to the left-hand side of her face and neck. He was to state that she was otherwise a healthy nineteen-year-old female.

The local press waited in the hallway of the morgue while the autopsy was being conducted. There were men from the *Newsletter*, the *Sunday News*, the *Belfast Telegraph*, the *Belfast Morning News*. There had been little serious crime since the war and the murders that had taken place had been domestic incidents, sordid and easily solved. The journalists recognized the possibilities of the Curran case. They struck various poses in the hallway. Some affected indifference. Others bent over notebooks. The air filled with cigarette smoke. They wanted to convey a knowledge of the futility of human endeavour. They hunched their shoulders slightly to give the impression of men burdened by their duty to the truth.

In the aftermath of the murder and the subsequent trial of Iain Hay Gordon the press were in general compliant and unquestioning.

Their only source of information at the morgue was an attendant. He was a young man with a fleshy face. He wore a white uniform, slightly soiled. Reporters huddled in corners with him while he delivered lurid tales of dissection, bloated corpses, foetuses dredged from the Lagan, those dead from car crashes, accidental poisoning, loneliness and loss of fortitude.

'The da and the brother took her in,' he told the reporters. 'I hear tell the brother keeps telling the doctor she's still alive and her stiff as a board.' The man's tone was laconic. It seemed to imply that in the glassy and cold environs of death a tone of wry perseverance was required.

They asked him how long the autopsy would take, when the findings would be available. They kept looking towards the metal swing doors leading to the dissection room.

'I'd say the professor'll take her handy on this one. Judge's daughter and all. He'll be taking a good look at her, make sure that the boy that done it had never tasted the goods before he bought them, if you're with me.'

The reporters continued to question him. Who had

accompanied the body to the morgue? Had he seen the judge? Why had the body been brought to the morgue at night? Had he seen Desmond? Why did the policemen who had been photographed that morning appear thin-lipped, forbidding?

The man began to succumb to the drama of the questioning. Bodies being removed by stealth. Dark forces at work. Men whose faces were averted from the light.

'I'd say they'll be a long time getting to the bottom of this one. I'd say there's more to it than meets the eye.'

They questioned him long into the evening. He stood with his back to the wall, his face glistening with sweat, his shadow cast up upon the ceiling, crabbed and gesturing. His voice, laden with portents and comic doom, audible through the metal doors, and down the corridor to where Professor Wells bent over Patricia Curran's corpse, straightening every so often to stretch his back and noting, not for the first time, the way Patricia's lips were pursed as though to utter a hard and unforgiving word.

FIVE

When Gordon was notified of his national service he applied to serve as a radar operator. As a teenager he took solitary cycling trips and once came across the geodesic domes of a radar site. He read *World of Wonder* magazine about Russian nuclear-powered ice-breakers. He read about secret naval bases and spy satellites. He formed the word Soviet in his mouth. The Soviet army. The Soviet threat. He thought that if he could join a radar team in a secret installation he would be able to form a sense of them crouched in dense pine forests to the east: Eurasian, masculine, melancholic. He attended a concert at the Leeds Playhouse given by the Red Army Choir.

When he was posted to Whiteabbey he frequently travelled on the train to Bishopscourt, where he could see the great cold-war building on the hill. As night fell the listening station started to fade into the hilltop, the low buildings, green paint on bare metal. Men sitting with headphones. Listening in on telephone conversations, radio transmissions. Conversations coming in on crackling salvos. A structure on top of a hill, looming and darkly aerialled. Men wearing earphones sitting on metal-framed chairs with their weight on their elbows, leaning into the windy night. Shutting out the generator hum. Deft and capable. Men from industrial towns on the banks of great provincial rivers. The Humber. The Clyde. Accustomed to great movement. The hymnal of mass and tonnage. Sitting at their consoles. Bent forward to the night, its vast and enthralling distances.

In fact he was detailed as an accounts clerk to the quartermaster's office at Whiteabbey, although this did entail his signing of the Official Secrets Act, which others at the base took lightly but he regarded as a solemn and binding act giving rise to dire consequence. There was a part of him attracted to the lonely devotion of a spy. To be alone and friendless, your mind honed in pursuit of dark espionage. The concealed microfilm. The secret transmitter.

At first he could not find the courage to go up to The Glen. He would get the bus into Whiteabbey and walk down to the gates and look up the drive towards the house. He looked at the windows in the distance and wondered which room belonged to Desmond. One evening the Judge passed him, driving himself in a black Rover car. He was wearing a black suit and stiff white collar. Wesley had said that the Judge was known to be a cold and distant man but that evening Gordon noticed a small smile on the Judge's face as he drove through the gate, as though he was in the grip of a refined private amusement. Gordon wondered how a man could be a judge and send people to prison and perhaps to the gallows. Afterwards Gordon said that when he looked up at The Glen it never occurred to him to think about the women in the house. It seemed a house for men of serious purpose to live in. It possessed a severe introspective aspect. It faced north. It was shabby in places. It promised vigilance. It rose out of the dark forest shadow of its grounds as though it had prevailed over it.

When Doris was a teenager she wrote letters to herself from imaginary boys. She picked names out of phone books. When she received them she felt transformed. She held them to her nose for the scent of dusty mail sacks, the smell of provincial sorting offices at dawn. The authority the letters gathered to themselves.

The first time she saw Lance it was at a bachelors' dance in the Marina Hotel in Bangor. They had their photograph taken together. The other men in the photograph were out of focus, their sombre archetypal features barely visible. The whites of the women's shoulders and breasts rising from their dresses were all that could be seen of their pale and consummate flesh. Lance was looking directly at the camera. It was a plain, unafraid look and she thought of it when she saw how he looked now. His watery, corruptible stare.

She remembered that the photographer had a camera that you held at waist level and looked down into. The man's hands holding it delicately as though it contained something precious that might spill. She thought it was like a compass. She thought it was like a device men use to find their way by.

Her father had been a clerk in a shipping agent at the docks and had lost his job when the shipping line closed. He spent his days walking briskly about the town. He always carried a folder under his arm. It was intended to show purpose. It indicated a resolute approach.

Her mother had always kept photographs of outings, young men in blazers, fixed and ageless. She understood how adrift men could be and what they required to make their days navigable. As her mother got older she began to mistake them for people from the films. She told Doris that she often felt the presence of dead film stars in her room. She said they wouldn't leave her alone. John Gilbert. Leslie Howard. The silvery hands. The shrewd, astringent kisses.

Doris had never intended to live in The Glen. Doris dreamed of a house in Malone, a house in Helen's Bay. A house appropriate to their station, comfortable and with elegant dining catered for. However, one evening Lance came home from chambers and informed her that he had bought a house. Doris thought that she had misheard him.

'Sorry darling, what did you say?'

'I have bought a house. I have purchased a dwelling. We take vacant possession of it in a matter of days.'

'Oh, darling. What kind of a house is it?'

24

'Listen to me, Doris. What are our prerequisites? Proximity to the city. Room for a growing family. A home where we can entertain appropriately. That is the kind of house that I have acquired.'

'You have not considered anything, Lance.'

'I have considered everything.'

'Is there a garden?'

'Substantial.'

'What about the kitchen?'

'Newly fitted.'

'I don't like it.'

'You can't say that.'

'I don't like the house. I know it is cold and empty. It's not a house; it's a bone.'

'Please don't start this now, Doris. We will be moving to Whiteabbey at the end of the month.'

'You are a heartless husband.'

'You'll like it, Doris. It's the kind of house you always wanted.'

Doris turned away from him and lowered her head. Before she turned he caught a look in her eye. A child's look. Lowly, submissive, culpable. Remorse tendered in advance for what she was about to say.

'I don't like your fucking house.'

'I will not tolerate profanity in this house.'

'Your house is a bitch.'

'That is enough, Doris. Stop it right now. Stop it.'

'I will not be told to stop it in my own house by the son of an actual butcher.'

The Judge looked up and saw Patricia standing in the doorway. She was wearing a nightdress. Doris followed his gaze, looking through her fingers. That would just be Patricia, she thought. That would just be the type of her. To walk unseen into rooms. The Judge looked at Doris and when he looked again the child was gone, as though she had somehow reduced her substance.

The Curran family moved to The Glen on 14 March 1947. Judge Curran became Attorney-General for Northern Ireland in the same year. Judge Curran and Doris took the master bedroom on the right-hand side of the landing facing the front of the house. Desmond was given the bedroom on the left-hand side. Patricia was given the remaining large bedroom to the rear of the house. It was Desmond's third year to attend the law faculty in Queen's University. Patricia was fourteen years old.

Mrs Crangle, the housekeeper who had started work with the Currans that year, said that Patricia had told her that she was frightened to move closer to the city. When Mrs Crangle asked why, Patricia said that she used to sit up at night and see the red glow in the sky as the German bombers bombed the docks and that she was afraid. Mrs Crangle said that the war was over and that the bombers weren't coming back. Patricia said, but what if they came back anyway? Mrs Crangle said that if they came back they would only bomb the docks and the Antrim Road like the last time. Patricia asked why did they bomb the Antrim Road and Mrs Crangle said that was where all the Jewmen lived.

Doris grew to like the area if not the house. She became a member of the Whiteabbey Bridge Club. She participated in whist drives and charitable works in the area, although she dreaded having to come home to The Glen. She was often on her own at night. The Judge would be at the Reform Club or an Orange meeting. Desmond would stay in his room. She never knew where Patricia was although often she heard a car pull up outside in the dead of night and the sound of Patricia's shoes crossing the gravel at the front of the house.

Doris did not like to entertain and found it difficult to talk to other prominent wives. On occasions her nerves would fail her. The night before a dinner party at The Glen she would lie still in the bed and see herself entering the roomful of ladies like Audrey Hepburn, slight-framed, with a nervy grace that women hated but were forced to concede to. But on the night itself she stumbled from group to group, repelled and made small by the ladies' bony hauteur.

Spring was the best time in The Glen. Each season possessed its own timbre. Spring was full of expectancy. Summer and autumn were affable, tolerant. After that the year settled into a dutiful monotone until winter came, with the best you could expect being a cautionary silence of remembrance. During the winter she found herself walking through the house, opening and closing doors, as if she might find one that would open onto a different house, one less prone to ambiguity and mischance.

Alone in the barracks at night, Gordon pondered Desmond's invitation. He knew that prominent local families were expected to invite servicemen to evening receptions at their houses, but normally these invitations were issued through an NCO at the camp and responded to as a duty by both parties. Desmond's invitation was not one of those.

One Tuesday afternoon he took the bus from Edenmore to Whiteabbey. He got out at the stop nearest to the house, the same stop where, several months later, Patricia would alight from the bus and disappear into the driveway of The Glen to reappear the following morning as a drained corpse, stabbed many times, her murderer unfound, to be brooded over in coming decades as an exemplar of morbid desire.

From the gates to the house the avenue fell into a hollow then rose again as it reached the house. It was early summer and there was a feeling of rank vigour in the hollow but nothing more. When Gordon was remanded to Crumlin Road prison he looked back for an inherent drama that the hollow might have suggested to him but he couldn't find it. The narrative construction of Patricia's murder was painstaking, deliberated over. It moved in slow ellipses and the episode in the hollow had not yet been introduced.

He was surprised by the appearance of the house when he reached it. The front of the house had been rendered and painted and the paint had flaked and fallen away in places. The shrubbery in front of the house was unkempt and there were weeds on the driveway. There was no sign of Judge Curran's Humber saloon or Mrs Curran's Sunbeam. The stillness was cold and animate. The bell was a porcelain button inset into brass. He rang it. The door was opened by Patricia. She was wearing a dressing gown and had a towel wrapped round her hair.

'Excuse me,' Gordon said. 'I was looking for Desmond.'

'Come in,' Patricia said, 'although he's still at the bar library. You'll hardly see him tonight. Come in before I get a chill. I just washed my hair.'

Gordon followed her into the hall.

'You must be one of Desmond's disciples then.'

'Pardon?'

'One of his funny religious types. Where did you meet him?'

'At the barber's.'

'The barber's? Fruity Wesley's demon barber shop? Sometimes I think our Desmond's a homo himself. Does he strike you as a homo? Sorry, I forgot to ask your name?'

'Iain.' Gordon had followed her through the parquet-floored hallway and into the drawing room.

'I suppose that's not a fair question, Iain. They say women get on with homos like they were girlfriends. Do you think you could get on with me?'

It was a formidable room. There were long curtains that reached from the ceiling almost to the floor. The furniture was heavy and unyielding. Over the mantelpiece there was a large photograph of the Judge after his investiture. He was wearing his robes and wig. Doris stood beside him with the handles of a white patent handbag looped over her arm, a pillbox hat on her head in bridal white with a small veil attached, like a confounded innocent recently joined in austere matrimony.

'I don't know.'

Patricia let her hair fall forward over her face and rubbed it with the towel. 'Are you lonely up there in that big barracks? I'd say it's a lonely place.'

'Yes, I am lonely sometimes.'

Patricia lifted her head so that she was looking out from under the towel and smiled at him. 'I meet lots of lonely people. I'm a doctor of loneliness. A lonely specialist. Sit on the settee, Iain. I'm going out and I've got to dry my hair. I'm afraid I haven't time to talk any more.'

Gordon sat on the settee. The heavy carpet was worn at his feet. Patricia knelt in front of the fire, drying her hair, the nape of her neck exposed. The fire burning, Patricia's dark mendicant head bowed over the flame, her eyes downcast as though decorum were required. When he was younger, Gordon had wanted a sister, and now he imagined that somehow he had been adopted and that Patricia was in fact his sister. He thought about meeting his real mother. He knew there was a structure to such things. The exchange of letters, the meeting at a neutral venue. The mother a soft-voiced housewife with worn hands. A woman fearful for her own compact family, her small rooms worked at over years. The son confident, self-assured, gracious in the knowledge that he held the upper hand. Talking to each other over coffee, exchanging photographs. Look at them, her growing family. How fragile their lives, how easily destroyed. Hours spent working towards the realization that they had nothing in common. Then she would say, almost shyly, you have a sister, and show him a photograph of a girl like Patricia. It would be different with a sister. He thought about them lying awake at night exchanging secrets.

Patricia said that she was going upstairs to dress. She came down wearing a black cocktail dress with sequins. She said she had made the dress herself. Gordon said that he liked her shoes, which were black velvet with a Cuban heel. There was the sound of a car outside. Patricia went to the curtains.

'It's Desmond,' she said. 'Watch yourself. He'll be out to convert you. He likes to do conversions on a Tuesday night.'

He heard the front door open and close and a man's low cough in the hallway. The kind of cough a man makes when he feels himself to be alone. As the door opened, Patricia winked at Gordon and smiled.

Desmond was wearing pinstripe trousers and a Crombie overcoat. There was rain in his hair. He gave Gordon a curt nod, his eyes fixed on Patricia.

'Where are you going?'

'I'm going out, Desmond.'

'Could you not stay at home one night of the week?'

'Give me one good reason for staying in this place listening to you going on about God and the what, the subornation of the flesh.'

'Because it might do you good.'

'Going out would do me good.'

'Patricia, you are nineteen years old and I know the type of men you are associating with.'

'You know nothing about the type of men I am associating with.'

'I have to go,' Gordon said.

'Please don't. Forgive me,' Desmond said. 'I've been very rude.'

'No, I really have to, there's a curfew at the camp.'

'You mustn't . . .'

'For Christ's sake, Desmond, let the little man go back to his camp. Can't you see he has to get home. The last bus is at half eight anyway, isn't that right, Iain?'

'That's right, Mr Curran. I really have to get going.'

'In that case, allow me to walk you to the door.'

As Gordon passed Patricia she squeezed his arm.

'I enjoyed our talk,' she said softly. 'It's not often there is someone you can talk to in the house.'

At the front door Desmond reached into his inside pocket. Gordon thought that he was going to offer him money but Desmond gave him a small tract. 'Moral Rearmament' by Frank Buchman. It was published by the Christian Truth Society.

'Good man,' Desmond said. 'I'm sure you'll find something instructive in that. Until you come back to see us again. You will come back, won't you?'

He was standing quite close so that Gordon could smell Palmolive shaving cream. He had unbuttoned his overcoat to reveal the barrister's suit underneath, the pinstripe waistcoat and starched white collar. Gordon remembered Desmond speaking about the rigours of God's love, about sacrifice, and he noticed the small gold hairs on Desmond's forearms, the way the light in the hall caught his hair. He remembered little about what Desmond had said but through the years after Patricia's murder he could not forget the harsh sound of his voice.

He did not mention Desmond when he was first interviewed about the murder. He tried to tell them about the girl kneeling on the rug in front of the fire, the soles of her bare feet turned towards him. He tried to tell them how they had talked until the room was dark except for the light of the fire and then she had gone to dress and returned wearing a black cocktail dress that she had sewn herself with small sequins, and how they had talked about the sewing of the sequins, the minute stitches, while she put on her make-up, and how when he had left the house he had turned to see her standing at the window looking out into the night, her eyes dark and ravenous like a pre-figurement of woman lost unto death.

This was the woman that people wanted, dressed in black, her face pale and desirous. This was the woman that posterity demanded. Gordon would try to explain that this was not the woman that he met. That he could not have killed Patricia. He told Chief Superintendent Capstick that they talked about clothes, and going out to dances. He said they were like girlfriends. They had that improvidence with feeling.

SIX

Judge Curran once told Harry Ferguson that if he came back in another life he would be a horse. He said a horse had meaning. He loved them for the sound of hooves on racecourse turf, winter meets indexed in chalk on a bookie's board. The testamentary lists of the next day's starters in the *Racing Post*. During the evening he would read their names over and over. Less to establish form than to confirm their steadfast virtue. That they might prevail over long odds. That they might not be trapped against the rail or be fallers at three furlongs or find themselves holding a delicate limb off the ground, shivering with insight.

He loved winter racing from Aintree, Goodwood, the sky darkening at four o'clock and the last race running on through dusk, the going heavy, the colours muted, the horses taut, the winning post lost in drizzle as though their riders laboured them towards an abstract end.

Judge Curran played poker once a week at the Reform Club. Two or three times a year he flew from Aldegrove Airport to the Isle of Man to play pontoon and canasta in the Douglas Casino. Sometimes when he came back from these trips he would be silent for days and Doris would not dare to approach him. Once, before they moved to The Glen, on the day of his return he brought Doris to McWhirter's Jeweller's on Fountain Place in the city where he bought her a 21-carat eternity ring. That Sunday he drove Doris and the children to Portrush. Judge Curran sat in the car on the esplanade reading newspapers while Doris took the children onto the beach. It was a hot summer's day and towards the evening Lance Curran came down onto the beach and took photographs of his children. They are standing against the tin wall of an old bathing hut on the front at Portrush. The photographs are underexposed so that the children seem dark-skinned, exotic. Desmond is frowning a little, holding his hand over his eyes to shade them from the sun. His expression is reserved. He is holding something back as though he knows to distrust the counterfeit world of tender nostalgia that the photograph placed them in, the ersatz mid-century wash of regret and innocence lost. Patricia on the other hand is smiling broadly, her teeth white, her hair sun-flecked, convinced of the moment.

The poker games at the Reform Club did not take place in the card room. The Club reserved a small room at the rear of the building. The games did start not until ten o'clock, when the club membership had thinned out. The players left the main club by the front exit and went to the alley at the back. They waited in the alley at the back door until the club caretaker, Harold Mahood, opened the side door and let them in. The game seemed to need an air of illicit entry, the drawing back of bolts, the scrutinizing of faces in an uncertain light. They were prepared to go through with this for the sake of whatever small increment of the underhand that it brought to the night.

Mahood knew what they required in terms of ambience. He had been raised by two aunts who played poker with their neighbours on an almost nightly basis, bending to their cards with the faces delineated by the single light hanging over the green baize card table as though committed to it in a corrosive pact. The Judge's regular partners were his election agent, Harry Ferguson, a solicitor from Carrickfergus, Dr Alex McKee and Ivor McDowell, a property speculator from Donaghadee. McKee was a thin man, a nervous player. He was reputed to own slum housing in the Shankill and Falls districts of the city. Ferguson thought that there was always someone like McDowell in a Western. A man who saw himself as a representative of bluff townsfolk. A man who cheated his customers, who spent the last big hand wiping his face with his handkerchief, glancing nervously at the other players, always about to fold, to throw his cards on the table. A man whose presence was demanded as a stark archetype of human weakness and greed.

Ferguson was a year younger than Lance Curran. He had long noted that when on his own the Judge often had a small smile on his face as if he knew something that no other knew and that this knowledge amused him. Ferguson noted that the Judge was not a good card player, although he had an unhurried way of shuffling and distributing the deck that intimidated opponents. His face seemed exactly turned to the light, his eyes hooded, the angles of his jaw and forehead in relief so that you gained the impression of an exacting and rigorous cognition from which none were exempt. However, the Judge had a inclination for the crucial error, the subtle tactical omission. Ferguson did not hold to any belief that a man playing cards provided a template for his life or that such actions were open to appraisal and conclusion but he had noticed that there were instances in the Judge's life where he made similar bad choices, where it seemed he was driven to place obstacles in his own path so that he could entertain himself by attempting to circumvent them. Or that he felt compelled to scatter evidence of his own shortcomings so that those who might later examine his life would be able to detect those shortcomings and this might somehow exonerate him. Or simply that below the calm exterior there was a man prey to self-doubt and equivocation.

During the months that elapsed between Patricia's murder and the conviction of Gordon, Lance Curran continued to play poker, until at first McDowell and then McKee withdrew, following an incident involving McDowell. As the trial drew near, Curran sat silent at the card table opposite Ferguson, speaking only to request a card or to place a bet. He removed his hat but retained his dark overcoat with the collar turned up about a face that seemed cold and waxen. In his childhood Ferguson had listened to stories of men who played games of chance with the devil, with their immortal soul for stake, and those stories came back to him as he played with a sense that he was spectator to a ghastly commerce. He had an impression of the Judge locked in debate with an unseen adversary. Afterwards, with the knowledge acquired during the trial, Ferguson came to know the nature of that debate and the deadly aesthetic that informed it.

Patricia went to the International Hotel, the Orchid Blue, the Vogue Ballroom. At the Orchid Blue the men wore white polo necks under their jackets. The women wore cocktail dresses or slacks and jumpers with crew necks. There was a sense of post-war largesse. The men looked hardened, dark-eyed, given to predation. The women looked complicit in a bargain of melancholy sensuality. They danced to the Melody Aces. They danced to Ray Martin. Patricia went to the Orchid Blue with John Steel two nights before her death. Newspaper reports afterwards described Steel as her boyfriend and he was envied, but when they were alone together Patricia would do little more than hold his hand. Men and women saw her in different ways. Women saw the way she never really looked at you, that she always seemed to be engaged on a husbanding of inner resources. When no one was talking to her she possessed the athlete's middle-distance stare, a preoccupation with endurance. Men treated her with a wary respect and were attracted to her, her air of danger. Women saw a dangerous fatalism and afterwards they called her a menace to the married man, a slut, a bad end waiting to happen, and they were not one bit surprised by her end. Men saw a stern voluptuary. They mourned her dying as they thought fit; they struck poses of manly thoughtfulness at her funeral.

In retrospect, Steel thought you could see that night as a series of exposures, a social photographer's contact sheet. Patricia removing her shawl from her bare shoulders and handing it to him with a small shiver. Patricia standing at the bar with a whiskey and soda in her hand, her head thrown back in laughter. Patricia dancing with a tall man in evening dress – a barrister, a doctor, a man in his twenties leaning into her and murmuring something into her ear. A young man with the air of having already succumbed to a series of moral compromises.

They had a row. Steel had insisted on leaving the Orchid Blue and going on to the International.

'What's wrong with here?' Patricia asked.

'I'm fed up with it.'

'Please can we stay, John? You know you can't resist it when I say please.'

'Let's not have the kitten talk now, Patricia.'

'Please, please, please.'

'This music is giving me a headache.'

She approached him, reaching out her arms to hold his head between her palms, massaging his temples with her fingers, looking into his eyes. At the time he thought it was mockery but he later grew to think of it as tender, a manifestation of the thread of physical altruism that he knew ran through her character. He turned his back on her and left the Orchid Blue. He walked for a mile before hailing a cab in Shaftsbury Square and returning home.

Afterwards Steel regretted the row. He said that it made their last two days seem condemned, without hope of amnesty, even though they had made it up the next day and were on good terms until the time of her death. Inspector McConnell uncovered evidence that suggested that Patricia had accepted a lift home that night with a man in his fifties, a Catholic publican with a grown-up family. At first the man denied it then said: of course he gave her a lift, was the girl supposed to walk? He said that she told him off for not being at home with his family. He had dropped her at the gates of The Glen but he had only discovered afterwards who she was. McConnell asked the man if there had been any inappropriate contact. The man said that when Patricia opened the car door she leaned across the seat and kissed him on the cheek, a small kiss, cold and loveless. McConnell reported the man's tone as being one of regret, as of an opportunity missed.

Desmond heard Patricia's key in the lock that night, her footsteps crossing the hall. Desmond was often awake on these winter night-times as he slept under a single sheet and lit no fire in his room for purposes of mortification. As a boy he had made a model of Louis Bleriot's Albatross Mk II which hung on monofilament line from the ceiling so that the room smelt of epoxy resin. He heard the stairs creak and the soft sound of her stocking feet as she crossed the hallway to the bathroom, then the sound of the bath taps. Desmond had observed that she had an odd habit of taking a bath no matter what time of night she came home, though Desmond well knew that there were blemishes that would be removed by no earthly ablution.

The national servicemen based at Edenmore went to NAAFI dances at Bishopscourt, nurses' dances at the Balmoral in Shaw's Bridge. They went to the Dropping Well in Ballycastle. On the nights that leave was permitted, men stood in lines to shave in the sinks along the walls of the Nissen huts where they were billeted. There were men from Liverpool, Preston, Coventry. As they got dressed they talked about the night in front of them, each with a Senior Service or a Capstan hanging from the corner of his mouth. They compared Belfast girls and girls from the country. The Belfast girls were mill girls, Gallagher's cigarette factory girls, shirt factory girls. Most of the soldiers preferred them. They were girls who had been children during the war years so that rationing and malnutrition had left them dark-eyed and pallid. The decadence of their condition hung about them and seemed to betoken a sombre carnality.

Gordon never went out with the other men. He liked the way the barracks felt after they had left. The smell of aftershave that hung in the air. The smell of carbolic soap. He would sit on his bed and absorb the cold, authentic silence of desertion. Sometimes he walked over to Stores to talk to Corporal Derek Radford. Radford was what Gordon's father called a firm's man, which he explained as meaning a worker who was on the side of management. Radford treated the RAF's property as if it were his own. He spent many hours when the camp was quiet working on inventory. Gordon often helped him. He found these evenings restful. A sense of order prevailed. They worked mainly in silence. Radford moved along the shelves counting, then calling out the number of each item. Gordon wrote them down, then when they had finished a row Radford returned to the desk and transferred the figures that Gordon had written down into a cloth-bound ledger. His handwriting was tiny and detailed and resembled the written manifestation of an arcane practice.

Radford told Gordon that his father was an off-course bookmaker in Blackburn. The father referred to himself as a turf accountant. Radford said that it was like working in a hospital or a solicitor's office or an undertakers.

'All human life is there, my son, believe me.'

'What do you mean?'

'You see man in all his glory, my son, and you see him in all his stench and misery. I seen a proud man beg pennies in the street to bet. I seen a wife walk across the floor of the very shop and split her husband right between the eyes with an axe. Torrents of blood, my son, and they hung the murderess the 20th of November 1948 in Wormwood Scrubs prison.'

Gordon never forgot the scenes described to him by Radford. The rites of betting. A man staking his entire home on one horse to come home first. A man bound and unheeding, his wife pleading with him to leave, to come home. Scenes of classical grief that seemed rehearsed but no less devoid of significance for that. He said that when he thought of the grief of the Curran family he thought of the stories that Radford had told him, as they seemed designed to set a median by which other griefs might be measured, and that Radford's precise script seemed to set that measurement, making greed and helplessness tabulate.

Afterwards Gordon told Capstick that Radford had encouraged him to begin a Pitman typing course by correspondence. He agreed that he had been practising on his own for a City and Guilds examination on the night of Patricia Curran's murder. He agreed that he had been practising on his own and that no one could corroborate his story.

SEVEN

Sometimes Doris drove into Larne and parked in the middle of Soho car park, where she sat in the car until the light started to change. She liked large open spaces. Once she had been stopped by the police. One of them had asked her if she had been drinking and the other had said that she was Judge Curran's wife. The first policeman had hesitated and looked off into the night like a man adding figures in his head, then told her to drive on without looking at her. She thought she knew how he felt. How you thought there were things in life that you could hold in your hand and say, 'This is under my power and no other's,' and then you hear that name Curran spoke out loud like a command or sharp retort.

Soho car park was on the site of the old butter exchange. There had been a spur line from the railway that ran alongside the canal as far as the lock gates into the basin. It had been a place of narrow alleyways and wooden gangways. The car park tarmac had been laid over the old tarmac so that it was uneven and broken in places. Gantries with winch cogs rusted solid stood by the canal. She would park the car in the middle, as far as possible from other cars, light a cigarette, wind the window down a little so that there was no condensation. The place gave her an eerie feeling that she liked. The jetties creaking, the lights flickering. There was a sense of waiting for a drama to take place. Stealthy figures emerging; tragedy foreordained. She remembered stories of revenue men and cadgers. She thought of herself as a dry-eyed beauty watching men going to their fate, a pulse beating at her slender throat. Sometimes mist gathered over the water and she thought of boats coming upriver, rowing steadily, a spectral contraband borne in on the night tide. She knows she could alert them but she watches them and gives no warning.

From the beginning Patricia was an awkward child. Visitors frequently made reference to the fact that Desmond was a quiet boy as if to further say: why could she not govern her daughter? She had tried to lay stress on the virtue of politeness and manners but Patricia seemed to take pleasure in defiance. There were days when Doris could have wept in mortification. Lance said it was a period of his career when social status was of the utmost importance. She took tea with the Women's Institute, the Unionist Ladies Association and other bodies engaged in important charitable work. At these times Patricia made a point of exhibiting the most terrible behaviour involving tantrums. Doris took her to Professor Glenny in Altnagelvin hospital. He asked if Patricia was sexually precocious, to which Doris replied no, being uncertain as to the terms used. Professor Glenny told her that these were normal childhood phenomena but she knew in her own mind that he was in error. She also talked to the Reverend W. Speers of Killinchy Presbyterian Church after Patricia had lifted a hot poker from the fire and put it to Desmond's bare leg in shorts. The Reverend Speers said the child had an infection of the spirit, and when Doris asked her what he meant he said that there was a demon in the girl.

She spoke to Professor R. A. Whitfield at the Royal Victoria. She spoke to Nurse McKinney, who was a midwife to, among others, her friend, Mrs Rene McIlhone, wife of Captain Raiph McIlhone formerly of the Royal Greenjackets. She made it clear that no effort was being spared in the control and management of the girl.

At times Patricia was put to her room. Lance removed the light bulb despite all the fuss the girl would make.

Doris would lock the door and she would be left to reflect on her behaviour until morning. 'Reflection' was a favourite word of Lance's. He would call upon defendants in front of him to consider for a moment the weakness of their case, to reflect upon their course of action.

When Patricia was sent to her room you could hear her throughout the house, the drumming of heels, screaming, tears and other wilful actions.

Doris could not have coped if Desmond had been like Patricia. Fortunately for her, Desmond was an ideal son. He would come home from school and do his homework with diligence. When he had finished it he would often spread a board on the dining-room table and spend time making models, working at them with a sharp blade so well that Doris, who was awkward in herself and no good with things, called him the expert. When he was sixteen Desmond played rugby with the Wesley College XV. They reached the final of the Lagan Valley cup and all the parents went. Doris found it quite exciting. There was mud on the ground and the men shouted hurrah when there was a score.

When Patricia was fourteen Doris entered her own room to find the girl sitting at her dressing table with her cosmetics arranged in front of her. Doris had seen to it that she was fitted for a brassiere and other intimate garments, but particularly the brassiere, since an ill-fitting brassiere was the cause of many ailments. She did not wish to be seen as not providing to Patricia's feminine needs. But on seeing a lady's cosmetics put to such careless and brazen use, she overflowed with rage.

Patricia had been in her mother's room for over an hour. The dressing table had two mirrors, which you angled so that you could see the back of your head. She had put on the bedside light but not the main light so that someone passing would not see light from under the door. There were two drawers on the front of the dressing table with compartments in them. There were mascara brushes, foundation cream, lipsticks, concealer. Patricia had often watched her mother put on make-up with small intent movements. The way she turned her face in the mirrors. The way she rubbed her lips together. Essays in self-absorption. It seemed a duty of the old, a terrible observance. There were tweezers with bevelled edges, nail scissors with curved ends, a pair of eyelash curlers like a fetish toy. Patricia opened a compact and dabbed at her face with the small sponge in the lid. She unscrewed the lid of a lipstick.

This is the picture provided for us. The mother's feet coming up the stairs and down the landing. The daughter awaiting the mother in the dark room. Sitting motionless, the door opening. Seeing her as the mother sees her first, the child's face looking up at her from the mirror. The child's features still half-formed and apprehensive, yet the make-up sits on her face as surety of womanhood. The daughter awaiting the mother in the darkness.

The mother cries out. She strikes her daughter and her face reddens from the exertion.

In the dining room downstairs the Judge finished his evening meal. He folded his newspaper along the crease the better to read it. He heard the noise from upstairs. Desmond looked up from his model-making and their eyes met, then they returned each to their separate tasks.

Every Tuesday Gordon went to Wesley Courtney's to have his hair cut. He could have had it done by the camp barber but the man was given to elaborate hand-washing after touching Gordon, along with references to homos.

The second time Gordon went to Courtney's he asked Courtney about Desmond.

'You're sweet on that boy, that right?'

'I'm not sweet on him. He's a friend.'

44

'The likes of Desmond Curran is friend to no man, you take that from me, forby a friend to the like of us.'

'He's very Christian.'

'Christian my hole. I tell you what makes Desmond Curran tick. You see the sister? She thinks she's better than us because the da's a big judge and they live in this big house and all, and she's right, so she is. She's a nobby bitch but she's right. You see Desmond? He thinks he's better than us because he knows all about God and all. He thinks he's being charitable bringing the likes of you up to the house as if he gives any sort of a fuck about you. Mistake number one.'

'I think he just wants to be kind to people.'

'It wouldn't surprise me if that's what he thought too. When it comes down to it, your lawyer friend looks after himself. He'll drop you in it first chance he gets.'

One day Courtney turned to Gordon and said that he was fed up listening to him talking about Desmond and why didn't he go down to Whiteabbey Crown Court and see Desmond in court?

Gordon had never thought about this. One day in the barber's shop he met a solicitor called Bertie Hoare. Hoare was a balding, nervous man married to the secretary to the Minister for Home Affairs. Hoare told Gordon that Desmond would be in Whiteabbey court on the following Thursday. Gordon swapped a day pass with Radford and persuaded Davy from the fairground to go with him as he was too nervous to go on his own.

Davy had been inside a courtroom before. He told Gordon he had convictions as a juvenile for illegal street trading for which the Probation Act was applied. He adopted a posture of formalized hostility. He met RUC men's eyes and tried to stare them down. He spat on the courthouse steps.

'Fuckers would walk clean over you if you let them.'

The hallway was full of people. Barristers, solicitors and

their clients. The wooden floor gleamed. There was a strong smell of floor polish. Homely, waxen, but with chemical overtones. Gordon couldn't see Desmond in the hallway. He had been afraid that he might run into him and have to explain why he was there.

They saw a sign for the public gallery. They went in and found seats at the back. A smell of Jeyes fluid came up from the cells below. Davy pointed out the ushers, the judge's bench, the jury benches and the dock. He told Gordon how prisoners were led up from the cells under the public gallery, blinking in the light and running their tongues nervously around lips suddenly dry. He told Gordon about the many depraved characters he had seen in that very dock. Murderers, rapists. Men who had been led from here to a place of lawful execution. Men who shouted terrible obscenities at the judge as he performed his righteous and awful task.

'I never seen a man hung,' Davy said. 'I always wanted to see a man hung. I hear tell he gets this massive big horn on him.'

Gordon found himself staring at the dock. It looked like a place to preach from, or a teacher's lectern. It had panelled sides and a low rail that ran round its edge. It seemed a setting where you might be subject to mild appraisal and not the place of challenge and jeopardy that he had always thought a dock would be. Nor did he think that in months to follow he would come to know its properties or that he would attain the attributes of grim celebrity that it conferred.

Desmond walked in accompanied by another barrister. He was wearing robes and a wig. His face was stern. Gordon felt that he carried himself with dignity. When the judge entered and they all rose, Gordon suddenly realized that even the spectator in the court had a role to play. He composed his features to express devotion to the stern upholding of values, the punishment of wrongdoing.

46

Desmond's first client was a man in his forties. He was on his third charge of drink-driving while disqualified. The man watched the magistrate intently as he talked about a custodial sentence. He was wearing a blue shirt with blood on the collar where he had cut himself shaving. He shut his eyes and nodded slowly when the magistrate refused bail, as if the stern verdict of society was something that had been long awaited. Desmond said that the man's wife had left him and that he had lost his job. He faced the court with the calm of someone who had successfully identified all the landmarks of failure and had hazarded them in his own heart. It seemed that he had mastered his own decline and was glad to see life reduced to dreamy essentials. A policeman led him down the tunnel to the cells and Gordon could see the two men talking as they walked, their heads together as though they had much to unburden themselves of.

The next case was a young man arrested for grievous bodily harm. He pleaded guilty. A policemen told the court that he had struck his wife in the face with a glass while under the influence of drink. Desmond entered a plea for leniency. He spoke in low tones so that Gordon had to strain to hear what he was saying. He said that the young man had been motivated by jealous rage, that the young woman had indulged in relations with another man. He called it an occasion of adultery. He did not wish to condone the young man's behaviour but he had now forsworn alcohol and was involved in part-time duties with a Christian organization.

Gordon could see the man's wife sitting in front of him in the public gallery. She was small and blonde. There was a vivid scar across her cheekbone and nose and she lifted her hand often to touch it. Her husband didn't look at her. Desmond said that she had allowed herself to be seduced by an older man, a manager at her place of work. He said that her husband, an assistant in a hardware shop, had

47

seen them together in a bar on Amelia Street. The small blonde woman looked at the ground as Desmond went back over the details of her affair as though she knew herself on trial on grounds of betrayal and subversion of a plain man's yearning heart.

When the judge passed down a sentence of one year's penal servitude suspended for two years, the woman rose and quit the court without lifting her head, although Gordon saw her lips move as she passed him. He thought she was counting, as though disgrace was a thing to be tallied and made account of, or that she had henceforth been pledged to a recital of the lonely offices of the unfaithful wife.

'Fuckers is all the same,' Davy said. 'Can't trust any of them. You got to be hard on a woman. A woman likes to be curbed, so she does.'

Knowledge he had acquired in the fairground, an arduous sexual wisdom.

Later Gordon realized that the woman reminded him of Patricia. They both seemed beautiful, covetous of life, adept in the discourse of their own mortality. They exhibited beauty and a willingness to endure.

EIGHT

It is conceivable that his father's occupation may have accounted for Lance Curran's interest in the law. It is possible that he may have tried to reconcile his father's activities by recourse to legal precepts or that he sought to acquire moral boundaries that may have been lacking in his childhood.

It may simply have been that he chose the subject most suited to his intellect and that he would have taken any available path to avoid his father's route to the old abattoir, with its cracked concrete drains unable to cope with the volume of blood and offal, and where you were deafened with the sounds of cattle in terror, and your head pounded with the sight of the men at work and the carnage they engendered.

At the time of Patricia's murder the newspapers described Judge Curran's career as meteoric, unprecedented. He was a High Court judge at the age of forty-one. He was Attorney General three years later and then became Lord Chief Justice, a position he was to hold for many years after his daughter's death, his son's defection to the papist church and the committal of his wife to Holywell Mental Hospital. Lance Curran was also a prominent member of the Orange Order and the Royal Black Perceptory, a prerequisite to high judicial office.

Harry Ferguson became Lance Curran's election agent in 1936. He had heard about Curran. People said that he was the talk of the bar library. Ferguson met him at a charity dinner dance run by the Whiteabbey Bachelors. Curran was talking to a man called Gilchrist, who was prominent in Orange circles. Ferguson had procured an abortion for

Gilchrist's girlfriend, a Roman Catholic by the name of McAlinden. Affairs with Roman Catholic girls were not uncommon for men in Gilchrist's position. You met them in public bars. They worked behind the counters of cheap cafés. You saw them walking in the town. Shop girls. Factory girls. The watchful and adroit sexual persona. Ferguson knew the attraction. To be lost in the darkness and vice of their ardour.

He studied Curran. The young lawyer held his head to one side when he talked, one hand in his pocket, the other holding a cigarette. He wore gold half-moon glasses common in the bar library and looked out over the top of them as he spoke, an effect designed to unnerve a witness, to remind them that they were subject to unwavering scrutiny, a pitiless intolerance of falsehood. Curran had black hair receding at the temples, which he wore combed back. Ferguson formed the impression that Curran was aware of being watched by people in the room, that he possessed a sense of his own celebrity among these people. That he represented the qualities that they most wanted others to see in their society. Polished, urbane.

Ferguson was standing alone in the hallway when Curran came over to him. Curran put out his hand. His grip was light and cold.

'Lance Curran. I wonder could I have a moment of your time, Mr Ferguson?'

Ferguson suggested a drink. They went to the Culloden Hotel. The Culloden had oak panelling. It had leather-upholstered chairs. There were horse brasses on the wall above the bar. Even in the summer a fire burned in the fireplace. The furniture and carpets were heavy, dark-hued, rooms laid out according to the sombre integers of provincial government. These were rooms designed to tell men that their concerns were weighty, to remind them of the necessity for a stalwart life.

Curran ordered a whiskey and soda. Ferguson declined

a drink. Curran informed Ferguson of his political ambitions. He said he knew Ferguson's reputation as a shrewd political adviser. Curran said that he had identified a safe seat in Whiteabbey, and that he had confidential information that the sitting MP would retire at the next election. He said that he wanted Ferguson to act as his election agent. Curran was courteous, insistent. He outlined an agenda of structured public life.

'Do I have you right, Mr Curran? You have ambitions to be Attorney General?'

'I do.'

'And do you see this ambition in terms of service to the community?'

'I don't think that service to the community and personal ambition are incompatible, Mr Ferguson.'

Ferguson laughed at that. Curran leaned back in his chair with a small smile on his lips.

Ferguson agreed to act on Curran's behalf. They arranged to meet the following week to discuss strategy. As they were putting on their overcoats in the hallway, Curran turned to Ferguson and said, 'My wife finds the duties associated with her position to be onerous.'

It was the only time during their association that Curran ever alluded to what Ferguson understood to be Doris Curran's highly strung condition.

Ferguson later described Curran to his wife.

'He's what you might call a coming man, Esther. He's the sort of boy gets what he wants, to my mind.'

'And what do you receive for your help, Harry, out all hours of the day and the night doing that man's work for him?'

Ferguson knew there were major projects afoot. The New University was being planned. There was the M1 motorway and the new town at Craigavon.

'A man in the right place, Esther. A man in the right place.'

As he watched Curran's rise at the bar and in politics, Ferguson's mind often went back to those first days. He saw Curran going from group to group at the Round Table dinner. He saw him moving around the dance floor with the daughters of the wealthy Protestant middle class. He saw that night without sound, in a flickering documentary light. He recalled the conference with Curran in the Culloden and saw himself and Curran as an outsider would. A middle-aged man in a sheepskin car coat, faced by the younger, his arms moving as he described his plans for the future. The young man wearing gold-rimmed glasses, wearing a pinstriped suit and silver cuff links exuding, it seemed at this distance, a ghostly magnetism.

There was one other noteworthy thing to remember from that night. In 1949, Gilchrist was brought before Belfast Crown Court on a charge of statutory rape. The charge related to a fifteen-year-old girl from Rasharkin in County Antrim. Ferguson attended the trial. Ferguson saw the girl outside as she waited with her mother. She sat with her head down, her hair partly covering her face. On the first morning, Gilchrist's counsel requested a meeting with the judge in chambers. When they emerged, the judge halted the trial and dismissed the jury. They were told that evidence as to the girl's age at the time of the alleged offence had not been satisfactorily presented.

Ferguson also remembered the girl, McAlinden, whom Gilchrist had made pregnant. Ferguson had made the arrangements and had agreed to travel with her to the clinic. They had travelled on the ferry from Belfast to Liverpool. It was a night ferry, an old ship, pitted with rust, and it seemed to Ferguson as it slipped away from the quay that it brought its own darkness with it and was cargoed with shadow. Several young men approached the girl on the boat but she had spoken to no one and they had not pressed her. From Liverpool they travelled by Victoria station by coach, then by taxi to the clinic, where they arrived before dawn.

When they got there he had opened the back door for her and walked behind her carrying her bags. Ferguson felt people looking at him. She asked for her ward at the desk and he followed her as she passed down through distempered corridors. He felt like a ghastly escort attendant upon her dismay. When she got to the ward he set the bags down and she started to unpack her clothes into the small metal locker. He turned at the door of the ward to look back at her. He wanted her to look up at him. He felt like she was his daughter. When he looked back on that time he saw himself stood in the door like a monument erected to sorrowful parenthood.

On rare occasions Doris attended functions with her husband. Otherwise Ferguson had only seen her in public once. Ferguson and Curran had an appointment in the Stormont Hotel with two car dealers from Lisburn called Gracey and Whyte, who had made campaign contributions to Lance Curran's election as Stormont MP for the Whiteabbey constituency. Their wives sat together at the end of the table, talking to each other. They looked foxy and amoral. Capable of massive, disabling infidelity. The men drank and laughed loudly. Lance Curran sipped whiskey and soda and answered the men politely.

'I hear tell you'd be brave and fond of the ponies, Mr Curran,' Gracey said at the end of the evening.

'I beg your pardon?' Curran said. He turned his attention to Gracey as though he was according him true judicial attention.

'The sport of kings. They say you'd be a man for the races.'

'You'd be keen enough on the fillies yourself, Harry,' Whyte said. 'You'd be well got for a ride in the country.'

Whyte's wife looked at him from the end of the table, a dark look, talisman of wintry lives.

Ferguson watched Curran. He reckoned the two men's bonhomie interrogative, and knew they were waiting to see the stuff he was made of. Ferguson had caught glimpses of Curran's past in his character; although not enough yet to divine a patrimony of unknowing violence, it was enough to suggest a man closer to a command of edgy dialectics than the other two had yet suspected.

'Mr Gracey,' Curran said, 'have you ever found yourself playing for high stakes?'

'You mean big money?'

'I mean high stakes.'

'I wouldn't be a man for the gambling myself.'

'Perhaps you are among those who think that life itself contains enough of gambles?'

'I'd go along with that.'

'Excitement enough for you?'

'I suppose so.'

The Judge nodded as though confirmed in a long-held view. He rose and went to the bar. When he returned he had a drink for each of them. They thanked him. The Judge eyed each of them in turn with a kind of icy benevolence and raised his glass to them.

'Don't mention it,' he said.

'Don't mention what?'

Ferguson looked up to see Doris Curran standing behind her husband. The two women stopped talking.

'You said don't mention it. What are we not talking about today?' Doris said.

The Judge held up his hand as though to restrain others at the table from rising, although none had moved.

'My husband is an expert in not talking about things. I couldn't tell you the things we don't talk about in our house on a day-to-day basis. I couldn't begin to list them.'

'Doris, please.'

'Also there is the question of my husband's ambition to consider. His humble beginnings.'

'I wasn't aware that you were here. This is Mr Whyte and Mr Gracey. And you know Mr Ferguson.'

The two women at the end of the table were rapt. Doris was aware of the largesse she was bestowing on them. She bowed slightly towards the two men.

'Bridge,' she said, 'in the ballroom. A woman on her own in a ballroom. It would not have happened in our younger days. Men were gallant then. And my husband was gallant. You may not believe it but it is true. A gallant boy.'

'I'm going home now. You can come with me if you like,' Curran said.

'I've got my friends here.'

'I forgot.'

'I don't want to disappoint them, you understand. We make up a bridge four.'

'Of course.'

'Then I will rejoin my company.'

'Please.'

'Renew my acquaintance with them.'

'I'll leave the door open for you.'

'Please do.'

They watched her cross the floor, moving towards the entrance to the bar. She was aware of being watched, a sense of dense theatrics in the room. The two women exchanged artful looks. A mental case for a wife. After Patricia's death there was melancholy talk of electroconvulsive therapy, lobotomy, but at that moment she made her mad unhappiness seem a talent.

It gave Ferguson and Curran something in common. After he had met Curran in the Stormont he went home. Esther wasn't there. He woke at three and came downstairs and found her asleep on the sofa. Her hair hung into her face. She looked like a character in her own lurid fiction. Sex-crime blonde. Her mascara showed the marks of tears and her breathing was gentle, almost imperceptible, as though engaged in minute resuscitation. An alcoholic wife. At one time it seemed as though he would never get over the unwholesome glamour of it. He was aware of women watching him for signs of it. His nights filled with violent rage, her girlish and unstable lusts.

There was a glass in her hand. He had time to wonder again how she maintained her looks, her make-up perfect, her skin unlined. He had seen her earlier that day, from the window of his office. He watched her cross the street. He noticed the edges of her heels worn, a thread hanging from the hem of her skirt. A woman in her late thirties, subject to small-scale reversals, the world held unfaithful, not for the first time. He imagined evenings spent in remorseful calculation, a setting of limits for herself. He wanted to ask her to go away with him. To winter some-where. An old chalet. Weathered planks swelling with rain. A place of empty streets going up hills, closed shops. A place wind-scoured, depleted. Adequate for late romances.

He went into the kitchen to make tea. When he came out her eyes were open. She watched him moving around the room, pulling the curtains, turning off the lights.

'How was his lordship tonight?' she asked, and shiv-ered. 'There's a badness hanging round that family. I'm heart scared of it.'

Her eyes were bright. Often she woke at night in moods like this. Governed by a stern inquisitorial spirit. Vigilance against pain distilled into prescience.

'Curran's all right,' Ferguson said. 'He'd be a bit on the cool side is all. The wife's clean mad though, far as I can see.'

'Dear God, such a family,' Esther said. 'That Desmond has the head away with religion. The mother. The daugh-ter . . . this town has the poor girl's reputation gone to ruination.'

There was a pause while it seemed that Esther was

engaged in weighing out the pain involved, reckoning it in a lamentable assay.

He waited for her to speak again. That she might say something timely on the subject of making amends and moving on from the past. That they could construct a marriage with mute, pained understandings. That they could lose themselves in wonder at the damage they had done to each other. That she would get up from the sofa, take a shower and make coffee so that they could take part in a soft parley on the edge of remorse, her wet hair hanging round her face. It seemed a chance, but when he looked down she had drawn her knees tight up against her chest and was asleep.

NINE

In late May 1951, Patricia fell into conversation with a fifty-year-old man at the bar of the Penny Farthing, a pub close to Carlisle Circus. The man's name was James Fisher. He was a supplier of building materials to many prominent firms. He did not attempt to flatter Patricia. Instead he jeered at her.

'This is no place for a wee posh girl the like of you. Away on home.'

It was Friday night and the floor was crowded. The Melody Aces were playing. The crowd was made up of women from Gallagher's tobacco factory, men from the markets, the Pound Loney. Friday night was pay night and many had cashed their cheques at the bar. After the murder they recalled Patricia. The women remembered the way she spoke, her crisp, grammar-school accent. They remembered that they wore print frocks and silk stockings bought at Nutt's Corner market while Patricia was wearing ski pants and a lamb's-wool sweater. 'She was got up like some sort of fucking film star.' Like Jean Harlow. Like Jayne Mansfield. Brazen yet somehow redeemed by virtue of being shadowed, death-haunted. Looking back, the women found that the evening took on a funereal aspect. The men said that she had a word for everybody at the bar. They noticed the way she would meet your eyes full on. They said they didn't know that she was a judge's daughter but you could have guessed. They thought her forthright and humorous and found it hard to believe that she had been killed and a few of them said she was like your daughter. They said how they would have protected her if they had been there, and imagined her gratitude. Then they remembered again that she was dead and wondered what she might say to them, her sad and reproachful words, a rebuke from the darkness.

Fisher continued to speak to her. He was a thickset, swarthy man with curly black hair. He was wearing a gold wedding ring. His talk was knowing, intimate.

'I know what you rich girls is after in a place like this. A boy like me'd do you, so he would, a working man the like of me. Look at them hands.'

He held out his hands and turned them carefully. There was hair on the back of them. His fingers were callused. He looked at them as if they did not belong to him, as if they were possessed of a life apart, sinuous and virile.

'Them's sensitive hands, them hands are hands to play a woman like a piano.'

His talk was relentless, detailed. There were connotations of sexual violence.

'Why are you saying these things to me?' Patricia said. 'I don't know you.'

'You tell me this then, girl, and tell me no more. What are you doing in a place like this?'

'I came for a drink.'

'You did surely. You come to see what the natives was up to.'

'If you really have to know, I'm looking for a job.'

'She's looking for a job?' Fisher addressed the question to the bar, holding his arms out as a token of his disbelief.

'And what class of a job are you looking for?'

'A summer job.'

'A summer job?'

'Before I go to college.'

'A summer job. By fuck I'll give you a summer job. Can you drive?'

'I can.'

'Well, then you can drive a lorry for me.'

59

*

After the initial impact of the murder had been absorbed, the newspapers were unsure as to what Patricia's job might signify. At first it was seen as evidence of an independent spirit. There were overtones of land girls, cheerful female munitions workers, wholesome smiling women in wartime utility clothing and caps tilted over one eye engaged in communal enterprise. Then an uneasiness started to assert itself. Newspaper columnists started to detect a wilful disregard for social barriers. It was implied that Patricia had misled them into their original perception of her as hardworking and dutiful. There was a hardening of attitudes. They would not accept her at face value any more. There were columns devoted to the rearing of children and the anguish of fathers. Young women were reminded of moral dangers.

The following Monday morning Patricia had Steel drop her at the gates of Fisher's yard in Whiteabbey. There was a building supplies warehouse on the site, machinery parked in rows. Road graders, low loaders. An oily odour of bitumen hung in the air. Patricia found Fisher in a prefabricated wooden office behind the warehouse. A gas fire burned in one corner. Several months later in the same office, in a darkening November sky, Fisher would back Patricia against a desk and place his hand on her breast, sweating and hoarse, a look of bewilderment on his face as though the lewd proposal coming from his lips was not of his own making but a text dictated by another that he was compelled to narrate.

But that morning Fisher took her outside and gave her the keys to a flatbed Commer lorry and instructions to deliver several pallets of concrete blocks to Helen's Bay.

'Are you going to send someone with me?' Patricia asked.

'The way I look at it, you can either do the job or you can't,' Fisher said, 'and if somebody done a job for me, I never asked him questions what way he done it.'

Fisher regarded himself as a self-made man and was given to gruff homilies on the theme of self-assurance. He gave Patricia the invoice and walked to the office without looking back. Patricia drove the lorry to Helen's Bay.

Helen's Bay was a prosperous suburb. The women played bridge. The men kept yachts at Bangor marina. They wore peaked skipper's caps on Saturday and affected an air of briny affluence. Patricia had often played tennis there with schoolfriends. Long-legged blonde girls in tennis whites calling to each other in the ghostly dusk; the sounds of tennis on a summer evening evoked and returned to silence. This was the place where Patricia should have belonged and the girls' mothers shivered when they heard that she had been among them in the employ of a tradesman. There was a desperate need to believe that she had done it for reasons of high spirits, evidence of a rebellious streak, but they knew that this was not the case, and felt without understanding that something dire and marauding and irremediable had been among them.

Fisher was later questioned by Inspector McConnell as to why he had given her the job. He said it was because she had asked. It was suggested that he knew of her reputation for promiscuity and hoped to take advantage of her. Then they asked him if he knew of any reason for her sudden departure. He admitted that there had been an incident. He said that he had made a pass at her. He turned his face away as he said this, knowing that the phrase was inadequate to the baleful sexual advance he had subjected her to. He had pinned her against the desk in the office. He described the kind of evening that it had been. The onset of early dark. A squall that blew hailstones against the window. He said that he suddenly realized how young she was. She was watching him with a grave, child's look that seemed to force sudden self-doubt on him so that he released her and watched her walk out of the office, leaving him regretful and awash with the stormy residuals of the unreflecting life.

TEN

Gordon often felt heartbroken at the thought of his parents. He was an only child. His mother had not been well for a period of years. His father wrote to him and asked him if he had decided to stay in Whiteabbey. He talked about selling their house in England and coming to live there. His father wrote that his mother liked to be near him. He panicked at the thought. Mentally he placed them on a small estate somewhere on the shores of Lough Neagh, a place prone to inland gales, fogbound winters. Their heads lifting at small noises as they waited for news of him. The conviction that dogged and lonely vigil was a fitting end to their days. He wrote back to his father and told him that he did not think it was a good idea. He alluded to the deficiencies of the health service. He suggested that standards of public hygiene and waste management had not been maintained. The Gordons were people with a clear regard for effective local government.

Gordon had constructed a version of his childhood that portrayed his parents as small, unemphatic people, tending to their child with gentle hands. This illusion of their vulnerability was among the elements that contributed to his eventual confession to the murder. He thought that his mother could not bear any pain. In fact, following his conviction his parents sold their house, moved into rented accommodation, and set about attempting to establish his innocence with a calm-eyed and undemonstrative rigour that sustained them for many years through solicitor's offices and the waiting rooms of public representatives, until at first one then the other died and were buried in a shabby Glasgow graveyard.

In his letters home Gordon said that he could imagine his mother and Doris becoming firm friends. He described Doris as an ordinary housewife and mother. He told his mother that he believed that Doris was unsuited to her life as wife to a prominent public man. It would be like your only son becoming a general, he wrote. She is sensitive like me and I think perhaps artistic as well, which others do not easily recognize. Also she is not crude like many other women of her age. His mother replied that women of a certain age are often troubled by a variety of nervous complaints and she enclosed a family recipe for ginger root tea if Mrs Curran would be so good as to consider its use and beneficial properties.

Of the Judge he wrote that he is a '. . . very serious man but there is not much laughter where he works ha ha!'

To Mr and Mrs Gordon the Curran family residence was presented in their son's letters as a place where values were strictly adhered to. They thought that their son had a gift of writing and brought people alive. Mrs Gordon was particularly taken with the children. Desmond, blond, firm-jawed, occupied with matters of conscience. And Patricia, who characterized what Mrs Gordon regarded as the fiery, untamed feminine spirit. A girl who looked down her nose at unworthy suitors with a scornful toss of her head, yet prepared to risk all for love. There were sub-plots, uncompleted narrative threads. Doris as a woman unsuited to her role, an air of dutiful sacrifice, held to her married obligation by iron will alone. Mrs Gordon imagined her wandering the house at night after the family had gone to bed, sleepless and troubled by regrets, the wind moaning in the trees outside. Mr Gordon said that it lacked respect to think about the poor woman in that way.

It seemed, however, that the Gordons had uncovered something about the Curran family. Looking back at them, they seem invented, a construct put in place to serve the elaborate mechanisms of Patricia's murder. There is a fated nineteenth-century quality to their lives. Many aspects of their personalities seem overly vivid, their actions prone to exaggeration. The dark house at the end of the damp overgrown avenue, setting for a lurid tale of morbid erotics, madness and primogeniture.

The fairground at Bangor, despite every appearance of being a travelling show, never moved. During the winter, tarpaulins were draped over the roundabouts and dodgem cars. It was Davy's job to spread heavy axle grease on exposed machinery to protect it from the corrosive, salt-laden air. When this was done, Davy signed on at Bangor labour exchange. During the summer he slept in a shed at the fairground in order to keep watch on the machinery. During the winter he moved to an old railway carriage set into concrete above the dunes at Whitehead, several miles to the north of Bangor. To Gordon the railway carriage seemed a natural place for Davy to live. It seem to embody themes of mid-century transience, resilience.

Davy warned Gordon about Wesley Courtney.

'That class of a boy's just waiting to get something on you. I'm fucking warning you, son. That boy is pure poison, so he is. Don't be betting on him being a homo himself so as he won't put it over on you. You mind me.'

In fact there were rumours around Whiteabbey that Courtney had been connected to the suicide of the seventeen-year-old son of a prominent local businessman. He had hanged himself from the rafters of a derelict railway shed. A young couple had gone into the shed and the girl had brushed against his feet. They heard the sound of the rope chafing against the beam, then looked up in the half-light to see the body turning at the end of the rope. Afterwards local people would not go near the shed after dark. They said that the young man had been heard to say that he would kill himself and come back to haunt the town. They said you felt his presence in the shed. They said you heard a mournful creaking in the darkness.

'I think he's just lonely,' Gordon said. He had read an article in *Readers Digest* explaining the lifetime importance of thinking well of people. The article had explained how to interpret other people's unattractive characteristics that were often a cry for help.

'Lonely your arse,' Davy said. 'The man's clean wicked at heart.'

Afterwards Gordon discovered that Davy often drove a van to the border for the man who owned the amusements to pick up a consignment of cigarettes. Gordon went with him once for company. It was just before dark when they reached the town and drove under the railway bridge towards the border. They stopped at a lounge bar called the Roadhouse, just short of the customs post. Davy lit a cigarette and leaned on the roof of the car looking north towards the line of low hills and the military installation on the top of the largest of the hills overlooking the border. He told Gordon stories of cement and oil being smuggled across the border during the war. He told him of hijackings and beatings and the seizure of contraband. Gordon thought that it had been a mistake to come. He wondered what Desmond would say. He imagined being cross-examined by Desmond in court, words of sorrowful reproach falling from his lips. The roadside here was lined with threadbare businesses. Carpet warehouses, fuel distributors. The strained, hopeful faces of the small businessman. There was little sense of frontier, although in Gordon's mind it seemed that every inch was mapped, storied. With nightfall however an eerie and compelling narrative began to emerge, fictions with a dark edge. The border incursion, the dumped body.

Gordon thought that the railway carriage was homely. He admired the way that Davy could do things with his hands. Davy put up curtains and installed a kerosene stove. Gordon bought a book mail order from the *Daily Telegraph, How to Improve Your Confidence in 99 Easy Steps.*

'Quit your worrying, for fuck's sakes,' Davy told him. 'There's you up to the two eyes in books and me never opened one in my life. All I'm fit for is mending and running after some other fucker's money.'

During his trial and interrogation, Gordon frequently thought about the evenings he had spent in the railway carriage with Davy, the east wind carrying gusts of freezing sleet in across the north channel, the hiss of the Tilley lamp creating an airless and sensual languor, with Davy engaged in a skilled domestic task so that the air seemed full of companionable affinities, unspoken and replete.

During this time, Gordon would see Patricia on the Whiteabbey bus. Often she was on her way to college on her own, her hair pulled back from her face in a way that made her seem withdrawn into a severe interior state. However, if she saw him she would give him a small wave, half-smiling, her face pale and ironical. On Saturdays she went shopping in the city with Hillary Douglas. The two girls sat in the back of the bus, smoking and chatting. This was the side of Patricia that he tried to stress to Chief Superintendent Capstick during his interrogation. He tried to tell him that the Patricia he knew was not the lascivious figure that she had become, the gaunt and sex-haunted woman that had been created through the press. She was a girl who went shopping with her girlfriend on a Saturday.

One day Davy told him that he had seen her getting off the bus in Carlisle Circus. Instead of turning right and walking towards college she had walked up the street towards the bottom of the Lisburn Road. Davy followed her. He did not tell Chief Superintendent that he followed her. She turned left at the Four in Hand public house. She stood at the corner for a moment, looking up and down the street, then a man emerged from a doorway and she stepped into his arms.

The man was wearing a trench coat and a hat pulled down over his eyes. There were beads of rain clinging to the rim of the hat. At the time Davy thought that it was John Steel but after she was dead he was no longer certain. It seemed like a wartime assignation laden with consequence. There were overtones of the illicit, images of betrayal.

Patricia Curran and Hillary Douglas were close friends until they were eighteen. In her statement to the police, Hillary said that they began to grow apart during the summer that Patricia drove the lorry for Fisher, but that they would have grown apart in any case since Patricia had applied for art college whereas Hillary had decided that she wanted to teach at Ballymena Academy and had applied for teacher training college. Inspector McConnell pressed her as to whether she had noticed any changes in Patricia.

'I'm not sure what you mean by changes?'

'I mean, did she give the impression that there was something on her mind? Was she withdrawn?'

'You mean man trouble. Is that what you're trying to say, Inspector?'

'Well, anything that might be troubling her.'

'Are you asking me if she was a virgin? Is that what you want to know?'

'I believe the post-mortem will establish that.'

'Oh yes, of course, slippy old Professor Wells. I'm not sure Patricia would have approved of old Slippy poking in her bits.'

'Please, Miss Douglas. Your friend is dead.'

'Yes, yes, I'm sorry, Inspector. The answer is . . . well, the answer is I don't really know. Patricia wasn't a girl to tell you everything at the best of times.'

'So there is nothing in particular that you are aware of?'

'Nothing. As you know, John Steel was her boyfriend, but to tell the truth he never really had his fingers in the pie, so to speak. Do you mind if I take another smoke?'

'So her relationship with John Steel was not particularly intimate?'

'Well, you know, he was allowed in the garden but he couldn't drink from the fountain, if you follow me. Besides, Johnny had an alibi, or so they say.'

'So you didn't notice if she had changed?'

'I didn't say that.'

'You noticed changes in her?'

'I didn't say that either.'

At the start of the investigation McConnell had sat in on all of the interviews, which at one stage had been running from seven in the morning until eleven at night. After a week of this he divided them into those who had volunteered information and others who were directly involved with the case or who were potential suspects. He assigned two detectives from C division to deal with the first category. There were those who thought they had heard or seen something that night, a car parked in a laneway, a woman's pleading voice, lovers. There were those who felt that the hand of God had fallen upon Patricia Curran and crushed her for a harlot and a Jezebel. There were those who had received signs and portents and those who came to relate tales from their own lives that might prove instructive, or those who were simply carried there on the eerie psychic tide of the murder. People queued in the lobby of the police station. They looked around suspiciously, addressed each other in low, ominous tones. After a few weeks the two detectives felt themselves unable to distinguish one voice. They found themselves prone to elation, profound and elaborate utterances. Their wives regarded them with astonishment. They lay back in their seats and let the incantatory babble wash over them.

McConnell concentrated on those close to the family. He thought that he could detect subtle evasive tones in their voices. That there were aspects of Patricia that they were concealing from him. He kept arriving at these moments. A close friend of the family sitting in front of him, poised on the edge of disclosure.

'What are you trying to tell me, Miss Douglas?'

'I don't know, Inspector. I don't know what I'm trying to say to you. You know, when all the girls in school would talk about doing a thing and it would be just talk, Patricia was the one who would just do it.'

Hillary lifted her eyes from the table and met McConnell's eyes. He was suddenly very aware of the young woman who sat across the table from him, leaning forward, her lips slightly parted so that he would understand what she was saying to him. She told him about lying awake at night sharing secrets, the coded and allusive language the girls used when they talked about boys, the urgency, the way that everything was brought back to the group, the sense of communality, their erotic decorum. Hillary said that when Patricia's parents moved to Whiteabbey Patricia had joined the school but had remained aloof from the schoolgirls' breathless and encrypted sexual dogma.

'She told me she liked men,' Hillary said. 'Big, hard, sophisticated men.'

Patricia had a word for these men. She called them svelte. They watched out for them on their Saturday afternoon trips into the city centre. They went into Anderson Macauley's and observed them shopping with their wives. Patricia would give them coy glances when their wives weren't looking. Patricia said she was looking for signs of interest. She said that she wanted to see if they were bored with their marriage.

It was schoolgirl stuff, Hillary said. But then suddenly it all changed, and Patricia seemed a grown woman, someone in the distance who looked familiar, her just-visible features seeming darkly transcendent.

During late 1951 and early 1952, Patricia's relationship with Doris seems to have deteriorated. The housekeeper, Mrs Crangle, said that she often heard rows.

'The mother never gave over moaning at the poor girl. She never let up. She was always on at her about this or that. Mind you, Patricia could give as good as she got, so she could. The two of them were at it morning, noon and night. The other pair, Desmond and the da, you'd swear to God they never heard nothing the way they acted, the two of them sitting in front room then the Judge goes, I think I'll pop down to the club, and Desmond away with him then, looking to do a bit of preaching or the like.'

Mrs Crangle had little to tell about the detail of the rows. She said there were strong words about clothing, the length of skirts, modesty. She said that the slovenly upkeep of the girl's room was often a subject. Patricia called her mother a snob. However neither of these seemed grounds for the murderous anger described by Mrs Crangle, the gnawed-at familial rage that seemed to have acquired its own dark jargon. Modesty. Slovenly. Words that came freighted with the lore of past arguments. The spat-out words. Snob. Slut.

When he spoke to Mrs Curran, Inspector McConnell formed the impression that the lorry-driving episode was a key turning point in the relationship between mother and daughter. Doris Curran returned to it often. There was something about her daughter at the wheel of a truck. The heavy, leather-covered steering wheel. The burnished chrome, smells of aftershave, diesel, cigarettes. Men with tattoos. Men wearing gold jewellery. A sense of grizzled maleness to the whole business, men's unpredictable and deathsome elations. It seemed to Doris that her daughter could sense her fear, that she brought it into the house with her when she came home from work.

Doris told her bridge partners that Patricia had taken a job as a lady chauffeur, a job that in itself seemed to possess a swarthy transgender quality. Girls in trousers. Girls with caps at jaunty angles and pencil moustaches.

Whiteabbey had become a centre for the weaving and dyeing of linen in the early part of the nineteenth century. The shallow glen leading down to the sea attracted migrant workers from Scotland and the South. It was an industry of harsh, corrosive processes, chemicals, bleaches. The retted linen itself could strip the skin from a hand. There were many public houses and shebeens. The workers fought sectarian battles with hooks, knives. As the linen industry declined in the early part of the twentieth century, faction fights became more commonplace. In the post-war years when Lance Curran bought The Glen, the linen mills had closed and the population of Whiteabbey had shrunk. The murder of Patricia Curran did not want for precedents in the district. Her shed blood did not lack for lineage.

ELEVEN

A few weeks before Patricia's murder, Desmond invited
Iain Gordon to The Glen for Sunday lunch. Gordon ironed
and pressed his uniform. Radford watched him work.

'You're seeing a woman,' he said.

'Going to the Currans for lunch.'

'Going to see the sister. If you wet the material it's easier to get the crease.'

All his life Gordon was surrounded by men who were
steeped in the domestic, who had access to calm, wifely
virtues.

'Desmond asked me for lunch.'

'Getting all dolled up. You're after the sister.'

'As far as I can see Patricia's the only normal one in that
house.'

'What do you mean by that?'

'She'd go out of her way to make you feel at home, if
you know what I mean.'

'I've heard you're not the only man that feels at home
with Patricia Curran.'

'I don't know where you heard that.'

'Come here, you're making a dog's dinner of that.'

Radford came over to the mirror where Gordon was
putting on his tie. He tied it in a Windsor knot, smoothed
the shoulders of his jacket, tugged his sleeves straight then
stood back to look at him.

'You'd swear you was off to the palace to see HM the
Queen herself.'

These were the good things that Gordon remembered
about the barracks. The feeling of being cherished by men.
Being surrounded by these trim, masculine gestures.

Patricia opened the front door for Gordon.

'Oh hello,' she said, then turned to shout over her shoulder. 'Desmond, your little friend is here.'

She was wearing the same calf-length check skirt that she had been wearing on the night she died, with a short-sleeved white cotton blouse and black patent-leather pumps. There was a small clutch bag and a hymnal on the hall table, and two black umbrellas in the hall stand. For some reason he could not explain, Gordon's mind often returned to this scene. The parquet floor, the light shining through the stair window, the girl half-turned in the door-way. It always seemed artificial, extemporised, as if moments before the Currans had sought to lay out a pattern designed to indicate the parameters of untroubled lives.

'Go on into the drawing room,' Patricia said. 'The men withdraw there on a Sunday morning to read their papers. Terribly solemn.'

Desmond was sitting in a low sofa by the window when Gordon came in. He looked up from his paper and rose to meet him. The Judge was sitting by the fire, also reading a paper.

'I'd like you to meet my father. Father, this is Iain Gordon.'

It was the first time that Gordon had met Desmond's father. Radford told him that Judge Curran had pronounced the sentence of death on the murderer McGladdery from Newry. He said that Judge Curran had donned the black silk cap. They had hanged McGladdery. Radford said that a man stretched by up to a foot when he was hanged. Then they buried the body in the prison grounds and sprinkled it with quicklime. An unmarked grave. 'The quicklime burns them up in days,' Radford said. 'It burns them with a pitiless fire.' When he shut his eyes then, Gordon could envisage McGladdery hissing and spluttering in the cold soil. A man's body, long, white and incandescent.

In fact, Radford was trying to frighten Gordon. Judge Curran had never presided over a capital murder case.

The Judge looked up from his paper. Gordon tried to say something but nothing came out. Shyness had always been a problem to him. His mother had enrolled him for activities such as elocution and extempore speaking but he still often found himself in a grievous lack of words. She had bought him a book that said that shyness is a thief that robs us of our rightful ability to communicate with others. Gordon always thought of it as the thief. The Judge regarded him over the top of his glasses as though this were a hearing where Gordon was required to enter a plea in mitigation of his presence. Desmond asked his father if he would have sherry. The Judge continued his examination of Gordon without answering.

In retrospect it is tempting to see the moment as two antagonists sizing each other up for the first time. For it seemed that was what they became, ill-matched opponents: the powerful and subtle Judge, and the thin, nervous young conscript. One of them to attain dominance, the other to endure, their antagonism governed by death and the threat of death.

The Judge returned to his paper. Desmond left the room to get sherry. Gordon sat down on the sofa by the window. The fire crackled. Gordon felt that the Judge was not aware of his presence. In fact, later remarks made by the Judge concerning the apparent strangeness of his son's visitor seemed to show that the Judge had paid considerable attention to Gordon.

Desmond returned to say that lunch was ready. They followed the Judge into the dining room. Patricia and her mother were already seated at the table.

'God but you're a mournful looking bunch,' Patricia said.

'If you're going to misbehave when we have a guest, Patricia,' Doris said.

'But they are, three big sheep's faces.'

'That will do,' Judge Curran said.

'Sorry, Judge. The old dignity not holding up too well this morning?'

'We will have grace now,' the Judge said. They sat with their hands joined while Desmond said a simple grace. Patricia grinned at Desmond from the other side of the table.

'He used to do a ten-minute one but the Judge made him stop.'

'I would prefer to eat luncheon without this kind of schoolgirl giddiness.'

'The Judge likes to do this when we have guests,' Patricia said to Gordon. 'He's fond of acting the big Judge.'

'I will not abide any further discourtesy from my daughter in front of a guest,' the Judge said. Patricia stopped talking. She lowered her eyes to her plate and ate quietly for the rest of the meal. Judge Curran had not raised his voice and Gordon was surprised by how completely Patricia had submitted.

Gordon thought that Judge Curran was the most intimidating man that he had ever met. He was visited by the thief that he called shyness and found himself unable to speak at all. He later told Radford how the Judge 'dominated the room' and how 'there were hardly two words spoke the whole meal after the Judge shut Patricia up'. Desmond seemed comfortable with the tension in the room, so Gordon was led to believe that they often ate their meals in a similar manner. Neither did Doris Curran speak but Gordon saw her look at Patricia with a cold grimace, less a smile than an articulation of a small malice.

It was a scene that Gordon revisited time and time again, the figure of the Judge gathering authority to itself until it seemed less a Sunday meal than a dread assize over which the Judge presided and where the fates of

Patricia and Gordon himself had been adjudicated and measured and handed down.

Gordon's view of the meal was not reinforced by the reported comments of the Curran family in the immediate aftermath of the meal and during the trial. Judge Curran reportedly said that he found Gordon to be a 'strange little man'. And Gordon's empathy with Patricia, his assertion that she seemed to be the most normal member of her family, was apparently not reciprocated. Desmond stated that he had spoken to Patricia and his mother after the meal. He said they also felt that Gordon had something wrong with him and asked Desmond not to bring him back to the house. He then repeated his sister's concluding words. According to Desmond, Patricia's words were: 'After all, Desmond, you have to think of us as well.'

TWELVE

Desmond Curran's religious beliefs attracted a great deal of attention both before and during the trial. He subscribed to the philosophy of Moral Rearmament developed by the American evangelist Frank Buchman. He had come in contact with Buchman's thinking through the Oxford Group. Desmond had attained a double first at Oxford. Followers of Buchman were encouraged to pursue potential converts with 'loving relentlessness', and to elicit 'humble confessions of hideous personal guilt'. It was noted that Desmond had, for several years, been in the habit of haunting public houses, particularly those with a bad reputation, where he would attempt to make contact with those he felt to be susceptible to redemption. Many who had come into contact with Desmond found him strange. He never looked at the person he was speaking to. He sat in profile to them, listening intently, nodding, making occasional pronouncements. It seemed that these incidents foreshadowed his ordination as a priest. That he saw himself in a role as confessor, ministering to the lost. Tearstained young women. Homesick soldiers. That he saw himself leading a drive for souls, a stormy, God-willed mission.

Oxford group agents in America had been known to circulate in hospitals. Through a process of 'personal evangelism', a 'life-changer' would win the confidence of a potential convert, who was led to feel guilt over sin and confess their wrongs to the 'soul-surgeon'.

Desmond took Gordon to revival meetings at the Ulster Hall and to Bible Camp meetings at Carrickfergus and Shaw's Bridge. He attempted to inform him about the five

Cs of Confidence, Conviction, Confession, Conversion and Continuance. Gordon agreed that submission of the will to the Almighty was the way forward. That was the trouble with Gordon. He was eager to agree with everything you said to him. His commanding officer, Wing Commander Richard Popple, said that he found that Gordon was almost too obedient to orders. He never questioned anything. Wing Commander Popple also thought that the RAF was no place for people like Gordon. He thought that a state of dreamy compliance could be a handicap in time of war.

Gordon saw the barber, Wesley Courtney, at several of these meetings. Courtney was always on his own. Like the rest of the men, Courtney wore a sober suit and gleaming shoes. They adopted a military bearing, spoke to each other in precise, clipped phrases. When the ministers spoke they adopted expressions that indicated spiritual rigour. 'Fucking hypocrites,' Courtney said afterwards. 'The same boys'd be begging you for a good seeing-to of a Saturday night.'

There was no doubt, however, that Gordon must have resisted Desmond Curran's proselytizing. There was an unreliable element to his ideas and Gordon possessed a small core of flinty self-reliance and common sense. There was another factor. He wondered what his mother would think of Desmond's ideas. How she would have liked the way that Desmond spoke. That earnest voice.

Frank Buchman became marginalized within his own movement and died in 1961. Photographs of him show a thin man with intense eyes and a long, hooked nose like a Mesozoic bird, beaked and vehement.

Harry Ferguson was in Judge Curran's confidence regarding his reason for resigning from his post as Attorney General. He knew that Curran wanted to be Lord Chief Justice.

'I have no wish to be law agent for a government of fools and timeservers,' Curran had told his agent. Ferguson was worried when he heard that Curran was losing heavily at horses and at the poker table. Even if the stories were untrue, they would damage his reputation. He had met Ivor McDowell a few days beforehand in Chichester Place.

'I hear Curran's in trouble,' McDowell said. 'I hear he's borrowed against that house of his.'

'Judge Curran is nobody's fool.'

'There's a few men in this town making a fool of him with that daughter of his. He'd do well to put a curb on her. Or a bit and bridle before she's rid out.'

Despite this and other rumours, Ferguson decided that he would wait for Curran to contact him. He wasn't surprised when he went into his office one Monday morning to find Curran waiting for him. It was three weeks before Patricia's death.

'Good morning, Ferguson.'

'Good morning, Judge. I hope everybody's well.'

'Oh fine, fine. Desmond seems to be coming along well at the bar.'

'Are Patricia's studies going well?'

'She goes out in the morning. She comes back late at night. I do not enquire.'

'Is there something I can do for you, Judge?'

'Yes, well perhaps. I am in trouble, Harry. I am in over my head. Financially.'

Ferguson had seen Curran's face when a horse he had backed was running. Pale, the lips tightly drawn, the face of a zealot. He wondered how much Curran had lost.

Curran told him that he had remortgaged The Glen to cover losses. However the bank required the deeds of the house, and these had already been given to the bookmaker, Hughes, as security against another loan. He had gone to Hughes. It was a wintry Saturday morning. People flinched from the wind and the driven rain, and black cloud lined the horizon as far as the eye could see. Signage banged and lifted in the wind and litter blew down the road. When the Judge went into Hughes's office, the book-maker had a small gas fire burning beside his desk. There was condensation on the windows, a smell of rain-soaked gabardine. Hughes came around the desk to greet Curran.

'Judge Curran, good morning, good morning, come in.' The fucker's been at the ponies again, Hughes thought. He's after more cash.

'Thank you.'

'Nippy this morning.'

'Indeed.'

'I hope it's not too warm in here for you. My staff like a window open but I think fresh air is for the young.' Not that you were ever young, you dry shite, Hughes thought.

'A drink, Judge?'

'No, thank you,' the Judge said.

Hughes thought that this was a bad sign. 'What can I do for you then, Your Honour?'

'A delicate matter, Mr Hughes.'

A delicate matter, Hughes thought. Flowers is delicate. Children is delicate. As Hughes reached for the desk drawer and the chequebook, the Judge held up his hand.

'Nothing of that sort, Mr Hughes. You have in your pos-session the deeds to The Glen.'

'I do.'

'I require them for a small transaction.'

'I'm not sure about that.'

'They will, of course, be returned to you.'

'I don't think I can do that. Security, Judge, you under-stand. Our arrangement is unsecured.'

The Judge did not speak. He seemed lost in thought. The gas fire spluttered. The rain and wind beat against the window behind the bookmaker and would not relent. Hughes did not know what was going through Curran's thoughts then and said afterwards that he had no mind to know, but that he felt he was in the presence of a man who would not be contradicted or gainsaid, and he half regretted that he did not give him the deeds and be done with it, for he had known enough violent men to feel a stern pathology of hatred emanating from the man in front of him. The Judge then rose and turned towards the door. It was the last time that Curran was to be in the bookmaker's office.

Ferguson was appalled by the Judge's lack of discretion. Owing money to a bookmaker, he told his wife. A Catholic. Did the man have no wit at all? Esther pointed out that the Judge had more sense than Ferguson was giving him credit for. That Protestant professionals often went to Catholic solicitors when they didn't want their business known among their own class, so why should the Judge not go to a Catholic to borrow money? It seemed to be the function of an alcoholic. To act as a curator of sad wisdoms. Ferguson told Curran that he would deal with the situation.

Three days later the RUC raided Hughes's arcade and confiscated the gaming machines. A week after that he received a notice from the Inland Revenue announcing that his accounts were to be audited. Shortly afterwards, Ferguson visited Hughes in his office. He did not take off his hat and Hughes did not offer him a seat. Hughes removed the deeds of The Glen from a drawer and laid them on the desktop. The two men stared at the papers. Ferguson experienced an odd reluctance to reach out for them, and there would in fact be those who would argue after the murder that The Glen itself was subject to an innate corruption, an antique and rancorous malice, which made it an apt setting for violence and death.

In the end, Hughes lifted the documents and handed them to Ferguson. Ferguson walked towards the door and turned.

'You'll get your money,' he said. 'Every red cent of it.'

That September, Patricia Curran had enrolled as an art student at the Queen's University, Belfast. None of her fellow students seemed to remember her particularly well, although one student said that she seemed a pleasant, happy girl. Another remarked that she seemed self-possessed, more mature than her classmates. Because they were art students they thought that they should be more affected than others by her death. They cast around for a response. They struck poses of brooding inarticulacy. The more astute among them were able to detect moments of terrible poignancy in her last few weeks. The truth was that they barely knew her. What was in fact significant was that she had passed through their lives and left only a barely discernible trace, an intimation of young life wasted.

The week before her death she had attended her first life class. The class was held in an airy room at the top of the college. Patricia told Hillary about it. She said that the model was fat.

'Disgusting, a porker.'

'There was something lovable about her.'

'Don't be dense, Patricia. A big, lumpy thing.'

'No, honestly.'

'A hippo.'

'I think she fancies me.'

'Oh, Patricia, don't tell me the rotten thing has been making eyes at you?'

The model's name was Olga. She was sleek when naked, given to half-closing her eyes when posing. Patricia had been told that you felt nothing for the model when you were drawing them, that their bodies presented a series of problems to be resolved, but Olga seemed to defy this advice. In the heat of the room and the advancing afternoon her eyes seemed to sleepily follow each movement of Patricia's pencil and a kind of knowingness seemed to hang in the air, a sexual miasma.

Hillary remembered how Patricia had told her about this. She remembered it during the trial, when the pathologist produced the autopsy photographs to be shown to the jury and she thought for the first time about her friend in a mortuary, her body, nude and forlorn, surrounded by middle-aged men who bent to their task as though she still owed them unchaste servitude. As though an account had fallen due, as though they were to be indemnified in her very flesh. She had a glimpse of one of the photographs as a juror turned it in his hand, pale flesh against a dark background, with cutting instruments placed in rows alongside and a man's hand at the very edge of the photograph, as though to remind the viewer that claim was laid to this flesh, that this was not an abstract composition.

Patricia had told Hillary how she had seen Olga one night at York Street bus station with another woman, a thin and mannish creature, Patricia said, smoking a cigarette. When she saw Olga looking at Patricia the woman put her arm through Olga's arm and stared defiance at Patricia. 'What did you do then?' Hillary said, but Patricia seemed lost in thought and did not answer, for she remembered how she had watched the two women walk off together and how the thin woman had turned as they reached the roadway and glanced back over her shoulder, the skin of her face pockmarked under the streetlight, her eyes gleaming with hunger and sadness as though subject to a ravenous need that could not be assuaged.

During the summer, Patricia played tennis with Hillary, but as winter drew in she played badminton with Steel in the university courts at Curzon Street, to which she had access now that she was a student. It was a parquet-floored Victorian gym, a large and echoing place with tiled changing rooms, the foyer lined with photographs of flint-eyed female athletes engaged in feats of chilly prowess. Patricia wore a crisp, pleated white skirt and blouse when she played. A dress code was clearly displayed on the wall of the women's locker rooms.

'These knickers they make you wear,' she told Steel. 'I swear they'll cut off the blood supply and my legs will fall off.' She saw the expression on Steel's face. 'I'm sorry, Johnny', she said. 'I don't really mean to shock you.' She touched his face in the way she always touched him, with a wondering tenderness, as if she did not quite believe in the substance of him.

When she played badminton she did so with intensity. She was muscular and aggressive, throwing herself into serves and volleys, clenching the racket as she waited for his serves, with an ardent, undaunted look. In the following years he was to wonder why she had not attempted to fight off her attacker, and had sustained no knife wounds on her hands and forearms.

But what he remembered from these times was walking Patricia to the bus at night. It was autumn, almost winter. There was a sense of midterm lull. There were few students in the gym and the streets after dark were almost empty. Sometimes Steel felt as if he had been manipulated. That all the elements of these evenings had been set in place just as he arrived. The beautiful girl whose life was to be brutally cut short. The rustling of autumn leaves, the empty streets, the sound of footsteps and a young couple's laughter as they walk home late at night. They seemed like scenes that were the creation of an arch and brooding sentimentalist, smothered with lethal detail. The smell of wet earth in the park. A snatch of song from an open window.

THIRTEEN

Doris Curran had been brought up to express herself when she thought that someone was in the wrong. Her grandfather was a Lutheran minister, a stern-visaged rural evangelist given to sermons of bare and unpitying revelation. He said that a man who did not offer guidance to a sinner or try to prevent the commission of a sin was defiled by the same sin. He was much exercised by moral turpitude in society at large. Doris was often taken to meetings by her mother. Her grandfather preached in a big marquee that was set up in fields throughout the district. His congregation were attracted to the utilitarian outdoors feel of tent worship. They thought themselves to be sturdy and dependable, given to the stoical toleration of hardship. The tents gave an impression of pioneer privation that they liked.

Doris seemed to have spent much of her childhood in these tents. People sat on folding wooden chairs and benches. On winter nights the tents were lit by Tilley lamps suspended from the ceiling. In the dim, flickering light, their faces seemed etched and unforgiving. Doris sat among them as a child, isolated in the middle of stony formalists.

She often said that as a result she held strong views on matters of a moral nature. Her grandmother had told her that a young lady's deportment was a good indicator of her moral condition. She thought that a young lady's carriage was as important as her education. Doris often said to Patricia, 'Shoulders back, chin up,' for all the difference that it made. She had thought that college would bring maturity to Patricia but it had not, and to make matters worse she had chosen to study the subject of art, to spite her mother perhaps, because Patricia well knew that it would give scandal.

Things had been tense in The Glen over the previous few months. Judge Curran had been spending little time at home. Doris harboured a suspicion of financial concerns but she did not pry. Render unto Caesar was a saying she was proud to abide by. On the occasions when the Judge was at home, such as Sunday lunch, he had recently been given to disseminating instructions and rules regarding the household like a taciturn and guileful chancellor issuing edicts. For instance, one lunchtime he made Doris and the children place their keys on the dining-room table. He put them in his pocket and said that for security reasons he would only issue a key when needed. Patricia, to her mother's certain knowledge, possessed a second key, which she would use to let herself in late at night. Doris knew this because Desmond's bedroom was above the hallway and he would hear her effect an illicit entry.

As for Doris, she often had to climb through a downstairs window with a broken catch if there was no one else in the house, or if she had forgotten to ask the Judge for a key. She lived in mortal fear that one of the ladies of the Unionist Ladies Association or the Bridge Club would come up the drive when she was climbing through the window. Once, Mrs Hazel Grahame came collecting money for the Red Cross just as Doris was about to prise open the window, but Doris had the quick wit to frown and say, 'Oh, Mrs Graham, I seem to have forgotten my key,' and Mrs Graham was sympathetic and told her about an episode when she had also forgotten her key. Doris was a little flushed because of the untruth. She told Desmond about it later, however, and he agreed that it had been quick-witted.

'You must face up to these people,' Desmond told her.

One of Desmond's beliefs was that you must defeat the causes of your fear.

Desmond told her about Patricia coming in late and also other goings-on regarding Patricia, but she knew there were things that Desmond wasn't telling her through regard for his mother's well-being. However, there were also sly enquiries from other ladies in the district, asking as sweet as pie after Patricia although you knew there was always a false purpose to their questions. Doris did not blame them so much as she blamed her daughter. Lack of obedience and giving scandal were worse matters in her book than simple gossip.

Doris Curran's marriage to a prominent and respected man should have been a source of comfort to her. She remembered her pride on the day of their marriage. She often looked back to that day for an omen, something to foreshadow the dread that grew within her day after day. It seemed that she could no longer remember her happiness from that day. All she could remember was a ceremony performed in front of a congregation of ashen-faced elders. It was why she could never look at the newspapers in the weeks and months that followed Patricia's death. They kept using that photograph. The one of Patricia in the cowl-neck white dress like a wedding dress, looking out at you with terrible authority, as though death had rendered her a haughty and autocratic bride.

One day in November when she was in the kitchen she heard the front door. She heard Mrs Crangle's voice and a gentleman's voice. Doris wasn't sure if she was fond of Mrs Crangle. She thought that she might be a carrier of tales. Doris knew that she could not run the house without her and she felt that this was an unsatisfactory situation. Then Mrs Crangle came into the kitchen and said that Dr Wilson wanted to see her. A few days later Dr Wilson would be the first medical man to examine Patricia's body when it was brought to his surgery and it was Dr Wilson who thought that the knife wounds on her body were caused by shotgun pellets. Nevertheless he was a competent doctor who seemed surprised that Judge Curran had not informed his wife that he had asked the family GP to call on her.

'What does the problem seem to be, Mrs Curran?'

Doris didn't know. 'I don't know why my husband called you.' She felt helpless. This is what she meant about the world. The way it came up on you unawares. She thought that Judge Curran must have had a reason for what he was doing. She was confused.

Dr Wilson examined her. Blood pressure, pulse. He asked her gently if she suffered from spells of any nature. He said that he had heard that there were tensions between herself and Patricia as arose in any family. Afterwards Doris was ashamed to have unburdened herself but she told Dr Wilson that Patricia had been examined by Professor Glenny of Altnagelvin who had made enquiries after a condition he referred to as sexual precocity.

'You had the child examined by a psychiatrist?'

'She refused to behave, Dr Wilson.'

'And did Professor Glenny recommend any form of treatment?'

The professor had told Doris that the child appeared to be normal if somewhat withdrawn. He did not recommend any form of treatment.

'Why did you take Patricia to Professor Glenny?'

Doris Curran started to say something about her mother and then stopped. Her mother had been prone to turns which her grandfather ascribed to hysterics of the womb. Doctor Wilson did not make any further enquiries. Before he went he paused.

'If there is ever anything you want to discuss, Mrs Curran, please . . .' Dr Wilson did not finish the sentence. He was wearing a tweed jacket and carrying a leather bag with his initials stencilled on it in gold. He seemed the epitome of the kindly country doctor, silver-haired, solicitous, prudent. The attention to detail is meticulous. A minor character but one determined to imbue his role with an air of competent integrity, to make each action appear thought-out, crafted.

Doris Curran had avoided raising the subject of a row between Judge Curran and Patricia on the previous Saturday. Doris had arrived home from shopping in Hillsborough and had thought the house empty. She climbed in through the window with the broken catch and was on her way to the kitchen to make a cup of tea when she heard the sound of raised voices from the drawing room. Already the moment seemed to be gathering dramatic elements to itself. The raised voices. The overheard conversation. The stealthy approach of the listener. From the corridor Doris could see the dining-room table. Patricia and the Judge were standing in front of the fireplace, beside the table. Patricia had a brown envelope in her hand. There was something in Patricia's stance that Doris well recognized as defiance. They were staring at each other as if harsh words had been exchanged.

This is a side to Patricia that has not yet been seen. Her father's daughter. Her father's equal.

Doris had noticed before that her daughter and husband both had full mouths that turned down at the corners. In Patricia it was the look of a person who had smeared lipstick, a grubby, carnal look. In the Judge it was an expression of subtle satisfaction as of bitterness assuaged. Doris was too afraid to move. She was convinced that they would turn and see her in the hallway but they stared at each other without moving and when the Judge came to speak it seemed stern beyond the moment, as though he carried within him a timeless authority of admonishment between father and child.

'You are my daughter. It is not your place to adjudicate on my affairs.'

'It is my place if my home is concerned.'

'Your home was established by me, is supported by me and will be disposed of by me if and when I see fit.'

'You've spent all our money, haven't you? The Judge has spent all the money and that's why you have the deeds, to get more money. I know what you are doing.'

'I don't doubt you know more than you should and that knowledge does not become you. To hear bar-room gossip from your daughter in your own house.'

'My father the Judge. The bar-room gossips say that Mr Justice Curran lost a whole year's salary in one night in the Reform Club. Is that the knowledge that doesn't become me?'

'It is of no consequence to me what your companions and hangers-on might say in their slops, what you might overhear in the middens you frequent.'

'The Reform Club is a respectable place, is that what the Judge says?'

'Please give me the deeds, Patricia. They are very important legal documents.'

Doris could see Patricia hesitate. The Judge's tone had changed. His voice was gentle with a note of weary indulgence. The father addresses the child after a long day. A tone of wry regard. The fond, roamed-over territory between fathers and daughters. Doris could see that Patricia did not know what to do. You may plead with her, Doris thought. You might as well plead with the wind.

'No, I will not.'

'Give them to me or you will not see one shilling from me for tuition or upkeep. Give them to me or you will leave The Glen and house yourself in some slattern's kip, for it is what your reputation demands.'

Doris watched as Patricia handed over the documents. She gave them as if she was relinquishing all rights and bequests of her line. Doris knew that the Judge's threats had not forced her hand. She understood that Patricia had withheld the deeds so that she could elicit the response that she had, that she should plumb the full depths of the Judge, who was now bent over the deeds, going through them with a kind of greed as though he was besotted with the parchment itself, the smooth vellum, its historic linkage of name and place, the fidelity that it represented. Patricia watched him. That downturned mouth.

The mother looking on from the hallway. She thought that she had witnessed something that it was unseemly for her to see. She thought that Patricia had reduced her to a spy in her own house, as though she had been dispatched on a mission, a perilous and unwholesome espionage on the things that passed between fathers and daughters.

Hillary Douglas said that Patricia rarely talked about things that happened at home, although there were occasions when she was quiet and Hillary thought that she seemed upset. If she did talk about anyone she talked about Desmond. 'My sainted brother.' Hillary thought that Desmond was 'funny'. He made her uncomfortable. Patricia told her stories that Desmond wore hair shirts and got up at four o'clock in the morning to lash his own back with a whip while reciting prayers the way that Catholics did. Hillary was sure that Patricia was joking but she could not help thinking about it when she saw Desmond, and remembered what Patricia had said about his risen body pale and cold in the 4.00 a.m. darkness. The mortified flesh. Hillary asked her father, the Presbyterian minister, if it was true that Roman Catholics did indeed mortify the flesh. Her father replied that if they mortified the flesh more and pleasured it less they would make better citizens. Desmond was modern and peculiar in his practices sometimes but he was not a Roman Catholic.

Sometimes Hillary pictured Desmond naked, his body cold and refined, as if engaged in the practice of a cold, bloodless sexuality that both frightened and attracted her. She knew that her mother thought that Desmond and Hillary would make 'a nice match'. Patricia laughed at her when she confided this. 'Imagine our Desmond coming at you on your wedding night. Poor Desmond,' she said, 'he wouldn't know what to do.' Hillary, however, was not so sure. She could see him coming towards her, a prayer on his lips, a cold, cloistered smell. Patricia said that her mind was warped with being brought up in damp church property. 'Besides,' she said, 'you don't look like a homo.'

'Do you think Desmond is one?' Hillary asked. 'Do you think he's queer?'

'I don't know,' Patricia said. 'Better hope for your sake he is. I'm not sure. He's got a lot of homo friends, though.'

'So do you,' Hillary said. It was true that some of the men who went to the Orchid Blue made a point of being seen with Patricia. They allowed her to adjudicate on their disputes, offer romantic advice. They hardly knew why they were drawn to her, although after her death they maintained that they had seen it in her, that she would die young, that she possessed a calamitous flamboyance that made it inevitable. Wesley Courtney laughed at them. 'Bunch of fucking fairies,' he told Gordon. Gordon thought they seemed gentle and unworldly.

On the night following Patricia's confrontation with her father, Patricia and Hillary were in Hillary's bedroom. Patricia used the mirror then sat on the bed while Hillary applied her make-up. In the mirror Hillary saw that Patricia was weeping in a discreet, self-absorbed manner. Hillary thought that Patricia cried like somebody in the pictures. It disturbed her. She had never seen Patricia cry before. She seemed to achieve a soft-focus quality, the glistening eyes, the single tear rolling down the cheek. The face turned upward with a pleading look, gently aspirant to noble causes of the heart. Hillary was afraid to disturb her at first, to break into her reverie, but when Patricia kept on crying she sat down on the bed beside her. She did not place her hand on her hair or her shoulder. There was a formality in their relationship, a well-bred Victorian reserve in physical matters.

'Patricia?'

'I'm all right.'

'It's too rotten to see you crying, Patricia.'

'I'm all right, honestly I am. It's just the Judge was mean to me today.'

'Silly old Judge. What did he say?'

'He called me a slattern.'

'Oh, Patricia. Is that like a slut?'

'More or less. I think a slattern is a little more sophisti-cated. Fewer men of better quality.'

'Then you're definitely not a slattern.'

'No?'

'No, you're obviously a slut.'

They began to laugh, abandoning themselves to the laughter like children, a rhythmic hilarity with a hysteric edge working their way back to innocence, a pre-teen wholesomeness, making inelegant snorting noises, their bodies shaking, tears running down their faces.

Afterwards they lay on the bed, side by side, staring at the ceiling, prey to a nostalgia that neither of them could define. They had planned to go out that night. Instead they went to the attic and dragged down a tea chest of Hillary's old clothes and emptied it onto her bed. They took out old dresses, school uniforms, drab utility clothes they had dyed with cold-water dyes, summer hats, scarves, stockings beaded with nail polish where they had been repaired. They held them against themselves. They tried them on and posed for each other: water-spotted, sun-bleached, frayed, timeworn. They worked their way into a hapless and sentimental frame of mind. They began to realize what they had lost with these badly made wartime garments, poorly stitched, threadbare, began to detect a bare subtext to them, a plaintive theme involving loss of innocence, the inevitability of lapsed friendship, loss, betrayal.

Their mood became quieter. Gradually they abandoned the clothes on the floor and draped on the bed. Hillary went downstairs and returned with a box of photographs. They sat beside each other on the bed and opened the first album. Hillary showed her photographs of her grandparents, the Lutheran preacher and his wife: grim, etched, northern. Her grandfather was given to speaking in tongues, delivering himself of a gnarly bespoke jargon culminating in something that sounded like a devout static, a refrain of sonic howls and crackles. There were copperplate engravings of her ancestors from the middle of the last century: cheerful, self-made looking men with muttonchop whiskers, who seemed to grasp the essence of engraving, the idea of processes, fine tools, the presence of toxic fumes.

Hillary remembered that Patricia seemed to know little about her own father's past. She said that her grandfather was a 'bloody old butcher' from Larne. She said she had never seen a photograph of him.

They looked at photographs of Hillary's parents next. They were hesitantly approaching the melancholy subject of themselves and their girlhood. Hillary's parents on their wedding day. The girls wondered at how young and awkward Reverend and Mrs Douglas looked. They were surrounded by untrusting and watchful elders, devotees of a sect centred on stoic vigilance. There were photographs of Hillary as a baby, her parents leaning over her in her cot, Hillary as a girl wearing heavy black shoes and a knitted cap, looking stocky and sensible, given to long country walks, the study of fauna. 'Sensible Sam,' Hillary whispered, 'that's what they used to call me.' Then they came to the pictures of Hillary and Patricia, which started when the Currans had moved to Whiteabbey. They barely spoke now as they looked at these. From the start there was a sense of girlhood complicity, of coltish plenitude about them. They looked at themselves on the beach wearing swimming caps and old-fashioned bathing costumes that flattened their hips and breasts and gave them the bulky stance of long-distance swimmers, the sense of fleshy endurance. 'Two big puddings,' Hillary said. There were photographs of them at a motor car rally in Lady Dixon's Park, on an excursion by train to Portstewart, standing beside the Reverend Douglas's car on an outing to the country, and finally on their way to their debutantes' ball, the dress that Patricia wore with hand-sewn sequins, Hillary's hair up like Grace Kelly, the kid gloves that reached the elbow, a sense of achieved womanhood as they stood together on the front steps of The Glen, fixing the camera with that Vogue look.

Too gorgeous, Hillary said. They stared at these for a long time. Eventually Patricia got up from the bed. She looked pale. She told Hillary that she had decided to go out after all. 'I have to say,' Hillary later told McConnell, 'I threw a smallish wobbly. Father would never have let me go out so late. I got in a snit,' she said. Patricia left. A violent disagreement, McConnell wrote.

It was to be the last time that Hillary saw Patricia. Two weeks later she was dead.

However she heard that Patricia had indeed gone out that night. She had been seen in the Orchid Blue, the International Hotel and later at the Belvedere on the Lisburn road. Those who saw her reported that she looked as if she was going to a ball, or a debs, costumed rather than dressed, even though there were no such functions on in the city that night and if there were surely she would have been accompanied; others maintained that there was indeed an escort, one that accounted for her deathly pallor, the way she drank and refused conversation with others, and that, at the end of the night, she was seen in the middle of the dance floor on her own, dancing with jerky reluctant steps as though she took her lead from a sure-footed and macabre suitor.

FOURTEEN

12 November 1952. It was to rain all day, events taking place under cover of low cloud and drizzle. The rain offered concealment, scenes of dripping leaves, early twilight. At The Glen, Lance Curran was the first to rise. Mrs Crangle carried tea into the dining room, where the Judge was joined by Desmond. Patricia came downstairs just as they were finishing breakfast.

'Can you never be on time?' Desmond said. 'What time did you come in last night anyway?'

'I'd say you know that anyway, nosy Dessie, lying awake at night waiting for his little sister to come home.'

'I'd like to know the owner of the car that took you home,' Desmond said, 'and what it was doing parked on the drive for over an hour.'

'God, you're so nosy.'

'I don't think strange cars should be in our driveway at night.'

'It felt nice and safe with my brother guarding us.' Patricia leaned across the table as the Judge got up and walked to the sideboard to pour more coffee.

'We were having nookie,' she whispered. 'I wish he'd shaved though, my chin is raw.' She could see Desmond's face turning red.

'You are a spiteful girl,' he said. 'Spiteful, commonplace and licentious.'

The Judge returned to the table. 'Patricia, please ask your mother to come downstairs. I have something to say.'

Doris Curran often stayed in bed in the morning. When they moved to The Glen she took a bedroom at the rear of the house. The Judge slept in the main bedroom. She said that she slept badly. She said that dark things came to her room at night and that she only really slept after dawn had come. Patricia, whose room was across the corridor, often heard her voice at night. She sometimes lapsed into her old accent when talking in her sleep. 'Take thon hand off me. You've no mission in this here house.' A fearful nocturnal dialect.

That morning she met Patricia on the stairs. Patricia informed her that the Judge wanted to speak to the family. They went into the dining room and sat down and Judge Curran informed them that he would be selling The Glen. No one spoke. Doris looked to Desmond but he was silent and she realized that Judge Curran must have already informed Desmond of his decision. Patricia sat white-faced.

'Our financial affairs have not been proceeding as I might have wished,' the Judge said. 'We shall have to move to a smaller house and effect some economies. I am afraid, Patricia, that we can no longer afford your tuition fees.'

Later that morning the Judge's black Humber car left The Glen with Judge Curran driving and Desmond in the passenger seat. Shortly afterwards, Patricia was seen waiting for the Belfast bus at the bus stop just before the entrance to The Glen. She was carrying an art portfolio and several books. She was wearing a yellow Juliet cap and a yellow silk scarf belonging to Hillary Douglas. Doris Curran stayed in the house until lunchtime and then she too left, taking the two o'clock bus into the city. Mrs Crangle was the only person to spend the entire day in The Glen.

When she was asked afterwards if she had noticed anything unusual, Mrs Crangle said that she hadn't paid much attention. They were all quiet with each other, she said, but they were all that odd anyhow that she never paid it too much mind. She thought that Mrs Curran was, if anything, more talkative than usual after the others had left. She was like that, Mrs Crangle explained. Sometimes you couldn't look sideways at her with the big cross head on her and not two words to say for herself. Other times she would talk the two ears off the outside of your skull and it would all be 'Do you really think so, Mrs Crangle?' and 'I'm sure I agree, Mrs Crangle.'

Judge Curran was presiding at Larne Assizes that day. He dropped Desmond at the law library in Chichester Street and drove to Larne. Mr H. J. Jones, the clerk of Larne court that day, later said that the Judge's bearing did not seem any different. 'You know Judge Curran,' he said. 'You wouldn't exactly read him like a book.' Meanwhile Desmond defended the case of a youth who had gone to the house of an elderly man on the outskirts of the city with the intention of robbing him. When the old man had resisted, the youth had beaten him and fractured his skull. Before the case was heard Desmond went to the cells below the courthouse. The youth was in the cells on his own. Desmond handed him a tract entitled 'The Priesthood of All Believers'.

'What the fuck is this?' the youth asked.

'You may find it helpful,' Desmond said.

'What I would find helpful is for you to get up on your two hind legs in that courtroom and get me out of here, you sideways-looking fucker,' the youth said.

Patricia Curran spent that morning in the life room on the top floor of the art college choosing drawings for an upcoming assessment. She met John Steel for lunch and told him that she couldn't concentrate and that she was going to take the drawings home in her portfolio. She arranged to meet him to play squash later that day.

Harry Ferguson had arranged to meet Judge Curran for lunch at the Stormont Hotel. He said that the Judge appeared to be in good form. Curran could be like that, Ferguson had found. Some days you would find him animated, sardonic. He had a gift for mimicry and would caricature those appearing in front of him in court, and their counsel. It was to be the last time that Ferguson was to see that side of the Judge's character. There were those who argued that the events of that night were to weigh almost unbearably upon the Judge, that he was never the same man after that. Others maintained that the Judge merely adopted the persona of a man burdened with sorrow by the death of a child. That he deliberately slowed his step and bowed his shoulders to give him authority in court. A man who had lost his daughter. They said that he drew an authority from it. It was the kind of thing referred to often by those who saw him at a distance. His housekeeper, the newsagent who delivered his newspaper. The man was never the same after it.

There were some who suspected that his troubled disposition was genuine but that it was not caused by the loss of his daughter alone, but by the circumstance of her murder and his own involvement in the events of that night.

Iain Hay Gordon spent that morning typing requisition forms for the Stores. His typing was slow and laborious and he had recently begun a Pitman typing course in order to improve it. Every half an hour or so, Radford came in to see if the requisitions were ready.

'Hurry up, Gordon, for God's sake. The RAF's at a bloody standstill waiting for you.'

Despite Radford's interruptions and his own slowness, Gordon enjoyed the work. The black Bakelite case of the typewriter. The oiled gunmetal keys. He liked the precision and sureness of the instrument. The sense of well-engineered components, hair's-breadth clearances. He was alone in the typing pool that morning. There was a portrait of the Queen above the fireplace. A strong smell of paraffin came from the heater in the corner of the room, steam rose from the wet coats on the coat stand inside the door and the rain ran down the outside of the window beside him. You had a sense of obscure clerkship, small deeds on the periphery of an empire in slow but inevitable decline. Gordon finished the forms just before lunch and carried them across to Stores.

'About bleeding time,' Radford said. 'We would've lost the bleeding war if you'd have been in the RAF then. It'd be all "Yes sir, Mr Hitler," if you'd been about, ain't that right, Gordon?'

After Radford had checked the forms he locked the Stores and they walked across to the canteen for lunch. Radford complained about the weather.

'Fucking awful. Mind you it probably suits a miserable bastard like you. Happy to get rained on.'

In the canteen the men were talking about the NAAFI dance that was to take place that night. The dance was held once a year in a hangar at the Bishopscourt base. As they talked it emerged that everyone at the base except Gordon was going to the dance and would not be back at the barracks until 2.30 a.m. Some of the men tried to persuade Gordon to come, but he refused politely. Politeness costs nothing, his mother said, and the price of rudeness is too high to pay. He felt that if he was going to be unhappy and alone he would rather be in the barracks instead of at a dance: the smell of cigarette smoke and perfume in the air, the interplay of glances and laboured-over impression of feminine mystique. It was not that Gordon did not like to be around women. It was the dismissive dance-hall look that he disliked. The look that slid over you: objective, appraising, feral.

He preferred the barracks when everyone was gone. The steel-frame beds and long tiled corridors. The smells of boot polish and Brasso. He liked the brown blankets on the beds and the crisp cotton sheets folded tight at the top. There was a sense of manliness about the place, of utilitarian virtues expressed and formalized. Sometimes when he was alone in the sleeping quarters he would lie on his bed and breath in the smell of Brylcreem and Palmolive Brushless and underneath it all the rank-scented odours of all the men's bodies that had lain on the narrow horsehair mattresses, their pale conscript limbs and narrow torsos.

Ferguson spent the morning in court. He had a small solicitor's practice in Carrickfergus. Afterwards he went back to the office. He signed letters, legal aid forms. He had specialized in criminal and family law. It seemed to meet the criteria for atonement he had set himself. Everything else was in hand. The office window looked across a narrow street into the upstairs windows of an electrical contractor. The two upper floors were both full of brown cardboard cartons containing deep freeze cabinets, washing machines, televisions, with long corridors in between. He remembered that Esther would always save the packaging when she bought something. She folded the cellophane carefully, replaced the packaging in the exact shape of the object, replaced staples and carried the box carefully to the attic as though by such action she could preserve a taintless memory of the object itself and confer indemnity against spoil.

The two secretaries moved around the dimly lit office. Typing up letters, photocopying statements, applying for injunctions. Files were removed from cabinets, files were returned. He recognized the details of each folder, each separation, committal, neglect, mindless battery as acts of heartsick transcendence. And he knew that the two women moving from filing cabinet to desk in the glassy light of a back-street office would move with the same unremitting fluidity if they were not in his office but in an annexe of a dispensary of human accountability, where their job was to assign the crime to be committed, the vow to be broken.

It was a slow day in Wesley Courtney's barber shop. Thursdays were always slow as most working men were not due to be paid until the following evening, so that there was no spare money. Courtney sat at a high stool with a leatherette seat at the window and watched people going past. Occasionally a man walking down the street would look up and see Courtney's fleshy full-lipped face staring at him from the window like a licentious and malodorous fetish placed there as token of a half-remembered malice. Most of the time the men would look away but sometimes their gaze would be held as though an awful and ungovernable sentiment within them had responded to Courtney and they were helpless to avert their eyes.

At four o'clock Courtney moved away from the window. The school buses from the city arrived in Whiteabbey at four o'clock. Several years before a Sergeant Annett had taken to positioning himself across the street from Courtney's as the schoolchildren got off. Courtney had taken the hint. He placed the cardboard CLOSED sign on the window and took off his blue nylon jacket. He had heard that the NAAFI dance was on that night. He stepped out onto the rain-blown street and closed and locked the door behind him.

Doris Curran went shopping that afternoon. It was the era of department stores. Brightly lit shops with elaborate chandeliers and wide curved stairs with mahogany handrails and authoritative names. Robinson & Cleaver's. Anderson Macauley's. These shops were constructed to convey a sense of strong values, moral purpose. They were dedicated to commercial dynamism within limits, and to this end management staff wore dark suits and were seen on the shop floor. Doris did most of her shopping at Robinson & Cleaver's, where they had an account and the saleswomen knew her by name. She had a dread of false accusation of theft or of being asked to please step into the office, Madame.

Doris Curran took a taxi back to The Glen. She didn't have a key and climbed in through the bedroom window. She later told Inspector McConnell that she had arrived there 'sometime after six'.

Patricia had arranged to play squash with Steel that afternoon. They met outside the Carlton cinema and walked up to the gym. Patricia had brought an umbrella so they shared it, pressed close together, as they walked. Patricia seemed to accumulate images about her that day. The kind of images that photographers look for when they are attempting to find a study of grimy, mid-century atmospherics. The elegant young couple walking together under an umbrella in the rain. The cigarette smouldering in the ashtray, lipstick on its tip. McConnell later asked Steel if he had 'noticed anything different' about Patricia. Whether there appeared to be 'anything on her mind'. To Steel it appeared that the policeman wasn't asking for evidence of a crime but for a sign that she was already in the vicinity of death, that she was within its spectral confine and had conceded part of herself to it, a faint odour of ashes about her, of grave cloth. Steel said that there appeared to be nothing wrong. They had walked as far as the gym where they were told that there was no squash court available.

'That's a bit of a nuisance,' Steel said.

'I'm glad, to tell the truth,' she said. 'I'm tired out. Je suis fatiguée.' Dark-eyed with fatigue, her cheeks hollow.

'What do you want to do?'

Patricia decided that they would go to the park. When they got there they sat in the bandstand and she leaned her head against his shoulder. He bent his head to kiss her. She didn't move.

'I'm tired,' she said. Ashen-faced. Quietly spoken. After some time they left the park and walked slowly back towards York Street bus station. Lighting-up time on 12 November 1952 was at 4.52 p.m. but the rain and low cloud made it seem dark and many cars were using their lights as they passed in front of the City Hall. When they got to the bus station Patricia said that she had half an hour to spare. They went into the Sorrento Café for coffee.

The young couple sat in the window. You could not see them clearly from outside because condensation had formed on the inside of the window but you could make out the figures of a young man and a young woman. Sometimes the girl makes a gesture, an awkward shape with her hand bent at the wrist. Sometimes the young man leans towards her but we cannot hear what he is saying and there is no way of finding out. No one asked them at the time and now John Steel is dead.

They left the café shortly before five. Patricia gave her books, folder and squash racquet to Steel to hold. She went to a kiosk to buy cigarettes. The bus terminus began to fill with servicemen in uniform, shoppers, people travelling home from work, bound for the outlying towns of Whiteabbey, of Greyabbey, Glengormley, Larne, Lisburn. The hiss of brakes. The sound of provincial destinations being called over the Tannoy. Newcastle, Dundrum, Kilkeel. York Street bus station was a Victorian building, constructed along the lines of a railway station with a vaulted ceiling of glass and wrought iron, which lent a middle-European dignity and import to the small towns that the station served. You lose sight of Patricia Curran in the crowd but there are other self-possessed young women there. They are wearing berets and smoking cigarettes and there is a *fin de siècle* air of mild intrigue.

Wednesday night was Judge Curran's poker night at the

Reform Club, and normally he would not be home until after midnight. However on 12 November he took a taxi home. When the taxi arrived at 6.40 p.m., Judge Curran was waiting on the steps of the club. When they arrived at The Glen, Stevenson, the taxi driver, noticed that the Judge couldn't open the front door with his key, as it appeared to be bolted from the inside. Stevenson said that as he drove off he could see Judge Curran going round the side of the house.

Patricia returned with her cigarettes and took her books and squash racket back from Steel. They walked slowly towards the bus. Steel kissed her and she joined the queue.

'You don't have to wait,' she said.

'That's all right,' he said. 'I'm in no hurry.' He stood against a pillar with the collar of his trench coat turned up against the rain. Every so often she looked up from the queue and gave him a small smile, then she mounted the steps of the bus. As the bus pulled off Steel saw her sitting towards the back of the bus and he expected her to wave to him but she seemed lost in reverie. He looked at the clock, which said it was five o'clock. In fact it was ten past five as the clock was running ten minutes slow.

It took forty minutes for the bus to reach Whiteabbey. The bus was full leaving the terminus and people were forced to stand, but by the time it reached Whiteabbey it was almost empty. The conductor, Harold Hamilton, took a seat at the front of the bus and began to tot up the total fares for that evening to reconcile them to the tickets issued. The bus slowed as it approached the stop outside The Glen and he looked up as Patricia, who had been sitting at the back of the bus, passed him to get off. She held on to the edge of his seat as the bus came to a halt. She was carrying an umbrella and squash racquet in one hand and books and a small folder tied together with a leather strap in the other, which made it awkward for her to hold on.

Asked if he was sure that it was Patricia Curran, since

she was standing with her back to him, he said that when she got off the bus she stood on the pavement to put up her umbrella and as the bus drove off she looked up and her saw her white face caught in the light.

Five forty. There was a small gatehouse at the entrance to The Glen, a low-roofed white building, slated in Bangor blue. Like the house to which it belonged, the gatehouse had paint that was starting to peel and there was an air of general neglect. The low stone pillars of the gateposts were crafted in Italianate style but they too were dirty and unkempt. Patricia stood by the lodge. She lit a cigarette because her mother had forbidden her to smoke in the house. The match flares in the darkness. If the story told by her father and brother is to be believed she is minutes from death and is therefore worthy of scrutiny. If the version of events heard in court is to be accepted, a man awaits her on the avenue and she will submit to his grisly embrace and will be forced to the ground and stabbed thirty-seven times. As she stands on the unlit verge of the road beside the entrance to The Glen, it is easy to construct a gothic fancy whereby death lures her towards it. But as she draws on the cigarette so that the glow lights her face and exhales the smoke and leans against the wall in a worldly pose, it is equally easy to imagine that she herself is inviting death, beckoning to it like some death-haunted and artful coquette.

FIFTEEN

November 13th 1952, 1.45 a.m. Constable Edward Rutherford had been on duty at Whiteabbey RUC barracks since ten the previous evening. A coal fire burned in the hearth of the whitewashed duty room. An unshaded sixty-watt bulb in the centre of the ceiling cast long shadows. It had been a quiet night. There had been several incidents involving soldiers returning from the NAAFI dance, which he had logged in the incident book, but the continuous rain had kept most people inside. Also logged were an elderly widow who reported an intruder in her garden and a traffic accident between a car and a lorry on the main Belfast road. Small incidents documented in Rutherford's meticulous hand. It was a cell-like room and there was something monkish about Rutherford's scratchy handwriting, of studious men with failing eyesight and the making of records to offset against the darkness, the chaos, the trans-European hordes swarming with fire and swarthy vigour.

The telephone rang at 1.45 a.m. When Rutherford answered, Judge Curran was on the other end.

'This is Lance Curran. My daughter has failed to arrive home from the city. Mrs Curran and I are extremely concerned.'

'Good evening, Judge Curran. I have no report of anything untoward. Might she have stayed with . . .?'

'We thought there might have been a road traffic accident involving a bus?'

'No sir, there's been nothing like that tonight, sir.'

'She was at college today. Normally she returns at approximately six o'clock. I have been informed by one of her friends that she had taken the five o'clock bus to Whiteabbey. It is now almost two o'clock and we have had no contact with her.'

'I tell you what, Sir. I . . .'

'I would be extremely grateful if you came to The Glen immediately.'

'Certainly, your honour.'

Rutherford replaced the phone in the cradle. He recorded the call in the night book and took his coat from its peg. As he did so, Constables McCulla and Tweed entered the station following their late evening beat. Both of them were wearing oilskins over their uniforms, and exuded a burly authority.

'What a fucking night,' McCulla said. 'How come you've got the coat on?'

'I got a call from Judge Curran. He says the daughter's missing.'

'From what you hear tell,' Tweed said, 'it's not the first time that one's gone missing in action. Far from the first time, if I heard it right.'

'I'm serious, boys. He sounded worried, so he did.'

'Get on up there, then. We'll hold the fort here. Go on to fuck.'

As Rutherford was fixing his cap the phone rang again. Rutherford had been a policeman for fifteen years and had once had ambitions to be a detective. He had craved the glamour that attached to it. The clandestine meetings with informers. The grudging respect between criminal and policeman. He often imagined himself as a craggy individualist, a man troubled by dangerous knowledge, moral ambivalence, given to dour, unsung heroics. It was not something he dreamed of any more and yet the two phone calls he received that night seemed to belong to a congruent fiction of felony and murder by night. When he lifted the phone he heard a woman's voice. Her voice was shaking. 'This is Doris Curran. Something terrible has happened . . .'

The phone line went dead. 'As if someone had put their finger on the receiver,' Rutherford said afterwards, carried along by the current of intrigue. He would speak the phrase thoughtfully, tailing off into silence while his listeners waited respectfully, recognizing his right to dramatic pacing, the appearance of pained reverie.

He told the others what had happened.

'I hear the mother's bad with the nerves,' Tweed said. 'Fuck me, what a house. The Desmond character playing on God's team and the daughter on the flat of her back with the rakes of the country. There's not much breeding there.'

'You'd better mind yourself up in that place,' McCulla said. 'I wouldn't take a pension to go near The Glen this night.'

Constable Rutherford cycled along the unlit railway track until he reached the main Whiteabbey road. He stopped and dismounted at the gates of The Glen and left the bicycle leaning against the gate pillar. He recalled that he heard a church bell strike two. Something moved in the trees. Rutherford had the sense of elements being put in place. An impression that a dark choreography had been set in motion. The rustle in the undergrowth. The tolling of bells. He heard gravel scuffle underfoot in the driveway. He looked up to see Judge Curran approaching him. He was wearing a judge's white tie and pinstripe trousers and his face was white in the gloom, so that he resembled a pallid and hollow-voiced compere come to announce the opening of a desolate festivity.

The Judge and Constable Rutherford exchanged a few words at the gate. Judge Curran told the policeman that he and his son had searched the driveway and had found nothing. The following day's newspapers recounted how Rutherford and Curran had then heard 'a cry' from Desmond Curran. They hurried down the driveway and located Desmond a few feet in from the edge of the drive.

He was looking downwards. The two men followed his gaze and saw Patricia Curran lying on the ground at his feet. He shone his torch on her. She was bareheaded but otherwise dressed. He was aware of the Judge standing behind him and Desmond at his elbow. She was lying on her left side and her right arm was raised, the wrist flexed as though in an overwrought gesture of farewell, although it was to be some time before a more sinister meaning was established from the position of her arm. Her clothing, from her neck to her thighs, was stained with blood.

Rutherford looked nervously at Desmond. He was staring at his sister and his lips were moving. Although Rutherford couldn't hear any words he formed the impression that Desmond was praying. Rutherford sank onto one knee and touched Patricia's shoulder. The blood on the shoulder of her coat was hard and crusted. He placed the back of his hand against her cold cheek and Rutherford knew then that Patricia Curran was beyond any absolution that Desmond's prayers might bring. As Rutherford began to straighten up he heard a car engine at the entrance to The Glen, then headlights on the drive. The car stopped on the drive beside them and a man got out. Rutherford recognized him as Malcolm Davidson, a local solicitor. He saw that Mrs Davidson was behind the wheel. She didn't look at him. She stared straight ahead, gripping the wheel. Malcolm Davidson approached the small group of men gathered round the body. He was a florid man who moved with a sense of his own import and he approached them like a man entering a funeral home, ready to shake hands and murmur obsequies in their ear.

'Dear God, Lance,' he said, stopping beside Judge Curran. As the man spoke, Rutherford felt Desmond begin to shake beside him.

'She's still breathing,' Desmond shouted. 'I saw her breathing.' He threw himself to the ground and began to

lift the girl's body. The corpse was so stiff that she was rel-
atively easy to lift. Rutherford waited for Davidson or the
Judge to stop him. Instead the Judge and Davidson bent to
help Desmond. Rutherford stepped back as they bent forward over her like men determined to press a depraved
suit upon the corpse. They managed to lift her and they
began to move towards the car, supporting the body
between them, its right arm still raised like a tormented
mannequin.

Inspector McConnell asked Rutherford why he hadn't
stopped them, since the girl was obviously dead, and
Rutherford knew the importance of preserving a crime
scene. By putting this question McConnell was clearly
observing a formality. He knew that an ordinary constable
would not dare to challenge the authority of a man of the
Judge's stature. Rutherford replied, 'I would not take it
upon myself to tell any of the men not to touch the body,
especially with a car so convenient.'

The three men attempted to put the body into the car.
The rigor mortis meant that it could not be placed in a sitting position and when they placed it lengthwise the feet
protruded so that the door could not be shut. In the end
they placed her across Desmond's lap with her feet
through the open window. During this entire procedure
Mrs Doreen Davidson remained at the wheel and did not
turn to see what was happening behind her. Rutherford
could see the whites of her eyes and a gold locket at her
neck rising and falling with her shallow, rapid breathing.

Davidson got in at the other side of the car so that the
girl's head was supported on his knees. Rutherford
could not see any signal being exchanged but Mrs Davidson put the car into gear and it lurched forward. She
turned over the muddy verge until the car was pointing
the direction it had come. The two men in the car kept
their eyes fixed frontwards as it started down the drive
towards the main road, like passengers intent on fulfill-

ing a gruesome itinerary. Curran turned back towards the house, saying that he had to tell Mrs Curran what had happened.

Rutherford returned to the station, where he telephoned Inspector McConnell at home. He told him that Judge Curran's daughter had been assaulted in the grounds of The Glen and that the body had been taken to Dr Wilson's surgery. It was now 2.30 a.m. After he had replaced the receiver, McConnell stood for a moment in the hallway of his home. From the hall window he could see across the lough to where car headlights were moving along the Whiteabbey road, sparse and remote. Then he lifted the receiver and asked the operator for the home number of Sir Richard Pim, Chief Inspector of Constabulary.

After he had telephoned Inspector McConnell, Rutherford went to Dr Wilson's surgery. He met the solicitor, Davidson, at the door.

'Is there any word of the young lady's condition, if you don't mind me asking sir?' he asked.

Davidson looked at him. 'No, I don't mind you asking Constable, and the plain answer to your question is that the girl is dead. Shot, as far as Dr Wilson is concerned.'

Rutherford telephoned Whiteabbey RUC station to pass on this information and then returned along the railway line to The Glen. He was uncertain as to what he should do so he decided that he would post himself at the gates of the house until the arrival of the Inspector. He could see lights burning in The Glen through the trees and he thought of the Judge and Mrs Curran waiting alone by the phone for news of her daughter.

Through the night and into the early hours of the following morning, people started to arrive at the house. Shocked relatives, legal and political colleagues, policemen. However, in the hours following the removal of Patricia's body, only Judge Curran and Doris Curran were in the house, and no record was made or notation set down as to what may have taken place between husband and wife during those hours, or what might have been covenanted between them.

At approximately 4.00 a.m. Inspector McConnell arrived, accompanied by Constables Tweed and McCulla. The two men were left at the gate and Rutherford accompanied McConnell in an attempt to relocate the spot where the body had been found. Rutherford had left his lit torch on the ground after the body had been lifted in order to find the spot, but the battery had run out. The two men cast around in the darkness for the site. They heard a car coming up the drive. It stopped and Desmond got out. Rutherford could see that it was the solicitor's car and that his wife was still at the wheel. She was stiff as before, but this time she turned and stared at him, and her eyes seemed to glitter, so that he felt that exposure to terrible events had burdened her with an unexpected and bitter grandeur. Rutherford regretted then that he had not become a detective. He thought that he could have got to the bottom of it. He imagined interrogating her in a windowless room. Look at me, Mrs Davidson. Did you hear anything suspicious in the car? I said look at me, Mrs Davidson.

Desmond and McConnell spoke quietly together and then they set off along the driveway again with Rutherford following. Desmond led them to the place immediately. McConnell shone his own torch on the spot and then in a direct line towards the driveway. He saw an object on the ground and moved closer.

'Those are my sister's college books,' Desmond said. McConnell saw the books and folder, held together by the leather strap, sitting neatly on the leaf mould. Desmond moved forward, past the books, and lifted another object.

'And this is her scarf,' he said, holding up the yellow scarf she had been wearing that day.

'Please don't touch anything at all, Mr Curran,' McConnell said. 'This is a crime scene.' He spoke softly. He knelt to examine the books and the folder. The edges of each of the books, and of the folder, were aligned as though they had been placed there rather than fallen. The other two men stood at the edge of the pool of torchlight. McConnell stood and took the scarf from Desmond. The fabric was only slightly damp and the scent of a woman's perfume rose from it. Patricia liked a heavy French perfume called Clair de Lune. Intended to be musky and melancholic when worn, it now exuded a brassy mystique that seemed dissipated. Desmond turned to Rutherford. In the torchlight his face looked pinched and guileful.

'Thank goodness there was no sexual interference,' he said.

In the early morning, the body of Patricia Curran was transferred by ambulance to the morgue at the Royal Victoria Hospital. A morgue attendant wheeled her into the cold-room and prepared her for the autopsy, which was to be performed by Professor Wells in the morning. He then covered the naked body with a sheet and departed. There was only one body in the morgue that night, presiding over that empty domain with a glassy imperious stare.

SIXTEEN

The early morning papers the next day all carried the Curran murder as the front-page lead. JUDGE'S DAUGHTER SHOT, the *Belfast Telegraph* said, going on to describe it as a 'sickening crime'. Dr Wilson's initial error in assuming that the stab wounds were in fact caused by shotgun pellets, and the subsequent correction of the error by the pathologist, was one of the major contributing factors to the sense of doubt that began to grow about the case, the undertone of stealth, concealment. Other newspapers printed the same error. Some hinted at IRA involvement, the presence of stocky monosyllabic men with concealed firearms, amoral designs on civil society.

The morning papers carried few photographs. The *Irish News* had a smudged shot of The Glen taken from an estate agent's brochure. The *Newsletter* showed Judge Curran at his investiture. The tragedy for the family was commented on. Police determination to hunt down the killers was stressed. The evening papers carried more detail. Inspector McConnell described the events of the previous night. He also stated that Patricia had been stabbed rather than shot. The phrase 'frenzied attack' was used in editorials. All the papers carried a small indistinct photograph of the murdered girl. It had been clipped from a society magazine and was poorly printed so that her eyes and mouth could not be distinguished from each other. They formed a single calamitous maw.

Ferguson heard the news that morning as he was shaving. He went into Esther's bedroom. She was sleeping. She had not removed her make-up and her hair was still half pinned up. He thought to himself that she did these things deliberately so that she could see the full extent of her degradation when she looked in the mirror in the morning. Sluttish, culpable. It was part of a resourcefulness she possessed in the field of self-hatred. He shook her gently by the shoulder. When she woke he told her that Patricia Curran had been murdered. She sat up slowly in the bed.

'The poor girl,' she said. 'Her poor mother.' She took his hand. She had a talent for simple, correct gestures. Later she would begin to rearrange the event in line with her drinking, labouring towards the alcoholic's stringent doctrine of self-reprieve, but for the moment her sympathy was genuine.

'Do they know who did it?' she asked.

He shook his head. 'They're still looking. McConnell's in charge of the investigation.'

'Where was she found?'

'On the driveway. She didn't come home and Desmond and Lance went looking for her.'

'Desmond and Lance.'

'They phoned everybody she knew first.'

'I'd no idea they cared so much.'

'Well, if your daughter didn't come home.'

'It wasn't the first time Patricia didn't come home.'

'I suppose that's true, Esther. The poor creature.'

'Will I come with you?' She was looking up at him. He knew how much a visit to the Currans would cost her. The hand that was sitting on the bedclothes was trembling slightly. He could picture her pale, driven face in the Currans' hallway, made ascetic and unworldly by terrible need, tucking her hands into the sleeves of her dress so that no one would notice the tremor. He shook his head. He kissed her on her forehead, as if her skin was a patinaed and reverenced icon. Something filled with ancient virtue, hard-won wisdom. When he left the room she was looking into a hand mirror with a kind of wondering revulsion.

*

It was Judge Curran's task to formally identify his daughter's body at the morgue. Ferguson drove to The Glen to bring him into the city. The small group of people standing at the entrance to the house stared at him, trying to establish his identity, to assign him a role in the narrative, some distinctive persona. A detective. A pathologist. A hard-eyed professional with experience of painstaking investigation. A policeman recognized him and waved him on. On the driveway two men in plain clothes and a uniformed policeman were examining the ground just off the drive. He thought that this was the place where Patricia's body had been found. About ten yards from the road he saw that a canvas cover had been erected over a piece of ground as if it had undergone dark consecration.

There were several strange cars outside the house and the front door was open. Ferguson went into the hallway, where he heard voices coming from the dining room. He looked in and saw Judge Curran, the solicitor Davidson, and Inspector McConnell. He waited in the hallway. He noticed a pair of girls' tennis shoes under one of the chairs and thought that they must belong to Patricia. He had seen her play at the Douglases' once. She had not wanted to stop when it started to get dark. The two girls played on into the dusk until they could barely be seen, moving like distant monochromatic figures of early film, stately and elegiac figures.

McConnell came out into the hall.

'A terrible thing,' Ferguson said, rising to greet him. 'Everyone must be most distraught.'

'Terrible indeed,' McConnell said, 'but there is a matter I must raise with you, Harry. The Judge won't let us search the house.'

'Why would you do that?'

'There's a good chance our killer was a burglar. There

might be some sign of his presence in the house. The murder weapon might have come from the house. God knows. I just think it's a good idea to have a look.'

'Better do what he says . . .'

McConnell turned to see Doris Curran standing at the top of the stairs. Her hair was uncombed, standing out in a halo round her head, and she was wearing a long floral nightdress so that she resembled an illustration of sorrow from an ancient book of days. Saintly. Resigned. The heartbroken mother. Ferguson wondered if she was aware of the authority of her position. She stared down at them for a moment then moved out of sight without speaking. The two men nodded at each other. McConnell put on his hat and walked towards the door. Ferguson went into the library.

Judge Curran greeted him as though it was Ferguson who had lost a child. 'Terrible news, Harry, terrible news. Can I get you something? A drink?'

However, Curran did not speak on the way into the city. He sat with his head on his chest and his eyes half closed, and once Ferguson thought he heard him mumble something to himself, but when he looked the man's lips were tight shut, his eyes seemed sightless and his face inanimate to such a degree that Ferguson thought that he may as well have had carriage of a corpse. They drove to the back of the hospital and were directed towards the morgue. As they approached the morgue gates were opened for them and then they shut behind them. The yard was of red brick and was paved in stone. An ambulance was backed up to the doors of the morgue and two men were unloading a reusable coffin of black enamelled steel from it. Wispy smoke drifted from the top of a cylindrical chimney on top of the building as if those within were engaged in a dreadful process and Ferguson held back, but the Judge strode into the building as if all of the day and night that had gone before had granted him right of audience in any charnel house or ossuary. Ferguson stood by the car and waited.

The judge stood alone in the viewing room. He could hear the approaching rattle of a gurney bearing his daughter's body.

If you look at the Judge's face as he looks down at the body of his daughter, you may see evidence that the body has struck a chord of remembrance regarding his own father's desolate expertise. The Judge would have recognized much about this building. There was a smell of blood that would have been familiar from his father's work, redolent of the familiar instruments and places. The cleaver. The hook. The blood tank. The doors opened as a porter pushed the gurney into the room. The director of the morgue followed him. He looked at the Judge to see if he was ready, then plucked the cloth from Patricia's face.

The funeral was held four days later. Patricia was buried in the graveyard of the Presbyterian church in White-abbey, yards from the gateway of The Glen. Men and women attended the house before the men left with the coffin for the cortège to the church. Ferguson saw the Judge talking to the Minister for Home Affairs. He recognized Desmond's blond hair as he moved through the crowd. He saw a young man in an airman's dress uniform. He did not recognize him then but he would later come to know that it was Iain Hay Gordon. Ferguson saw the young man approach Desmond Curran and speak to him briefly. Ferguson had seen Desmond earlier that morning. He seemed cold and aloof and his face appeared to grow colder as Gordon spoke to him. Ferguson had the impression of a suitor soliciting a favour. He thought that Desmond had the look of a minor Germanic prince, haughty and disdainful. He turned his back abruptly on Gordon and walked off through the crowd.

Ferguson saw Patricia's friend Hillary Douglas. She was wearing a large hat and white dress and her face was grey-pallored and otherworldly as though it was Hillary and not her friend who had been promised in deathly betrothal.

'There's no real side to that girl,' Esther said when he got home. 'She wasn't fit to deal with what happened.'

He was surprised to see the bookmaker Hughes at the door, come to offer his condolences. Ferguson moved quietly to his side.

'I'm sure Judge Curran would be glad of your condolences . . .'

'I'm not here to add to the Judge's sorrow, Mr Ferguson,' Hughes said. 'I am here to express my sympathy at the passing of his daughter.'

Doris Curran was sitting in a chair by the fire. Now and then people would approach her to offer their condolences and she would murmur something without looking at them. Something kept most people away from her. She seemed a severe presence, about to deliver herself of a stern admonitory address. Mrs Douglas sat across from her. Mrs Davidson stood by the fireplace, her hand resting on the back of Doris Curran's chair, her face filled with sympathy but also a kind of authority as though she had been granted dominion over the mother's grief. It was these three women that Ferguson was to see last as he followed the funeral down the drive, the women, as was customary, not accompanying the men to the graveyard. He turned then and followed the cortège towards the graveyard, where the Reverend Douglas was to exercise his dismal jurisdiction.

SEVENTEEN

Gordon told Davy that he could not get over the fact that someone he knew had been murdered. He cut Patricia's photograph from the *Belfast Telegraph* and stuck it on the inside of his locker door. On the morning of 20 November, Corporal Radford met Gordon on the steps of the Edenmore billet. Gordon was wearing full uniform.

'Where you off to, then, all done up like Lord Muck?' Radford asked.

'To the funeral,' Gordon said.

'What funeral's that, then?'

'Patricia Curran's funeral.'

'What? The girl that got killed? You think you know them people so well, they'll want to see you at her funeral? You think they want to see proof the girl's been hanging round with squaddies and so on?'

'She was a lovely girl.'

'A lovely girl. Hark at him. A high-class tart was what she was.'

'I'm going anyway.'

'Suit yourself, your lordship. But if I was you I'd look out for the coppers. They see you at that funeral they'll be wanting to know what you're doing there. And then look out, my son.'

Wesley Courtney, however, was happy to talk about the murder.

'I hear tell she was used goods,' he told Gordon. 'They say your man had a go at her. The knickers was near tore off her.'

Some of the girl's clothing had in fact been torn but it appeared that this had happened as her body was being dragged from the edge of the driveway into the woods. But Courtney was not going to be distracted from the lurid vocabulary of the murder, its melancholy sexual idiom of semen stains, the tearing of intimate garments, the overtones of unspeakable acts. Frenzied attack. The sating of dark lusts. It was an area that Courtney could claim some expertise in. He was able to draw from a knowledge of sexual crime in the Whiteabbey area going back over several decades. The molestation of schoolboys. Married men exposing themselves to women in public places. He told Gordon that if the police came to him he could 'show them where the bodies were buried'. There was much talk about stamping out homosexual activity in the general Whiteabbey area. It was widely believed that they could be singled out by their high-pitched effeminate speaking voices, their weak handshakes, their poor eyesight. There were calls for the civil service to be vetted. In internal documents, police talked about the possibility of blackmail. People were alert for well-dressed men behaving with studied casualness in public parks.

In police files from that time, Wesley Courtney was described as operating what was called a 'homosexual ring'. In fact he thought of himself as a recorder of the secret sexual history of the town, an archivist of terrible need.

On the morning following the funeral, Inspector McConnell received a phone call from the office of Sir Richard Pim. A meeting was arranged for the afternoon following Patricia's funeral. At the funeral Ferguson remained at the back of the church. The front row was reserved for the men of the Curran family. The *Belfast Telegraph* recorded that 'many prominent figures in the judiciary and public life were present'. Pim sat in the pew behind the Curran family. Ferguson thought that the man didn't look well. He had lost weight and his skin had a yellow hue, giving him a pinched and wrathful look. When he stood to follow the coffin from the church he moved carefully with an old man's conscientious regard for anatomical disarray, the skeletal frailty.

Pim occupied an office in Commercial Buildings at the centre of the city. The hallways were distempered. Glass doors bore faded gilt signs for loss adjusters, shipping agents; in the basement there were rows of filing cabinets behind fireproof doors filled with dockets, contracts, invoices. There were buildings like this all over the city. Monumental, begrimed. Repositories for the lore of empire. McConnell could understand why a man like Pim had chosen this place for his office instead of one of the castellated government buildings on the outskirts. 'Mind yourself dealing with that creature,' the election agent Ferguson had said to him quietly after the funeral. 'He'll have no time for the likes of us. As far as he's concerned you're a native.'

Pim was sitting at a roll-top desk when McConnell entered. The room seemed to belong to another time, full of stagy Victoriana, the dense period theatrics. A tin of Robinson's pastilles was open on the desk and he saw a blue bottle of Milk of Magnesia on top of a filing cabinet. A fountain pen sat on the blotter in front of Pim with a bottle of Quink beside it, as though Pim had been interrupted in the act of filling his pen. McConnell noticed that there was ink on Pim's fingers, adding to the impression that McConnell had always got from such English public-school types, men who did not seem to have left those days behind them. They had an air of schoolboy cruelty about them, of inky heartlessness. He got up to shake hands with McConnell and the policeman noticed that his face was yellow and jaundiced and that there was a sweet, acetone odour on his breath that made him think of visits to the Natural History Museum when he was a child. Pallid objects in glass jars of formaldehyde. The millennial stink.

'You needn't tell me, McConnell. I smell of the morgue,' Pim said. 'I suffer from diabetes. There is damage to the liver.' He leaned backwards in his chair and joined his hands. 'There is whiskey and soda on the table by the wall. I am not permitted it.'

'No, thank you.'

Pim arranged the documents on the table in front of him. 'What's your opinion of this affair, Inspector?'

'Too soon to say, sir. Could be somebody followed her off the bus. Could be somebody waited on the avenue for the girl.'

'Judge Curran informs me that the girl was afraid to walk up the driveway on her own.'

'There was no sign of a struggle, sir, in any event. We have to consider the possibility that her killer knew her.'

'The press are hinting at some subversive involvement. The IRA striking at a prominent man.'

'Those boys would be on the blower to the papers to say what they done, sir. They wouldn't try to hide it.'

'You haven't considered any other possibilities, Inspector.'

'No, sir.'

'Then don't.'

'I'm not sure I understand . . .'

'There are also ugly rumours regarding the girl's moral probity, Inspector.'

'Someone gets murdered like this, sir, there's always rumours.'

Rain blew against the window outside.

'Inspector, there seems to be some public unease about the number of foreign servicemen still posted in the Province.'

'To be honest, sir, in my experience it'd be our own servicemen that cause trouble.'

'Still, Inspector, it has been my experience that the foreigner does not possess the same restraint in sexual matters as our own men.'

'That may be true, sir. But, begging your pardon, there's been a lot of local girls cried rape when their man came home from the war and they were up the spout from some Frenchie or some such.'

'It was our Polish allies I had in mind, Inspector.'

'No better or worse than the others, sir.'

'You will be aware that the situation regarding the Free Polish army has not been resolved.'

'I never thought much about it, sir.'

'Some of them are resisting repatriation. The Communists have control of their country. There is a degree of unease that large numbers of Polish men settling in the Province might upset delicate balances.'

'I don't see how, sir.'

'They are in the main Roman Catholics. The girl was stabbed, wasn't she?'

'Yes, sir.'

'The knife is a cowardly weapon. I cannot see one of our own men losing control in such a loathsome way. The facts point firmly towards the involvement of a foreigner certainly, a Pole in all probability. There has been much talk about the girl's sexual history.'

'I haven't heard anything about a sexual history, sir.'

'Find out about it.'

'Yes, sir.'

McConnell knew that care was required. Pim was a personal friend of Winston Churchill. All the way through this case, McConnell was to be aware of forces moving beyond his control. He had a sense of men in poorly lit offices such as these, timeless and unhurried functionaries moved according to the dictates of some unknowable mandate. He could not help turning for another look at the man as he closed the door behind him. Pim was examining a document on his desk but when he felt the policeman watching him he lifted his head, and McConnell saw the other man's eyes filled with a colourless exaltation. McConnell realized that these men were bred for such work and dispatched to administer territories across the empire. He realized that he could have been in any part of the world and seen the same disease-haunted face.

At five o'clock that evening, McConnell was called to Whiteabbey RUC barracks. He was informed that a witness had been found. The witness was an eleven-year-old paperboy called George Chambers. The outer office at Whiteabbey had been converted into an incident room. It reminded McConnell of wartime strategy meetings that he had seen in films, meetings carried out in concrete-lined secret rooms far beneath the ground where young women of authoritative beauty wearing crisp blouses moved armies across maps using pointers. There was the same intense concentration on establishing the terrain of the dead, to assign cartographic values to its mapless interior.

Detectives in shirtsleeves were compiling lists of people to be interviewed. A blackboard had been erected in the middle of the room with details relating to Patricia's day. The time of her departure from Whiteabbey to the City. The time she had bought cigarettes at the kiosk in York Street station. The blackboard was taking on the appearance of a text, gathering narrative authority to itself. McConnell read down the list of places that Patricia had been seen. Queen's gym. York Street bus station at dusk. Bus tyres on the tarmac of the station, the Tannoy sounding out place names in the fume-laden vestibules of the station. The sounds of a squash ball on parquet. Rainy and autumnal evocations of the girl's last journey. The men in the station seemed to have caught this mood. They had already placed photographs of their wives and children on their desks and allowed themselves to be seen staring thoughtfully at their daughters. They spoke to each other in tones of gruff fatherhood. It seemed to be an accepted protocol to stand at the window smoking and staring sightlessly out into the night. Experienced detectives were solicitous with their colleagues. The men gave each other leeway in the practice of melancholia.

McConnell was shown through to the interview room where George Chambers sat with Constable Tweed. The boy was wearing a thin sweater with holes in it and a man's boots tied around his ankles with string, and the room was filled with his sourish, smoky odour. He had given an address in Irishtown. McConnell thought that you saw boys like Chambers at work more and more often as though they had come into their own in an era of industrial decline. They were sent into waste pipes with cloths tied to their bodies to clean them. They were rag-pickers, they sold newspapers, they pushed bone carts and fish-meal carts through the town shouting the criteria of their verminous calling in strange, husky, back-alley voices. They were small, dark-skinned boys. McConnell thought that they looked like foreigners, the unwanted offspring of sailors come to port. McConnell was wary of their steady, untrusting eyes, their air of being privy to caste secrets.

The boy and the constable were laughing but they stopped when McConnell came in. Tweed stood up.

'Who do we have here, Constable?'

'Boy by the name of George Chambers, age eleven years six months, sir. Works as a newsboy for Irwin's. Says he seen something the other night delivering the Judge's paper.'

'Heard something, more like,' the boy said.

'Sit down, Constable. We'll hear what he has to say for himself. Go ahead, George.'

Chambers described how he had collected his papers from Irwin's shop and had started his round at four o'clock. He said that it was quarter to six when he started up the drive to the Curran house.

'How did you know the time?'

'I must've seen it in the stars.'

'You'll get my boot drove so far up your hole you'll be farting teeth, wee lad, you start talking shite to the Inspector.'

'That's enough, Constable. How did you know the time?'

'I heard the mill hooter.'

'And what happened then?'

Chambers described how he heard sounds in the bushes on the side of the driveway.

'What kind of sounds?'

'Sounded like feet, so it did. Like following me, so they were.'

'Were you worried?'

'Scared out of my shite, so I was.'

'Did you see anything?'

'Never seen nothing.'

'Did you hear any voices? A woman's voice.'

'No.'

'But you were sure there was somebody in the undergrowth?'

'There was somebody there, mister. I could feel the hairs on the back of my neck stood up.'

'You ever listen to stories about the avenue up to the Judge's house.'

'Them's only stories.'

'What kind of stories?'

'Stories about the men the Judge hung up in Crumlin Road prison. They say Judge Curran'd hang you as soon as look at you. They say he's Pierrepoint's man.'

Albert Pierrepoint. The last hangman. Twenty guineas to hang a man. Twenty-five guineas to hang a woman, wed or unwed. 'A man's easy hung. It is the circumference

130

of the neck, do you see?' Pierrepoint would say, demonstrating this with his thumb and forefinger. 'You better take care. A woman's voice is as hard as a band saw, but her neck is like a twig.'

'I hear tell you can see them hung in rows from trees and twisting in the wind with the head all swole and the tongue stuck out.'

George Chambers would have passed up the driveway of the Curran house twenty-five minutes after Patricia had got off the bus at Whiteabbey. However, there was little in his evidence to suggest that what he had heard was the sound of the girl being attacked. The boy's evidence would be used to some effect at the trial and meant that the time of death was never challenged. McConnell turned away from the boy and spoke to Tweed under his breath.

'This isn't much good to us. The boy's head is full of old yarns he hears running about the town.'

'Still and all, sir. He heard something.'

'He heard leaves. He heard a bird. He heard nothing.'

'I hear tell she was rid,' the boy said.

The two men turned to look at him.

'What was that?' McConnell said.

'I hear tell he rid the girl before he killed her.'

The following day McConnell issued a statement to the effect that he believed a foreign national, 'probably a Pole', was being sought for the murder of Patricia Curran. He referred to the fact that a knife had been used and that such a weapon was the usual choice of a foreigner. He said that all servicemen stationed in the Whiteabbey area were to be questioned immediately. In the aftermath of this statement several members of the Free Polish Army were attacked and beaten in local bars. After that they were confined to barracks for their own safety. Newspaper photographs showed them behind the wire fences at

Whiteabbey, Ballykinlar, smoking, talking softly to each other, waving across the fence with ironic half-smiles on their faces. They knew that many Polish soldiers who had returned to Poland from the war had died in labour camps, and there seems to be an awareness among them that they are already lost and that they will lie awake at night as their barracks creak in the wind and whisper one to another news of the dead.

When he looked back at the events of that first week in November, it seemed to McConnell that most of the early witnesses had been children. The children seemed to have some access to the murder that was denied adults. They seemed to regard Patricia Curran as a fabled figure, a dainty and two-dimensional heroine who was subject to a dark enchantment. The drugged apple. The poisoned needle. They understood from what they heard from adults that it was something she had brought upon herself, that she had somehow transgressed and wandered off the path. A shining, golden-haired figure in a long dress disappearing into the forest murk. The day after George Chambers had been interviewed an eleven year-old girl was brought to Whiteabbey barracks by her mother. Marcella Devlin said that she walked to school along the Whiteabbey road and said that she had often seen Patricia in the company of a young man with a scarred face. She said she had once seen them in a car and had once seen him jump out of the trees at the gates of The Glen and stop Patricia roughly. The little girl persisted with her story but the man with the scarred face was never found. The newspapers acknowledged the dramatic appeal of Marcella Devlin's story. They succumbed to the cautionary image she had offered them. The beautiful girl. The malformed suitor appearing from the forest or the well or some other mazy, spellbound backdrop to an unforgiving and cautionary tale.

EIGHTEEN

Gordon was working in the typing pool when the OC called parade in twenty minutes. Within fifteen minutes all the men in the base had assembled on the parade ground. Warrant Officer Collins called them to attention as the OC came out. This was an aspect of the RAF that Gordon disliked. The sound of Collins's shouted orders, the brutal forced squawk. When he wrote to his mother he spoke of the use of unnecessary foul language. His mother wrote back to say that men without the civilizing influence of women were as beasts unrestrained.

The OC informed them that the police would be coming to question every man at the camp and that full cooperation was expected from all of them. He said that Judge Curran had been a 'good friend to the RAF', and he then called for a minute's silence in memory of Patricia Curran.

The men stood to frozen and dutiful attention in the thin icy wind blowing in off the lough, and their boots shifted on the cinder surface and the flag cracked stiffly and they fell silent as though engaged in a thoughtful and sleety commemoration of fallen comrades: men lost in cold northern latitudes. Scapa Flow. The cold formalism of the event seemed inclement and unconnected to the murder, the haphazard sexual drama of a woman's body sprawled in the dreamy undergrowth. When the minute was over the OC turned and walked away and the men put their caps back on and started to move back towards the buildings without even a pretence of solemn thought-gathering or suggestion that the act of remembrance lasted one second longer than it had.

Back in the canteen, Corporal Radford noticed that

Gordon was still shivering. He clapped him on the shoulder and told him to get a cup of hot tea into him. It was a moment he was later to recall. 'Gordon was shivering and shaking like I don't know what. I says to him, "What's up? You got the flu or something?" And he says, "They're going to be asking questions and I was here in the barracks on my own, on account of everybody else was at the NAAFI dance." So I says, "Somebody must've seen you here," and he says no. He was in a rare old state. So he says to me, "I have to get an alibi," and I says at him, "You needn't look at me, mate." You got to remember, the whole country was all of a commotion. You ask me, he was afraid they'd think he was a fruit, that was what old Gordon was worried about. He were dead peculiar but he weren't the type to go stabbing women.'

Both Desmond Curran and Judge Curran returned to practice before Christmas.

Desmond's colleagues had not expected to see him back that term and he was closely watched as he crossed the bar library and sat at his desk. With its dim lighting and barristers' robes hanging on nails and wigs sitting on a wooden desk, the place bore resemblance to a tribunal of last inquiry. Several of the men wanted to approach Desmond to express their condolences at his loss but something stopped them. It seemed to them not that Desmond's manner had changed but that they suddenly recognized it for what it was. That immobile face. The blue eyes that never looked at you. That he seemed affixed to the library and its doings like a talisman of harsh pieties. There were murmured conversations behind the library shelves. People fell silent as he approached and stared at his back as he passed, but without comment, as though his passing had taken the form of a bare instruction to the sinful and depraved.

There was comment in the newspapers about Judge

Curran's character before the murder. He was referred to as humane. He was referred to as progressive. Before the death of his daughter he was said to be the kind of Judge who had an affinity with those before him. He was given to trading wry jokes with defendants in the dock. Criminals were said to accept stiff sentences from Judge Curran without rancour. Judge and defendant seemed to accede to archaic notions of fair play while kindly policemen looked on. It was implied that the criminal underworld had offered to help in tracking down the murderer. It was implied that hardened villains had been moved to outrage over such an affront to public morality. Phrases such as 'common standards of decency' were used. Phrases such as 'shared values'. The Judge's role in the public narrative was established early. He was to be the good man bowed low by parental grief. He was applauded for returning to his position on the bench so soon after the tragedy. It was felt that the administration of justice was safe in the hands of men such as Curran.

In fact, Harry Ferguson thought that the Judge looked terrible after the murder. His eyes were sunken and sleepless and his hair had turned grey at his temples, so that when Ferguson met him some days after he had returned to the bench he thought that he was faced with a cadaverous and antique figure of judgement from an ancient manuscript. For months now the Judge had been given to fits of temper in court. The Judge's tipstaff informed Ferguson that the Judge was consuming large quantities of Bisodol, Andrews Liver Salts and other proprietary remedies. The tipstaff said that there were food stains on his shirt and his jacket, although he did not seem to eat. In mid-December Ferguson was called to the chambers of the Lord Chief Justice, Harold McDermott. The Lord Chief Justice told him that he was afraid that Curran's appearance might give rise to scandal. That he did not resemble a Judge of the High Court but rather some sunken-cheeked revenant.

Ferguson told the Chief Justice that he would speak to Curran and persuade him to put aside the weight of his duties for the following term, but he found himself unable to approach the Curran house. However, the Judge was to provide the opportunity by attending the Tuesday night card game at the Reform Club three weeks after Patricia's funeral. Ferguson had arrived first and Mahood had unlocked the door for him. He sat down at the green baize table while Mahood added more anthracite to the Baxi fire. Ferguson looked up and saw Judge Curran at the door. He handed his coat and hat to Mahood and the man stood there staring at the Judge as though he were a shuffling visitant come to lay claim to his very soul.

The Judge crossed the room. Ferguson rose and shook hands with him. Curran sat down opposite Ferguson.

'They want me to stand down,' Curran said.

'The Chief Justice suggested that you might take a short sabbatical. He thinks that you are under strain.'

'Why should I stand down, Ferguson? You know that I won't. There is no reason for me to stand down.'

Ferguson did not answer him. The two men sat in silence until the door opened again and Dr McKee entered. McKee took Judge Curran by the hand.

'My dear Lance,' he said, 'my dear Lance.' You could see the doctor's eyes behind the glittering lens of his glasses. The dull orange of the glass-fronted fire was reflected in them, and he stood for a full minute with his hand on the Judge's shoulder, expressing his solicitude.

Ferguson wondered about the doctor. 'That man's like a jackrabbit,' Esther had said to him once. 'He'd get up on the table if he thought he'd get a stir out of it.' As for Esther, the doctor had offered Ferguson a white powder one day. 'It's bromide,' McKee said. 'You could slip it in her tea. If she ever drinks any.' He said it was important to curb the physical impulse in the advanced stages of alcoholism. Ferguson presumed from this that the doctor had slept with Esther. Ferguson imagined McKee and his wife in a darkened hotel room. The woman's face turned away, the doctor labouring over her, ashen-faced, as though in the act of administering an appalling physic. Ferguson felt an unexpected pity for his wife. He had the urge to take her by the hand.

As the doctor turned to sit down, Ferguson saw the property speculator McDowell come in. The man saw the Judge then scanned the whole room, his eyes moving from side to side. Ferguson could see that the man was afraid to be here, that he had absorbed the mood that Judge Curran had brought with him, the dark taint and spoil.

'I see we're four-handed tonight,' he said, 'now that the Judge has decided to join us.'

'If you consider it bad for business, McDowell, or offensive, then you may go home.' The Judge's voice was reedy and precise like a wintry elder delivering judgement on a difficult cause before him.

'Not at all, not at all,' McDowell said. 'It's good to see you out and about so soon after the tragedy.' He pulled up a chair and sat down at the Judge's right hand.

'Here, Mahood, get us a brandy and port from the bar like a good man, and something for the Judge here. Whiskey and soda, or whatever it is that he's drinking these days. Sit down, Ferguson, for Christ's sakes. You're stood there over me like a hangman.'

Ferguson sat down. He caught the doctor's eye in acknowledgement of what the night ahead was to hold. The doctor picked up the deck of cards and began to shuffle.

McDowell drank heavily all evening and into the night. He became red-faced, casting glances at the Judge. Once, when the Judge had got up from the table to take another drink from the tray that Mahood had placed on the sideboard, McDowell leaned towards Ferguson and whispered, 'They say she rid a squad of boys on the one night. Soldiers. Poles.' Ferguson thought that the Judge must have heard but he gave no sign of it. He returned to the table and sat down. Shortly afterwards it became clear that McDowell was losing heavily. Ferguson looked at Curran but the Judge had eyes only for the game and for the cards in front of him and for the growing pile of bank notes that sat at his right hand. It seemed that each time McDowell put down a stake the Judge doubled it or trebled it and Ferguson and the doctor turned their cards face down on the table. The Judge sat with his back to the wall and as he won each pot he drew it in and tallied it and stacked it neatly to his right. The shadows in the room grew longer as the fire burned down, and looking at where Curran was hunched over his winnings it seemed to Ferguson that the Judge sat in a strange counting house where righteous and exacting account must be rendered to him without regard for consequence.

Ferguson thought that if he were McDowell he would throw down his cards and quit the game, but he did not, and neither man spoke except to call for more cards or raise the stakes. Towards midnight McDowell asked Curran if he would accept his IOU and the Judge assented. The game went on. The colour had drained from McDowell's face and he had long since stopped sweating. Such was his complexion that the doctor glanced at Ferguson and then stepped forward and said to McDowell that he had better stop for the sake of his health, but the man shook him off and continued to play as though to quit was to invoke a hellish forfeit.

But in the end McDowell began to gasp for breath and call for water. McKee loosened his tie and forced a capsule of nitroglycerine between his teeth and pronounced the game over, with a look of rebuke at Curran. Curran sat there without moving as McKee led McDowell away, then he turned towards Ferguson, gesturing towards the pile of money and IOUs, and his eyes were clouded as though he was stricken with cataracts.

On the same evening, Gordon was alleged to have approached several men in the Edenmore barracks to ask them if they had seen him on the evening of 14 November. None of them had seen him. Corporal Radford, when interviewed following Gordon's arrest, quoted Gordon as saying, 'If I had a friend, a good friend, and he was in trouble, even to the extent of murder, I would be prepared to lie for him.'

Radford's statement continued, 'I remember vigorously attacking him for having such a funny conception where murder was concerned.' There is a great deal of this kind of language in the records of the case. In some statements you find policeman's argot put into the mouths of those who are supposed to be independent witnesses. In this case Radford's statement has the appearance of having been dictated by a professional, a solicitor, or a prosecutor. Vigorously attacking. Funny conception. There is an authoritative middle-class ring to the statement. A stalwart upholder of values is asked to compromise himself. Civic virtue is assailed. It was not known who was responsible for coaching Radford, but it seems more likely that it was someone with legal training, a man wearing the black coat and white cravat of his profession imposed upon the corporal, a dandyish and subtle charlatan. There is a sense of compromises devised, unspoken rules. There is an understanding of false testimony.

In the end Gordon found his alibi. Airman James Connors agreed to say that he had seen Gordon in the Edenmore base between five and six o'clock on the night of Patricia's murder. At Gordon's trial he told how Gordon had asked him, and he had agreed to lie on his behalf. Many years later Connors was interviewed about the

Curran case. He was a heavyset man in his sixties with a pronounced stammer. He is sitting in an armchair and behind him you can see ornaments on a varnished wooden shelf. A porcelain dog with a barrel round its neck. Two brass candlesticks. Connors is wearing a warm cardigan over a shirt. You have a sense of a man moving within kindly boundaries that he has set for himself, hard-earned comforts. A man with minor heart trouble and three or four fair-haired grandchildren. A small-boned wife with a worn face will have taken up a wary stance just off-camera. You expect him to address the past with wry benevolence, an understanding of how life faces men with untimely misapprehension, and be willing to dispense makeshift absolution to all those remote figures from the past, most of them dead. He should really sit there in the philanthropic gloom of his room with a half-smile on his face and deliver a few well-intended and vague opinions about the entire matter, but it seems there is an unspecified bitterness about him that builds during the interview. And at the end of it he is asked what he thinks of Gordon and he is barely able to get the words out at all. He struggles to speak his final word on the matter. Iain Gordon was stupid. His voice rising on the first syllable of the word, the second syllable spat out.

Ten days after the murder, McConnell interviewed Wesley Courtney. He knew that Courtney had a bad reputation, but that he had no convictions. The local constables said that they kept an eye on him. He'd be hanging round playgrounds and that, they said. He said afterwards that it felt like interviews he had done with convicted men in prison. Courtney was deceitful and knowing. He was given to small, secretive smiles. There seemed to be aspects of human sexual appetite that were apparent to him alone. When McConnell came in to the interview room Courtney was sitting quietly at the table. Courtney started to talk.

'Who do you think could have killed her, Mr McConnell?'

'I don't know, Courtney. Who do you think killed her?'

'A pervert, I'd say.'

'Why would you say that?'

'You hear tell he was at her. He had the knickers tore off her.'

'You'd better mind your tongue, Courtney. This is a Judge's daughter we're talking about here, a young lady who was brutally murdered, and I expect full cooperation from you and your like.'

It was 1952 and policemen felt themselves entitled to attitudes of stern condescension with those they believed to be criminals.

'I didn't mean nothing, Mr McConnell. It's what people are saying, is all.'

'Where were you on the night of the 12th of November?'

'I locked up the shop at five o'clock, went to the British Legion. Plenty of people there, so there was.'

'Was there now?'

'There was.'

'All right. We can check that.'

'I got an alibi, Mr McConnell, as long as he done the terrible crime at the time the papers says he did.'

'What does that mean?'

'Just using the head, just using the bap. Nobody seen her killed, and I hear tell the autopsy never proved nothing as far as time goes.'

'How'd you hear that?'

'Peelers got to get their hair cut too, Mr McConnell.'

'They do a lot of talking in that shop of yours.'

'A man the like of me hears a lot.'

'What do you hear then, Courtney?'

'Hard to say, Mr McConnell. There's people saying

Dessie went mad with her, her being out for the ride and all.'

'That's enough, Courtney.'

'I'm only saying.'

'Never mind what you hear. What do you think?'

'You want my opinion, Mr McConnell, you'll throw the eye over them national service crowd. Some of them servicemen's clean perverts, so they are. The national service boys wouldn't be like the regular soldiers.'

'There's something here you're not telling me, Courtney.'

'I swear to God there's not. I swear on the Holy Bible, so I do.'

'Don't bring the Lord's name into it. There's no place for your profanity here.'

'I never meant no offence, Mr McConnell. I'm just saying, that's all.'

'If I find out you know something about this and you're not telling me . . .'

'There is one thing I know, but I think you know it too.'

'What might that be?'

'There was something not right up in that big house. There's a twist in that Curran family, that's what I'm saying.'

McConnell kept returning to that interview during the weeks of the trial. The squat little man sitting at the table across from him. He had noticed that Courtney had dark, curly hair protruding from his cuffs and the collar of his shirt, and that his head seemed too large for the rest of his body. Courtney's attitude was respectful, eager to please, but all the time the eyes never left your face and the unchanged tone of his soft voice, whispery and mean. It did not seem so at the time, but later he was to think that it was the day that things began to turn against Iain Gordon.

*

On 20 November McConnell had received a phone call from Pim requesting him to consider the possibility that a mental defective from the area may have been responsible for the attack. On 30 November McConnell conducted the questioning of a sixteen-year-old boy from Whiteabbey who was given to violent epileptic attacks. On 2 December he conducted an interview with a fourteen-year-old who suffered from mild encephalitis. As the series of interviews continued, McConnell felt himself beginning to resemble the superintendent of a lightless infirmary with red-brick institutional walls and a tendency towards archaic practices. He could not meet the gaze of the women who watched him as he attempted to interrogate their idiot sons. Their dark-rimmed watchful eyes, scarves tied about their heads. The other policemen treated the women with gruff suspicion, as though there hung about them the taint of an unnamed degeneracy, and the women bowed their heads.

At the end of that week, McConnell received the instruction from Pim that every male person in the Whiteabbey area was to be interviewed. Resources were allocated to him from other divisions and rotas were drawn up. School gyms, libraries and other public buildings were to be used. Members of the public volunteered premises and the police were aware of a stern mood of civic virtue. On the first few days the station was filled with solicitors, doctors and other community leaders who wished to be seen as leading by example. People wanted to be perceived as tolerant in the best traditions, but able to dispense steely justice with stern-jawed rectitude when boundaries were crossed. After those first few days the shopkeepers of the town came forward, the postmen, the bank tellers, the casual traders. The town seemed to have looked into its heart and come to a conclusion as to the order in which they would appear, to have worked out a dismal etiquette involving an increasing scale of suspicion. On the third day the interviewees looked as if they were attending an audition for a role as epitomes of shabby provincial diligence. The men were being interviewed in relays by inspectors from outlying districts, with McConnell taking over those that he thought might be promising. Where were you on the evening of the 12th of November 1952 between five o'clock and seven o'clock. Who were you with? Between five and seven. Can you prove that? Did anyone see you?

Those were the times that had been established at the start of the inquiry and they were never challenged in court, though there was reason to doubt them. Patricia left the city at five o'clock. Doris Curran arrived home at six o'clock. Judge Curran arrived home at seven and they said that Patricia had not appeared. The Whiteabbey bus dropped her off at the entrance to Glen House and went on, its textual remit fulfilled. The fact that the investigation was fixed on events that occurred in two hours excluded all other possibilities except that Patricia had been killed on the way up the avenue. It seemed that the idea of a man lurking in the trees was too strong, the presence of a primal figure in the undergrowth overcame any suspicion that she might have died at any other time; it was accepted that her body was already lying there through ten o'clock, eleven o'clock, through suspenseful midnight and on into the bone-chilled morning hours. But the possibility should have been considered.

On 31 November McConnell took the testimony of a man called Arthur Hanna. Hanna had been at Mons, Ypres. He wore his decorations to the interview. He entered on crutches and the leg of his right trousers was pinned neatly together above the missing knee. He had the ghostly authority of those who spoke for the dead. He had the air of a man who had come to deliver a summons on their behalf.

'I'm sure I won't have to detain you very long,'

McConnell said. The other man said nothing but stared at McConnell. He could not be over fifty, McConnell said, but he had the eyes of a rheumy ancient. You often saw veterans on the streets of Whiteabbey. Men who would approach you without bidding and give account of themselves. Harrowing tales of field amputations, gas attacks. The naming of the dead, their ages and birthplaces. You saw them standing at war memorials, staring into the sentinel dark.

'They tell me her arm was up in the air and twisted like a swan's neck. I seen plenty like her in the war.'

'I don't doubt it, Mr Hanna. It was a terrible business.'

'You're not hearing me.' The man had lung damage, McConnell realized. His voice had sunk to a terrible gassed wheeze.

'My uncle was at Verdun, Mr Hanna. Many's the tale he told.' McConnell's uncle had survived Verdun but he had not returned as the same man. He sat on his own before the fire, staring into it, and his lips moved as though in an attempt to tally the countless dead.

'The girl's arm was in the air. They say it was froze like a swan's neck. I seen that before.'

McConnell nodded. It was a detail that had been picked up by the press. It had appropriate overtones of tragic grace for the death that they wished to portray. There were overtones of juvenile eroticism.

'You know where I seen it? I seen it in the backs of lorries when men would be took back from no-man's-land dead. I seen it when men was threw into graves with no coffin or nothing.'

'As I said, Mr Hanna, it was a terrible war.'

'Listen to me.'

'I'm listening, Mr Hanna.'

'It means that she wasn't killed where you found her.'

'How do you work that out?'

It means that she was killed lying on her side and was

left lying there till her arm got stiff, then she was lifted and threw down on the other side. She wasn't killed in the place she was found.'

McConnell discounted Hanna's statement. New theories were advanced every day. However when the pathology photographs were examined many years later by a forensic pathologist, the same conclusion was drawn. The dying swan, the wrist bent in a self-dramatizing valedictory gesture.

On Saturday 31 November, McConnell interviewed the bookmaker Hughes, who was regarded as an influential figure among the Roman Catholic community of the town.

'Did you know the Curran family?' McConnell asked.

'I did.'

'What was your relationship with them?'

'I lent money to the Judge. He run up a fair tab with me on the horses on top of it. Well you may look at me, Inspector McConnell. You never knew the Judge was a gambling man?'

'It hadn't come to my attention, no.'

'What else would he be doing with the like of me? Jesus Christ, McConnell, I get you now. You haven't talked to any of them, have you? You never done any interviews with them, Desmond or nothing?'

McConnell had in fact spoken briefly to Judge Curran, Desmond and Doris Curran on the morning after the killing, but since then, despite repeated requests, Pim had refused him permission to approach the Curran family.

'Did you ever meet the girl, Mr Hughes?'

'The girl. You sound like one of them. The Currans. You notice the way they never say her name. The da always talked about "my daughter". Desmond would talk about "my sister".'

Hughes thought that they referred to her in this way to make a stranger of her, as if they had already seen her receding away from them into bleak abstraction.

'I asked you if you'd ever met her.'

'She used to say hello to me in the street. A big cheerful hello.'

'Did you ever have any contact of an intimate nature with her?'

'Catch yourself on. Look at the cut of me, McConnell. I'm a fat old man. What would I be doing with a girl like Patricia Curran. Hold on a second. I see where you're coming from, now. I see what this is about. I see what the way of it is, now. I'll have no hand, act or part of ruining that child's name. There'll be no smut from this quarter. Leave her and her memory be. She was a lovely child and you'll have no aid from me in dragging her through the mud. It'd be the best part of your play to leave her alone and catch the man that killed her.'

At night McConnell examined the case file. There was a diagram of the crime scene. The body was located eleven yards from the edge of the drive. Patricia's scarf was beside the body. Her right-hand glove lay six feet away. Forty feet away her shoes were located. Black patent shoes with a Cuban heel. At the edge of the drive police found her books and folder, her handbag, her yellow Juliet cap, an unposted letter. McConnell studied it for hours in the belief that there must be a relationship between these objects and that that relationship would yield meaning to his appraisal. That there was codified in these bare objects the means whereby she met her end. The shoes were side by side as though in her extremity Patricia was victim of an ill-timed fastidiousness. They were like a pair of shoes placed at the end of a bed at nightfall. Then it occurred to him that the killer may have placed the shoes there. McConnell closed his eyes and saw the single glove lying on the leaf mould. One day he went to the evidence locker and removed the glove. He kept it in the drawer of his desk and laid it on the surface when the others had gone. A white cotton glove that reached to the elbow, the palm slightly soiled. At first it seemed a dramatic object, a long white glove, faintly scented. It suggested large themes, an operatic sweep to the case. But as the days wore on he began to see that the glove represented something else. Close-fitting, intimate.

Weeks later he went to the evidence locker to look for the unposted letter that had been found with the books. He found the unaddressed white envelope and returned to his office. He felt a strange reluctance to touch it, as though he feared that it might form part of the correspondence of the recent dead, their wistful parlance prone to envy of the living, a tone of mute grievance. When he opened it he found a simple note to a pen friend in Switzerland written on unlined Basildon Bond. In it Patricia complained about the weather. 'The weather here is dreary,' she wrote, 'The wretched damp gets into your bones.' She said that she loved snow and adored the idea of skiing. 'It must be such fun.' She said that she had bought tulle and velvet to make a new dress for Christmas.

McConnell did not associate the idea of pen friends with Patricia. There was a grammar school primness to it. The idea of a pen friend. Young women of equal social status writing to each other across the adolescent reaches. Somewhere in Patricia's room there would be a photograph of a teenage girl standing beside a long-fringed pony, squinting into the sun. Patricia had probably been writing to her for a long time, McConnell thought. Part of being pen friends lay in the endurance of the relationship, the nurturing of girlish sentiment over years.

In the letter Patricia said she had asked her father for money to go on a skiing trip but he had refused. McConnell wondered if this was the reason for her taking the job driving the lorry during the summer. 'Do you stop at inns and everything like that for hot punch?' Patricia asked in the letter. McConnell could see the appeal. Rosy-cheeked alpinists. The ersatz cheerfulness of log fires and mulled wine, the snow piling into drifts outside the window, the shadows lengthening under the pine trees.

He went through the list detailing the contents of the girl's handbag. A Rimmel lipstick, a powder compact, a lace-edged handkerchief, mascara, bus pass. He noted that no keys were found. He noted that there was nothing personal in the handbag, a photograph, or other cherished item that a woman might be supposed to keep in her handbag. The bag itself was a simple clutch purse with a gold clasp. He thought about the suicides that were taken from the water at Whitehead, or at Larne. More women than men because after the war many women had been abandoned by GIs. Many of these women had gone to great lengths to remove any means of identification from their clothes. Often their bodies lay in the morgue unclaimed for many weeks, and it seemed to McConnell that this was the very thing they had sought – the chill anonymity, the dreamless plenitude.

Iain Hay Gordon was interviewed by Detective Sergeant John Harrison on 7 December in the gym at Edenmore. Harrison came from a mountain area east of the city. He attended a small tin-roofed Pentecostalist church each Sunday evening with his father and his brothers and forty other men. They exhibited an unbending faith in the congregation of the faithful and the doctrine of predetermination. You could hear their hymn-singing through the timber walls of their hall at night, the plaint of an abandoned people sounding out their desolation. They had a view of themselves as deadpan, unhurried, inexorable. He was a member of the B-Specials, a black-uniformed rural constabulary with an ethos of late-night house raids, border checkpoints, religious zealotry.

After the interview Harrison wrote that the subject appeared nervous and agitated. Before Harrison could begin the questioning he announced that he was acquainted with the Curran family.

'With the whole family?'

'Yes. I've met them all and I've had Sunday lunch with the family.'

'How did that come about?'

'Me and Desmond share an interest in religious matters.'

'I've heard it said that Mr Curran is a religious man.'

'That's right. I can help you with this. I can give you information.'

'What sort of information?'

'You know . . . information.'

Gordon wasn't the first interviewee to behave like this, people edging themselves closer to a great event, pretending to know more than they actually did, sometimes believing it, craving complicity. There was a terrible inner need to be close to public figures, to connect with their vivid affairs. The love letter from the condemned cell. The obsessive photographing of starlets.

Gordon's interview was full of innuendo, significant glances, meaningful gestures. Harrison had the impression that he was witnessing a performance.

'Where were you between five o'clock p.m. and seven o'clock p.m. on the 12th of November this year, Airman Gordon.'

Harrison noted that for the first time Gordon seemed genuinely nervous, looking down into his lap and muttering something about another airman seeing him in the typing pool.

'Can I have the name of the other airman, Airman Gordon? Your alibi?'

Harrison asked the question to see how Gordon would react. Whether the use of the word alibi would produce a reaction. It was not a term employed by policemen, in his experience. It was a term freighted with a lurid history, intimations of perjury. He noted that Gordon considered the word carefully, then looked pleased.

'Alibi,' he said softly, 'my alibi,' turning the word over to himself like a cherished possession. Seeing himself as a man who required something with the conspiratorial glamour of an alibi. Seeing himself as guileful and edgy.

In his report, Harrison noted that 'the interviewee appears to have known the Curran family on a social level. He appears eager to please and has a fascination for the case. He states that at the time of the murder he was in the typing pool practising for an examination, which has been confirmed by Airman Connors.'

Harrison's final comment was that the interviewee appeared to be of 'the nervous or neurotic type'. When he read the report, McConnell put a red question mark in the margin beside this sentence and the sentence noting his connection with the Curran family. He had read over a thousand interviews. The early interviews contained pensive marginalia, sentences, reflections on each subject's place in the case. As the case continued without a break the notes developed a plain, unadorned style, sparse and cryptic.

NINETEEN

Harry Ferguson had not been in contact with any member of the Curran family since the murder. He had called at The Glen several times and had rung the bell but no one had come to the door. All the windows at the front of the house had their heavy blackout curtains drawn, but Ferguson could see light around the edges of the front door. He felt that there was something contrived about the atmosphere about the house. Weeds on the gravel. Rain dripping from the dank eaves. The sense of being watched. He felt that an older, unresolved drama had encroached on the present. He recalled the family portraits belonging to the previous owners of The Glen that still hung in the hallway. Heavyset scowling men in stiff collars. Their daughters are frail women dressed in white. You know there are glass vials just out of reach. The eye watching you from behind the curtain. Glittery, unstable. There is a lace handkerchief twisted in the fingers, an expertise in the field of early pharmaceuticals.

Ferguson had met McConnell several times in the snug of the White Horse Hotel in Whiteabbey. McConnell had developed the habit of entering by the side door, and drinking several whiskeys quickly before returning to the station. McConnell had lost weight. He talked about the case incessantly. Interviews he had carried out. False leads followed up. It was inevitable that things should develop this way. There was a recognizable choreography involving the detective in charge of an unsolved murder. The drinking. The neglect of family and personal appearance. The pressure from superiors and the onset of premature ageing. McConnell was being avoided by his colleagues and he had responded in terms of mood swings, morose solitary drinking. He no longer attended morning service at Carrickfergus Baptist Church with his family, and his colleagues noted this with approval. Spiritual doubts were among the things they expected from a man in his position. It was part of a progression of failure and they felt that McConnell had been dependable in his obser-vance of it and they could comfortably await the next stage. An assault on a junior colleague. A transparent and doomed attempt to manipulate evidence or suborn a wit-ness.

Ferguson was aware of the pressure on McConnell and wasn't surprised when he was in the bar of the White Horse one night to see McConnell beckoning to him from the door of the snug like an aged and frightful relative, liver-spotted, trembling, about to subject you to a terrible family confidence.

'Come here, Ferguson. I got to talk to you.'

When Ferguson went in, McConnell was sitting at the bar, laying out sheets of paper with handwriting on them, smoothing them with rapid, nervy movements. Ferguson thought that the man was trying to appear energetic, on top of his job, ready to exchange hearty confidences in the interest of cronyish bar-room intimacy.

'Come in, Ferguson, for Christ's sake and sit down.' There was mucus in the corners of the inspector's mouth and his hands were trembling.

'I got something to tell you, Ferguson. Can you keep it to yourself? Can you keep the beak shut?'

'Take her handy there now, course I can keep the lid on something. Just take her easy there and we'll get to it. What have you got?'

'There's something I don't like going on here, Harry.' The policeman looked quickly over his shoulder. It was what Ferguson had dreaded. That furtive glance. The case had got to McConnell and Ferguson could see that he felt the whole room filled up with ferrety evils. Ferguson felt sorry for him. Once a man found himself prey to this kind of wholesale misgiving then a full life becomes impossible.

'Listen, Harry. There's something going on here.'

Ferguson nodded. Of course there was.

'I been looking over these statements here. The ones the Judge made on the night Patricia got killed and the one your man Steel, the boyfriend, made.'

Ferguson listened. He had noted the way the detective had referred to the girl by her first name. Identification with a victim. He could see past the moment to a date in the future when he would see McConnell briefly from a passing car, a shambling figure on the pavement, his head down and his lips moving as though he were saying the grey names of the paving stones.

'Get that expression off your face, Ferguson.'

'What expression? There's no expression on my face.'

'Come on, Harry. I can see what you're thinking, read it in your face, no matter how much poker you play. Or who you play it with. I got a real problem with these statements.'

'Tell me about it.'

'I'll ignore the tone in your voice, Harry, and I'll tell you. The Judge says he rang the boyfriend Steel at one forty-five a.m. to ask him where Patricia was.'

'What's the problem?'

'Steel says the call come at between five past and ten past two. I rung him and he's not backing away from it. His da answered the phone and he says the same thing.'

'What are you saying?'

'I'm saying that at five past two on the morning of the 13th of November, Judge Lancelot Curran was aware that his nineteen-year-old daughter had already been found and was on her way to a doctor's surgery. If Steel isn't lying through his fucking teeth for some unknown reason then Curran rang him and asked him if he had seen Patricia when he already knew that she was dead or dying.'

Ferguson looked at him. 'A Pole did it, McConnell, some Polish airman. A farm boy from some frozen back of beyond place. Never seen a beautiful woman before. Give me a kiss beautiful woman. Just a kiss. Stick to the Pole doing it. That was a far better story. Even if you never catch anybody.'

'That's the problem, Harry. They want me to catch somebody. They kind of insist on it.'

Later on that evening, Ferguson told Esther what McConnell had said. He knew that she had been drinking all day and he sat patiently, awaiting the moment when she would lie back on the sofa and indicate, with spacious empathetic gestures, that she was ready to talk to him. He brought her a fresh drink and told her about the phone call. He took the cellophane from her cigarettes and put them beside her. He said that McConnell had gone on to explain another anomaly involving the Judge's phone call to Steel.

'The Judge says to Steel that he had information that Patricia had got the five o'clock bus home from the city.'

'Yes?'

'The clock in the bus station was wrong. It was the ten past five bus that Patricia got home, even though the clock read five.'

The mind goes back to the bus station. The sound of bus tyres on wet tarmac. The Tannoy calling out place names that boom and echo in the high wrought-iron roof. Patricia went to a kiosk to buy a packet of Black Cat cigarettes. You look for fatal detail. The clock was one of those large white-faced clocks with black roman numerals, plain, with the manufacturer's name on it just below the hands. Stalwart, dependable. The clock had been in the same place for fifteen years and it had never been wrong, but it was wrong this night.

'I don't understand what you're saying to me, Harry.' There was a note of pleading in her voice. Be kind in the presence of my disarray.

'The Judge said he had information that Patricia got the bus home at five. There was no bus at five. The only person who thought there was a bus at that time was Patricia. So the Judge must have got his information from Patricia.'

'Before she was killed.'

'Before she was killed.'

Esther took a cigarette from the packet on the table. He lit it with a Dunhill lighter and as she dipped to take the light from his cupped hands, her eyes half closed against the smoke, he thought he saw someone she kept hidden from him. Her clandestine self, a tactile poise about her, an unguessed-at sensual aplomb.

'If it's true it means that Patricia went home from the bus.'

'It does.'

'There would be no man waiting for her on the drive.'

'Then whatever happened to her must have happened after that.'

'Something awful is going to happen here,' she said, 'and we're all going to be part of it.'

'There's nothing much we can do about it,' he said. 'What can we do?'

'Have you spoken to Lance?'

'What can I say to him? Why were you lying about your daughter's murder? Why did you ring her boyfriend and ask him where she was when you already knew where she was?'

'What is McConnell going to do?'

'He is going to put all of this in a report and give it to Pim. He's going to say that he has no other suspects and that they should begin to look at events in the Curran house that night.'

Esther shivered and wrapped her arms around herself.

She walked to the window and looked out into the dark. He wanted to put his arms round her but he knew not to go near her. She would not allow him to touch her. He knew that in her mind this was a kind of tribute paid to him, a dark bounty of celibacy.

'Who killed her, then?' she said quietly. 'Who killed the girl?'

'I don't know, Esther. They are a strange family. And it was a violent death. Stabbed thirty-seven times. The work of a madman.'

'I think I know,' she said.

He didn't say anything. She stood at the window looking out. She was not waiting for him to question her. She knew that he wouldn't ask. When she finally turned from the window he was gone. She heard the car door slam outside and the sound of the engine. She refilled her glass and carried it upstairs to her room.

Two days after he had submitted the report, McConnell walked into his office to find Pim sitting on a hard wooden chair just inside the door.

'I hope you don't mind, McConnell, my seating myself in your impressively tidy office. It's the legs, you see, the circulation.' He gestured with distaste towards his feet. His cheeks were sunken and his eyes were yellowed to an ammoniac hue, but his expression suggested a man bent upon the fulfilment of a covenant.

'I think you've done a wonderful job on this Curran thing, played a blinder, really.'

'Have you read my report?'

'We've realized that we have left you very much on your own with all this. Thoughtlessness on a major scale, really. There's a chap at Scotland Yard eager to assist you, straining at the leash rather. We thought you'd appreciate the helping hand.'

'The report, Sir Richard.'

'Chief Superintendent Capstick should be here by the weekend. I'm sure his experience will prove invaluable.'

McConnell afterwards told Ferguson that he felt something had happened over that weekend to make Pim alter the course of the investigation.

McConnell watched from the window as Pim crossed the station yard. He walked badly and looked as if he should be in hospital, but he seemed inexorable, adamant, as though he yet drew bleak sustenance from the murder.

McConnell admitted afterwards that he had in the end been relieved to have direct responsibility for the investigation removed from him, in the light of what happened. But that evening he was depressed and stopped as he was passing through the numbered roundabouts and artificial boating ponds on the outskirts of Larne. He got out of the car. It was a salt-marsh landscape, unproductive. It was a place where wildfowl overwintered. Unnamed species. In winter he could hear them fly over the house. Sometimes he stopped on one of the bridges and watched them wading in the mud. It was what he did now. The birds moved across the mud, leaving their footprints in it like a minutely reckoned calculus, then stood motionless in the early morning mist. Cold, iconic figures.

'You like living here,' his wife had once told him. 'It's the self-pity in the air you like.'

He had to acknowledge the truth in what she said. Something in the place attracted him. He was fascinated by its scattered housing estates, its compact industrial zone, its melancholy inner life.

TWENTY

On 14 December 1952, Chief Superintendent John Capstick of Scotland Yard was summoned to the office of Sir Ronald Howe, the Assistant Commissioner for crime. Howe told him that Sir Richard Pim had asked for their help. In his 1960 autobiography, *Given in Evidence*, Capstick records Howe as telling him, 'This is as ghastly a murder as any I've ever known.'

The autobiography in fact appears to have been ghost-written by a journalist called Jack Thomas. Capstick is presented as bluff, no-nonsense, intelligent. There are elements of grudging respect for the criminal. A certain amount of brutality is alluded to but you draw the conclusion that it was proportionate, appropriate to the manly values shared by policeman and criminal. You learn that Capstick was a member of the anti-black-market team during the war. The team was known as the Ghost Squad. You learn that Capstick liked to be referred to by a nickname acquired during that time. Charlie Artful.

Thomas's style is dramatic. Each case conducted by Capstick is given a title. 'Blood on the Moon'. 'Welsh Valley of Fear'. He works hard at setting the scene for a crime. In the case of 'The Judge's Daughter' you are introduced to the case via the paperboy, George Chambers. The darkened drive in Whiteabbey, the terrified newsboy hearing sounds in the undergrowth. The policeman referring to himself in arrogant asides. You can almost hear the detective's voice. You imagine him sitting in a comfortable chair with the reporter in front of him, hunched on a smaller chair, writing in shorthand. The tone is vain, self-justifying. You would not be surprised to find that some concern had been expressed over Capstick's methods before he left the force.

Later that evening, Capstick and Detective Sergeant Denis Hawkins flew from London to the airport at Nutt's Corner, fifteen miles from the city. The airport had a wartime air about it. Makeshift and apprehensive. The air crews looked tired, burdened.

Capstick was a tall, burly man who dressed in a double-breasted pinstripe suit and wore a carnation in his button-hole. There was a half-sovereign ring on the middle finger of his right hand. He smoked a pipe to give the impression of dependability. When he was working he affected a stoop. He wanted to demonstrate the weary burden of detection. They said he liked women. There were stories about the wives of colleagues. There were stories about parties at the police club in Essex. The languid narratives of the suburbs. Before Capstick sat down he carefully gripped the material of his trousers above the knee and hoisted the trousers up an inch. He cared about his clothes. His hair was swept back behind his ears. You thought of open-topped sports cars, the seduction of divorcees. He was experienced in dealing with the press and was capable of projecting the sense of hard-eyed melodrama in an imperfect world that was required by the press.

Capstick records that Hawkins carried the 'heavy murder bag'. McConnell met them at the airport and drove them to the International Hotel in the city. He tells how McConnell outlined the case in detail as they drove to the hotel. McConnell dropped them at the exit and said that that someone would be waiting to meet them in the hotel bar when they had put their bags in their rooms.

'What do you reckon, guvnor?' asked Hawkins. 'Think some kind of mental defective done it?'

Capstick didn't answer. He often saw police manuals

lying open on Hawkins's desk. Weighty books with well-handled covers that he had sent to him from American law-enforcement agencies. He knew that Hawkins enrolled on correspondence courses and repeated Spanish phrases from a cassette when he was in the car on his own. He described himself as a believer in self-improvement. Capstick often saw him driving along on his own, his lips moving, that earnest look.

When they went down to the bar, Pim was waiting for them. He sat in a wing chair with his back to the window. He reclined in the chair as if he intended to display a well-bred languor. But afterwards Hawkins said to Capstick that he doubted that Pim would have been able to get out of the chair without help. 'He's like the walking fucking dead, guvnor,' Hawkins said. 'He's like a corpse stood up.'

Pim ordered drinks and the two men sat down.

'Have you been appraised of the facts of the case, Chief Superintendent?' he asked.

'More or less, sir. Saw a bit in the papers over the past days. And McConnell gave us the low-down on the way here.'

'Ah yes, Inspector McConnell. The provincial police-man. He is, of course, at your disposal. And have you formed any conclusion, Chief Superintendent?'

'Not so far, sir. A frenzy of some nature. An animal. I've seen cases like it in the past. Can't contain themselves, so they can't, sir. Any evidence that the girl's virtue was interfered with?'

'McConnell says not. But the girl's underclothing appeared to be torn.'

'Usually the motive behind these things, sir.'

'I rather thought that a foreigner might be involved. Stabbing is rather a foreign modus operandi, is it not, Chief Superintendent?'

'Its a useful thought, sir. Plenty of stabbings in London

during the war. Spaniards, Arabs and the like. Stab you soon as look at you, some of them.'

'What about Poles?'

'The temperament is there, sir, no shadow of a doubt about it.'

Pim leaned forward. 'I believe our suspect is among those that have so far been interviewed, Chief Superintendent. I want you to find him.'

'And what if he isn't there, sir?' Hawkins said.

Pim turned his head to look at him. It was like a dead man looking at you, Hawkins said afterwards. He made you feel icy all over.

'He will be found among these men and he will be found quickly. And Chief Superintendent? No useful purpose can be served by further distressing the Curran family. There will be no further interviews.'

'Mum's the word, sir. We'll give them the old wide berth.'

'What do you make of that then, sir?' Hawkins asked as they entered the foyer. He's a rum enough character, our Sir Richard.'

'By all accounts he's got the ear of Winston Churchill.'

'You don't say, sir.'

'I'd say we keep our noses clean and find our man.'

'Basic investigative technique, sir. Start with the family. Look at them first.'

'We'll start where we're told to start, Hawkins. We start looking at the people who were interviewed.'

Capstick attempted to keep himself in trim. He knew he should stop smoking. He read extensively into the literature of premature hair loss, emphysema, a variety of sexual disorders. He practised energy techniques intended to prevent anxiety and promote ease of spirit, but he could not prevent a gnawing in the stomach. There were always those prepared to call down calamity on the head of an efficient detective. He worried about his health. He was concerned about what might be going on in London during his absence. Late at night Capstick would confide in women that he had cancer. He did it when he was drunk. He said they wanted to open him up but he wouldn't let them. He could not resist the grandeur and pathos of cancer terminology. Tumour the size of your fist. Riddled with it.

When he was sober he felt ashamed of the cancer lie. But when he was drunk he couldn't resist the tragedy of it, the dramatic sweep.

Capstick said that death held no fears for him. The pain of dying was different. He had never claimed heroism when it came to the pain of death. The truth was he feared the heart attack most. He fitted the profile. The survivors of heart attacks always said it was like a giant hand picked them up and threw them across the room. That was the phrase they always used. Giant hand.

The following morning McConnell took Capstick out to The Glen. It was a dark, overcast morning. In anticipation of Capstick's visit, massive battery-operated searchlights had been erected in the wooded area alongside the driveway and they were switched on. Press photographers were allowed onto the driveway to photograph Capstick investigating the scene. McConnell, Capstick and Hawkins were photographed together. Capstick is standing to one side, but he dominates the photograph. He is carrying a pair of white gloves. His jaw is set but the ghost of sardonic amusement hovers round his lips. A smile implying an understanding of the games played by murderers, the jests that accompanied their foul practices, the subtle devices of the ungodly. Hawkins is watching him with a similar expression. The impression that is given is that these are men who understand what is happening here, men who are not subject to dread, the deep psychic unease that was abroad regarding this murder. In the bottom left-hand corner of the photograph a hand holding a pen is poised above a notebook, suggesting that an informal press conference is taking place.

McConnell is also in the photograph but he doesn't appear to be part of the shrewd-eyed station-house camaraderie of the others. He is closer to the camera, almost turned away. His face seems very white, which may be due to his proximity to the flash. The same flash that shows up the three men in such detail has also left the scene behind them in total blackness, so they appear to be posed against a black backcloth. It is into this darkness that McConnell is staring, with an expression that suggests a melancholy prescience as to the outcome of the investigation.

There were no photographs of the scene under the trees. The lamps were set up on the dry ground at the edge of the forest and pointed inwards, and the policemen and journalists stood silently behind them as if they expected something to emerge from the forest, a movement in the undergrowth, breathing coming in harsh rasps. The damp earth and trees were bathed in the yellowish light, and rainwater striking the hot lens of the carbide lamps floated through the trees as condensation, ghostly fictions.

'Turn them off,' McConnell said. 'Turn those bloody lights out.'

The glare of the lights seemed to demand a literal interpretation of the scene in front of them, one lacking in misgiving and cerebral murk. One by one the trips were thrown on the lights and the scrubby margins at the edge of The Glen's driveway were returned to their air of rain-soaked mystery.

McConnell showed the two men where the body had been found and recounted the sequence of events from that night. He pointed out that there had been little blood on the ground, despite the severity of the girl's wounds.

'But this is the really interesting thing,' he said. He led the two detectives back to the driveway. A small area beside it had been cordoned off. He told them that Patricia's folder, books, handbag and cap had been found there at dawn the following day.

'What's interesting?' Capstick said, looking around him.

McConnell paused. At first he had the feeling that the two detectives were being polite, that these were necessary formalities being carried out by the local man.

'Is this stuff not in the report you gave us last night?' Hawkins said.

'Not this bit. I just worked it out and I kept it to myself.' McConnell explained that Patricia's possessions had been placed at the edge of the driveway with the yellow cap on top. He had worked out that they had been passed in close proximity at least thirteen times during the night, but no one had spotted them.

'People a bit sleepy round here then?' Hawkins said. 'A bit dozy?'

'No, that's not it. They weren't spotted because they weren't there.'

'Just saying they were there,' Capstick said, 'just saying, couldn't she have put them down there, gone into the bushes?'

'For a spot of slap and tickle, who wouldn't?' Hawkins said.

'If they had just fallen there then the folder and all would have spilled open.' McConnell explained that he had already carried out experiments to test that and that the folder would indeed have fallen open.

'So she must have put them there,' said Capstick. 'I think we'll follow that one up.'

'A little cuddle on the way home,' Hawkins said, 'things get out of hand. It's usually the way of these things.'

'That's not what I'm saying,' McConnell said. He was aware of how he sounded. Scholarly and earnest. 'I'm saying that the books weren't there that night. That someone must have put them there sometime early in the morning.'

'I'm sure with all the coming and going, the excitement, people would have walked past them,' Capstick said.

'It's natural enough,' Hawkins said.

McConnell started to name the people that had passed the books, starting with the taxi driver and the paperboy and including Constable Rutherford, who had searched the ground with a torch.

Capstick turned towards the journalists who were standing behind the lights. They began to call to him.

'It rained all that night,' McConnell said.

'See what I mean? In the rain people keep the head down,' Capstick said. 'Couldn't see their hand in front of their face.'

Hawkins and Capstick were moving towards the journalists. As they did so the men behind the lamps began to turn them again. McConnell put his hand up to his eyes to shield them. The two Englishmen lost outline against the harsh light, their figures became ill-defined, looming. McConnell spoke but it was impossible to see if either man turned back to acknowledge him.

'The thing is that it rained all night but all her things were dry. They couldn't have been there all night because they were bone-dry.'

The first time Capstick saw Esther Ferguson he knew that he would have her. There was always one on every investigation that he did outside London. The dissatisfied wife. The alcoholic wife. He sometimes wondered why these women came to him. There was something frightening about it, these shadowed women who undressed in the dark. Who sat at a hotel dressing-room mirror in the morning putting on their make-up with small domestic gestures, as though satisfied with the bleakness of the encounter.

Capstick and Hawkins had started drinking at the Europa Hotel where the English journalists were based. The man from the *Manchester News*. The man from the *Birmingham Argos*. The men stood at the same corner of the bar every night and the reporters gathered round them. The English journalists formed the inner circle. The man from *The Times*. The man from the *Telegraph*. The local reporters stayed on the outside, listening in to the knowledgeable talk of the others. They could hear the pleasure the others felt at using the words. The phrases that hung in the air between them. Murder weapon. Forensic examination. They savoured the words. Absorbed by their tainted imperative. Crime scene. Foul play.

'Here we go,' Hawkins said, when he saw Esther standing on her own at the end of the bar. 'Another Merry Widow.'

Capstick stared. She stood with one hand on the bar and the other holding a cigarette to her lips and she was looking at him with a steady, covetous gaze. He felt his chest tighten. At first he didn't move for he felt the woman an envoy of sexual havoc. He saw it in her ravished face. When the bar closed he took her to his room.

He had no illusions about himself. He knew that Ferguson's wife wanted from him confirmation of how bad she was. The little sounds she made, the little sexual polysyllables, were the language of her worthlessness. It gave her comfort, he thought, that she could call it an affair, that she could put a word on her dread, take comfort in its venality.

'Are you going to catch the big bad murderer?' she said, lying next to him in the bed, not looking at him.

'I expect so. Probably some pervert. It usually is.'

'I'm thirsty. Be a darling and ring room service. Don't you think the family are all a bit peculiar?'

'Never met any of them. Never want to.'

'Why not?'

'Get in the way.'

'Please call room service.'

'There's Scotch in my bag if you need it.'

'Don't be mean. You're tired of me now.'

'I've got a long day tomorrow.'

'I could cuddle up beside you. I'd be safe beside the big detective.'

'Not a good idea.'

'Suddenly nothing is a good idea any more.'

He turned to her. 'They say Patricia Curran was a bit of a slut.'

'Don't.'

'They say she was a tart. Would that be right?'

'Please don't.'

Ferguson knew where his wife was that night. He felt an obligation to keep a track of her and had followed her on several occasions. Shortly before Capstick's arrival she had disappeared. A friend who had been at Newry Assizes said that he had seen Esther in the foyer of the Maritime Hotel. Ferguson took the afternoon off. Driving down Chancellor's Hill, Ferguson could see the whole town of Newry laid out beneath him. The canal leading into the Albert Basin and on through the ship canal into the lough. The railway marshalling yard from which the rails had been removed for scrap, their alignment still visible and the tollhouse still intact as though a levy might still be demanded of some phantom freight. The section of the canal running along Merchant's Quay was silted and the warehouses there had collapsed, although there was still a smell of rendered bone meal from O'Hare's Mill. It had been late before he had been able to get away from the his office, so dark was beginning to fall as he drove past Solitude Park then turned down Buttercrane Quay and over the tram tracks into the Albert Basin. He passed the stockyard, the Shambles, the coal yard and the timber yard and darkness was almost complete when he turned onto Sugar Island in front of the Linen Exchange and looked down the canal and saw a vista of the roofless houses of unnamed merchants stretching into the distance beyond the metal bridge, the houses derelict and the windows empty so that you could see the sky through them and the shapes of roof timbers raised like the devices of an aristocracy of ruin.

Ferguson parked on Quay Street opposite the Maritime Hotel. It was a Victorian building with turrets, gaudy and complex. It stood alone on Quay Street. The buildings on either side had been demolished. He looked up and saw a woman standing at one of the windows. He went in. The foyer was the same as he remembered. Dark panelled walls. Heavy carpets. On the counter there were collection boxes for the blind, for the lifeboat service. Upstairs he heard a man's voice, a woman's laugh. The place seemed to lend itself to furtive encounters. The air seemed to ring with fraudulent declarations of love. There was no one at the reception desk so Ferguson opened the heavy register and turned it towards him. He ran his finger down the page until he came to Mr and Mrs Harry Ferguson. It was written in Esther's handwriting. He closed the book and replaced it. He went outside and sat in the car. He waited until at two o'clock a woman he had seen earlier enter the hotel on her own came to one of the bedroom windows and leaned out to smoke a cigarette. She was wearing a slip. She spoke to someone in the room without turning round and pulled on the cigarette. It lit her face. He could see the puffiness under her eyes, the lines at her neck. He could see the wariness in her eyes, the knowledge that this was an outpost on the peripheries of desire. She turned at the sound of a man's voice and let fall the curtain behind her. He stared blankly at the remaining windows. He wondered which one concealed his wife. He thought of her waking in the dark, reaching for a man with her long, ruinous fingers.

Following Patricia's murder, the female students at Queen's had organized themselves so that they did not go home alone. Male students walked them to their buses and trains. Their fathers waited for them in parked cars at railway station car parks and at bus stops. All over the city, men sat in their cars, smoking, their faces half-lit, alert to the noirish possibilities of the situation they found themselves in, acknowledging each other with curt nods as they drove past, participants in a grave male discourse. Sentinel figures waiting for their wide-eyed daughters to dismount from their buses and trains and run towards the car, moving awkwardly in heels, breathless, books clutched to their chests. They dash towards their fathers, who are happy to see their daughters explore a full range of girlish vulnerabilities under their supervision, then fall silent as the car turns into a suburban driveway, becoming breathless at the sight of their porch lights, the glittery and uncomplicated pledge of access to all that's full of promise.

The car is put in the garage and the tennis racket is left beside the hall stand and the intricate night is left to its own devices. Patricia doesn't belong to this world any more and there is a growing feeling that her name should not be spoken, as she might come slouching up the gravel path, her face turned away, shifty and underhand in death.

TWENTY-ONE

Doris Curran stayed in her room during the days and weeks following the murder. Mrs Crangle never saw her. She came in during the morning and cooked lunch before leaving. She was under instructions from Judge Curran not to go upstairs. Instead, either the Judge or Desmond would come home and they would take the tray from her wordlessly and carry it upstairs to Doris's room like a stern of purpose Victorian jailer. Mrs Crangle would listen to their heavy tread on the steps overhead, and the bedroom door opening. There would be murmured talk and then the door would close again and she would hear the footsteps returning till the house seemed flooded with terrible solicitude. Mrs Crangle said that she was walking down the drive one day and turned to see Doris standing in the bedroom window. She was wearing a long white nightdress. Her grey hair was uncombed and her eyes seemed to be fixed on the spot where her daughter had died. 'It put the heart sideways in me,' Mrs Crangle said, 'to see the poor woman stood there with the two eyes red raw with crying. She must've been froze stiff, for it was a cold house and there was no light ever put to the fire in her room.'

The housekeeper stood in the driveway watching, but Doris's gaze never deviated and she stood without moving as though fixed there.

One evening towards the end of December, Judge Curran had asked Mrs Crangle to stay late. He said that he was to have a visitor and that he wanted the fire in the drawing room lit and a tray of drinks left on the butler's table. A little after eight o'clock a large black Rover came up the drive. The driver got out and held open the door for a man in evening dress. He got out of the car using the door to support him.

'First off I thought he had drink took,' she said afterwards. But the man straightened himself and scrutinized the front of the house for a long time. The dripping gutters. The peeling paintwork. He was wearing a stiff collar and starched shirtfront and his hair was combed back and his face revealed decay commensurate with that of the house. 'God help me but he was the picture of an undertaker,' Mrs Crangle said. He climbed the steps carefully and rang the bell. 'It was like a film,' Mrs Crangle said. You expected an ominous sound, a sepulchral tolling in the depths of the house, the front door creaking open, a crabbed figure in evening dress climbing the steps as agent of a long-prophesied catastrophe. Judge Curran was waiting for Pim in the drawing room. Mrs Crangle followed Pim in to check the coal on the fire, but neither man spoke until she had left the room. The Judge standing at the fireplace, Pim standing beside him. Although Pim was smaller than the Judge and bowed by illness, the Judge seemed ill at ease with him and Mrs Crangle thought he looked like a man attendant upon some trial or inquisition.

Mrs Crangle did not see Pim leave. She heard the hall door close and then the sound of an engine. She went into the drawing room to fetch the empty glasses. The Judge was sitting by the fire. His elbows were on his knees and his head was bowed. On hearing Mrs Crangle in the doorway he lifted his head. He opened his mouth to speak but nothing came out, and his eyes were puffy and red.

Davy prepared the railway carriage for Christmas with decorations that he had cut from pink and blue crepe paper. He cut a fir tree from a small plantation on the embankment behind the caravan and put it up in the middle of the carriage and hung tinsel from its branches. There was an adroitness in matters of sentiment. He found a wind-up Victrola on the kerb where it had been left for the bin man. He dismantled and repaired it, working at night in the glow of carbide lamps he had fashioned himself. He worked quickly, setting out tiny machined parts on white tissue paper with deft movements.

Gordon was careful not to touch any of them. Laid out on the sheets of paper, each tiny part looked like a character from a lost language. You thought about a scroll unearthed in a cave, evidence of a civilization advanced for its time, now mysteriously vanished. You imagined the words set out on the scroll. Dry, precise, detailed.

He had been a dreamy boy and his mother had warned him about imagination. 'Imagination is all very well,' she said. What she meant was that you did not need to bring mystery with you when even the simplest of human transactions was knee-deep in perplexity.

But now Gordon was on the edge of a murder, and subject to its stark metaphysic allure.

'I think the papers is right. Some Pole done it. They're fucking perverts, that crew,' Davy said.

'I think there's more to it.'

'I hate when you do that.'

'Do what?'

'Go all mysterious on me. Letting on you know more than you do.'

'Maybe I do know more.'

'You'd better not be talking like that to any of them detectives, I'm telling you that for nothing. Them boys'll not be long in beating thon playacting out of you.' Davy knew that nothing good could come of Gordon's attraction to the case.

'I think I should call Desmond.'

'You're mad in the head. That boy's nothing but trouble for the likes of me and you.' Davy knew that the world was untrustworthy in ways that Gordon could not guess at. 'Just stay away from them peelers.'

'Maybe there's something I could tell them, would help them catch the murderer.'

'You don't mind yourself, them boys'll help themselves to you, so they will.'

Three days before Christmas, Davy finished the gramophone. Gordon brought him a packet of Victrola needles from Moneyworth's in Whiteabbey, and some records that he had borrowed from Radford. Davy put on 'Blue Christmas' by Jim Reeves. They listened in silence. Gordon thought about snowfall in America, a prairie hush, the muffled sound of hooves. He went to the window and looked across at the promenade. It was dusk but there were still couples walking, drifting back towards the lights of the town, and Gordon thought about the houses they were going back to, the smell of cooking, the fire lit, teatime. He thought about words for people like them. Homeward. Homebound. It made his life seem small, constricted, worried-at.

'What the fuck's up with you?' Davy asked. 'Who ate your bun?'

'Nothing's wrong.'

'There's something. Tell you what. I'll put on something we can dance to.'

'I can't dance.'

'What? What do you mean you can't dance. Everybody can dance.'

'I never learned.'

Gordon's mother had not approved of dancing and kept him from it until it seemed too late to learn. She managed to create an impression of unsanitary practices in the local dance halls. In fact, Gordon went along with her because he feared the local youths. Some of them kept razors under the lapels of their drape jackets. Others carried steel combs with the handle filed to a point and sharpened, giving them a lethal edge as well as an improvised jailhouse allure, even if few of them had ever been sent up to the damp coastal fortress that had been turned into Peterhead prison. On Saturday nights when he was a teenager, the streets of Dollar filled with young couples going to the Frontier Ballroom at the top of the town. After the dance, the couples moved into the alleyways behind the houses, into the doorways. When the hall first emptied there was talk and laughter. After that a silence descended apart from a murmured word, a small cry relayed through the dark. Lying in bed, Gordon thought that he could sense the intentness that was brought to the night by so many couples; eyes tight shut, he gave himself up to it: the lingered-over nocturnality, lost in the desirous gloom of small-town romance.

'Come on to fuck till I show you how to dance. That's fucking mad, so it is, man doesn't know how to dance.'

Davy found a copy of 'The Tennessee Waltz' and put it on. It was by the Carter Family or some other far west purveyor of kinship and downhome yearning. Davy liked Johnny Cash. The voice wintry, gravely lyric. He showed Gordon how to place his feet and moved him around the room. He played 'Begin the Beguine'. Gordon looked down and saw that Davy was wearing cracked leather dance pumps. Gordon thought that not even his father would have worn such shoes, that they looked like something from a portrait. Gordon enjoyed the easy-going country dances. Davy moved smoothly holding Gordon at arm's length, an old-fashioned upright dance style, his face turned away, with a kind of eighteenth-century dance master's decorum. As the light went down, Gordon rested his head lightly on Davy's shoulder. Gordon closed his eyes, thinking that even if this wasn't happiness it was near enough for him. The floor creaked under their feet and in the still of the evening people returning from the promenade could hear the drifting notes of a scratchy and timeworn dance tune, Gordon's good luck receding in two-four time.

Capstick told Hawkins to go through the interviews that had already been done. 'Pick out a few likely lads and we'll have them in. There's bound to be some squealing bastard out there'll help us get this sorted.'

'Who found the girl, anyway, the corpse?' asked Hawkins. 'I'll go five to one it was somebody walking a dog. There's always some bastard walking a dog. Sometimes I wonder if they're as innocent as they look. Maybe I should bring one in. Let the fucker sweat.'

'You weren't listening to the inspector. The body was discovered by the son after the girl went missing.'

'You going after a confession, sir?'

'What do you think?'

'To be honest, there ain't much more to go on, sir, as far as I can see.'

'A confession, full, free and frank, Hawkins. I want it settled quick as possible. There's politics in this.'

'Ain't there always, sir.'

'Right. Get a few of the local scribes in, butter them up, buy them a few drinks, whatever the fuck they drink around here, you know the score. Find out who the local perverts and lunatics are. By the look of the place, there's plenty of them. Homosexuals, saddle-sniffers, flashers. I'll take care of Johnny foreigner, see if I can't find a nice depraved Pole for our Mr Pim.'

'Mr Pim has it in for them Poles, sir.'

'All he wants is for them to go back to Poland where they belong. Hanging one or two of them would be the cat's pyjamas for him.'

For several days, Capstick stayed in the gym of the YMCA in Whiteabbey re-interrogating Polish soldiers who had criminal records. None of the charges involved sexual assault. They were mainly concerned with petty larceny, the theft of food, vegetables from people's gardens, chickens from farmers' coops. Others had been involved in fights with other soldiers. One had been arrested by MPs based in Larne for the theft of women's underwear from a washing line outside a Greenfinch hostel in Whitehead. He was a quiet, serious-minded young man who later proved to have an alibi. The language was an obstacle. The man would speak quietly to the Polish officer, sometimes for several minutes at a time, and the information would then be translated into English for Capstick. A story began to emerge that was elaborate, biographical, filled with the particulars of sexual awakening. A boyhood in a twenties apartment building in Warsaw. An aunt glimpsed undressing, silk hissing; her pale, Slavic face turned towards the watching boy as she stepped out of her slip, lifting one foot and then the other before reaching towards her stocking tops in a motion he had never seen before but that seemed composed of deeply formalized sexual mannerisms. He said he thought the woman was dead now, killed in an Allied bombing raid. He could not rid himself of his memory of her, half turned towards him. He said that his crime had been a sin of insurmountable longing.

The translating officer had a thin moustache and spoke a precise English, redolent of pre-war European aristocracy, vast estates, obscure codes of honour. But when the two men spoke Polish among themselves, Capstick found the language harsh, constructed of surly, obstructive gutturals. A centuries-old insolence seemed to have found its way into it. After a few days, Capstick instructed McConnell to take over.

Meanwhile Hawkins started to frequent the White Horse Hotel in Whiteabbey. He bought drinks for the regulars.

Gin and tonic, whiskey and soda. He started with the day-time drinkers. Men in their forties and fifties who had come to terms with the debased loyalties of the all-day drinker. Most of their stories were lies. They embarked on long sentimental stories on the general themes of treachery to their offspring, the radiant and wholly justified contempt they had earned from their wives, almost sobbing as they spoke. They took Hawkins by the arm and pointed him out to their friends. The successful London detective, a scale by which to measure their self-contempt. When Hawkins drew them aside as the afternoon went on and started to quiz them about the inhabitants of the town, they composed their features in expressions of spurious and unearned worldliness. They lowered their voices, anxious to tell him about the town. It was the first time he heard the name Wesley Courtney.

Capstick went to the law library and waited outside. He had a copy of the *Daily Mail* photograph of Desmond in his hand. When Desmond came out, Capstick fell into step beside him. He made no comment and Capstick realized that Desmond had recognized him immediately. Capstick didn't like the look of him. The way he never looked at people when they were talking to him. The air of privilege.

'You didn't think much of your sister's choice of associates, did you, Mr Curran?'

'I didn't regard them as suitable companions for a girl of her age.'

'For a man of Christian belief you don't seem all that upset that your sister was murdered.'

'I was never given to showing my emotions, Inspector.'

'Fair enough. But I tell you something, Mr Curran. If she was my sister I would care about the things that people were saying about her.'

'And what manner of things are people saying about my sister?'

'I wouldn't want to repeat them to you, Mr Curran, what with you grieving and all.'

'I didn't hear you were a man given to so much delicacy, Mr Capstick.'

'They're saying that her morals were not what they should be for a young lady of her station in the world. According to my sources she was seen with older men, married men.'

'I am aware that she had a vivacious nature, Chief Superintendent.'

'I'm labouring under the impression here, sir, correct me if I'm wrong, that you didn't approve of your Patricia?'

'My sister never sought my approval.'

'See? There it is again. There's a way you have of saying that, if you don't mind me saying.'

'I have a consultation at twelve o'clock, Chief Superintendent, if you're finished.'

'Would you have thought that Patricia was in danger, morally like? Would you have thought she was jeopardizing her immortal soul?'

'All our souls are in jeopardy, Chief Superintendent.'

'Spoke like a true brief, sir, and many's the one I've come up against in court.'

'I'm sure.'

'What I'm trying to say is that, if Patricia was putting her immortal soul in danger, flaunting her sin, so to speak, she'd nearly be asking to meet her maker, wouldn't she?'

'I believe our Maker usually requires us to attend upon His wish, not the other way round.'

'You've still got the hangman, here, haven't you? Always thought it was a deterrent myself.'

'Good morning, Chief Superintendent.'

'Right you are, sir. Right you are.'

Capstick stopped at the top of Chichester Street and watched Desmond until he had turned into the law courts.

He was like a clergyman, Capstick thought. His thoughts went back to the scene that McConnell had described to him. The body stiffened with rigor mortis being forced into the car, the headlights shining on the wet driveway; the Judge and his son, the movement through the trees of the small rain-slicked cortège. He remembered that Desmond had apparently found the body, stumbled upon it in the dark, throwing his hands up, crying out, his mouth a perfect circle of horror. Turning it over in his mind, Capstick saw a performance, grimly parodic, a study from an engraving of foul murder stumbled upon. Slipping into a detective's argot of dark promise, he told himself that he would keep an eye on Mr Curran.

Courtney recognized Hawkins as a policeman as soon as he came through the door. The detective placed his hat on the hat rack and swept the room with an incurious gaze that omitted nothing. Courtney turned back to the man in the chair. Hawkins yawned and picked up a copy of *Buy and Sell*. Courtney watched him in the mirror.

There was a sense of early positions being determined, character established, an audience settling itself in the darkness. Courtney addressed the man in the chair.

'Terrible thing, the murder of that wee girl. You could be living in the same town as the boy that done it, like as not.'

The man in the chair was elderly, weathered, a morose dockhand with a union badge in his lapel and one eye almost obliterated by a scar that ran from his jaw to his hairline. He was given to speaking in homely adages that were given the ineradicable force of scripture by the massive lesion on his face. 'You lie down with dogs you get up with fleas.'

'Still and all, she was only walking up to the house. There's some rare perverts in these parts.'

'There is. A woman would have to mind herself, so she would. As she sows so shall she reap.'

'I hear tell whoever done it had a go at her. Word has it the police haven't a notion. Word has it they're running around the place, fit to pick up anybody they like and stitch him up with it.'

'You wouldn't put it past them, so you wouldn't.'

'What about these English boys they brought in?'

'I'd say they're no great shakes either.'

'That's what I thought.'

The old man paid and left. Hawkins sat down in the chair and Courtney tucked a striped towel into the collar of his jacket.

'Shave or haircut, sir?'

'Haircut.'

Hawkins studied Courtney's face in the mirror. The bald head, the heavy, dark-framed glasses and white coat that made him look like he was dedicated to a frontier fifties technology. The nuclear reactor. The X-ray. There was a sense of objective scientific insight being brought to bear, barriers to progress being pushed back. On the shelf under the mirror a handful of combs were floating in a sterilizer. A cutthroat razor lay open beside it.

'You know what you were saying about somebody being fitted up for this murder?' Hawkins said.

'Yes?' Courtney said. Hawkins half turned in the chair so that he was facing the other man.

'Just make fucking sure it's not you,' he said.

'Oh, no,' Courtney said with a soft laugh, 'it won't be me.'

'The guvnor doesn't like fruits. Thinks they're unnatural. And he's right.' Hawkins looked in the mirror to see Courtney grinning at him. There was a fetid odour in the barber's shop. Hawkins could see things floating in the water of the sterilizer, rudimentary life forms, green filaments growing up from the bottom. As Courtney cut his hair, Hawkins questioned him about the town. Adulterers. Fornicators. Homosexuals. He took out his notebook and wrote down names. It was a record of provincial sexual misconduct. He put phrases in brackets after some names. Married woman. Likes boys. He took a list of locations in Whiteabbey and nearby towns. He asked about public toilets. He knew that they were popular meeting places. He asked about parks, areas within the town where people kept company. He asked about old houses and demesnes. It was his experience that illicit lovers possessed a weakness for places that were formerly inhabited, now deserted or overgrown. They could not resist the fraudulent appeal of such places, the bogus melancholia of overgrown rose gardens, tattered velvet curtains blowing in empty windows, deserted ballrooms.

'Place is a regular fucking hotbed,' Hawkins said when they had finished.

'Everywhere is, Sergeant. Believe me. Everywhere is.'

Hawkins had been with Capstick when the Ghost Squad was set up in 1946. The origin of the Ghost Squad's name is explained in Capstick's autobiography by Chief Constable Percy Worth, who explains to Capstick that 'As far as the underworld is concerned, you will have no more material existence than ghosts.' The purpose of the Ghost Squad was to combat the alliance of former black marketeers and ex-servicemen who flooded London after the war. The tone of the chapter is light-hearted. The black marketeers are presented as causing problems for the war-damaged economy while remaining spivvy and engaging. You get an impression of men in cheap suits and thin moustaches. There is an underlying theme of intimacy between police and criminals, mutual respect.

Every evening at five o'clock, Capstick and Hawkins would have a drink in the snug of the White Horse and review the information they had collected that day. They put a conference sign on the door so that no one else

would come in. After they had talked about the day's findings, the conversation would turn to the war years and the
years immediately afterwards. They regarded this as
being an essential part of the policeman's job, to reminisce
in a sentimental way, to show a forbearance towards
themselves and others, talking on into the evening light in
a context of self-forgiveness. Capstick often brought up
the cases of men who had been hanged for murder in
cases he had prosecuted. Peter Griffith, the 'mad moon
killer' of Farnworth, hanged in Walton prison in February
1948. Evan Haydn Evans, hanged in Cardiff prison for the
murder of Rachel the Washerwoman in November 1948.
At that time only the hangman, chaplain, prison governor
and prison staff were allowed to attend hangings. Capstick often speculated what it would have been like to
have been there. The murmured prayers of the chaplain,
the smell of fresh sawdust, the dread shadow. He imagined the murderer, pale-faced in the pre-dawn chill, coming over to shake his hand, a murmured thanks for being
there, grateful for the role that Capstick had played in creating this sense of things coming to their fitting end.

Hawkins did not agree with him. He remembered a
night in 1946, shortly after the formation of the Ghost
Squad. Hawkins had been drinking in the Lock Bar in
Camden Town with Capstick. A Post Office van had been
robbed earlier in the week and that day an informant told
them that the driver had set up the job himself. The driver
was called Chink Newell. They had gone to the Lock Bar,
where Chink had been seen buying drinks for a large
party. Capstick had waited until the bar was about to
close, then he had motioned to Hawkins and the two men
went out the back entry and waited there in the rain
beside Chink's car. While they waited Capstick occupied
himself by pulling a length of cast-iron spouting from the
wall beside them so that the water gushed from the broken spout at head height. You couldn't hear yourself.

Hawkins thought of the word torrential. Chink came out of the bar and walked down the entry without noticing them. He put the key in the car door and then looked up and saw Capstick standing and Capstick gave him no chance to speak.

Looking back on it, Hawkins thought it was like a scene stripped of sound and colour, taking place in a flickering documentary light, Capstick's arm rising and falling as though he were engaged in a great toil, and Chink looking up at him, from half under the car where he had tried to crawl for shelter, his teeth showing and his back bent in a theatrical cringe and his arms raised hopelessly against the blows until in the end he dropped his arms and looked away from the two men standing above him, seeming lost in reverie. When he saw this, Capstick threw the length of pipe aside and carefully went down on his knees beside Chink, lowering his head to put his ear to Chink's mouth, listening carefully and them climbing to his feet and walking off down the alley as though absolution had been effected and no further succour could be offered.

They went to Chink's house and Capstick got shovels from the shed and they worked for an hour shifting the ton of coal in Chink's back yard until they found the proceeds of the robbery in a biscuit tin, Capstick digging determinedly in the wet coal as though to dig was an obligation that had been vested in him in the wetness and blood of the alley.

'He never got over the kicking.'

'He never got over being a thieving bastard. I'd give money to know what happened to him.'

'The man couldn't walk the length of himself the rest of his born days. That's what happened to him.'

Hawkins remembered Chink sitting on the bridge at Camden Lock, summer and winter, in a wheelchair with a blanket over his knees as though he kept vigil in reparation for his breach of fidelity. Hawkins remembered that the man's head and hands shook and twitched in a kind of palsy, for he had lain all night in the freezing gutter where they had left him, but that his eyes were steady, without pity or blame, and he would watch Hawkins pass without expression or recognition until one night in drink Hawkins could take no more and stood before him and called him for all the crippled fuckers, all the while held fast by Chink's cold, insensate stare.

'He was a villain and that was the end of it,' Capstick said. He turned to look at Hawkins. During the trial of John Dand for murder, defence counsel, Mr Shepherd, referred to Capstick as being 'of rather frightening mien'. Capstick liked to be seen as a cultured man. In *Given in Evidence* there is a photograph of Capstick and his wife 'on the way to the theatre'. But Capstick was not a cultured man.

Hawkins lowered his head towards his drink. 'Yes, guvnor,' he said quietly.

They discussed Courtney. Capstick saw him as a 'likely tipster' but thought that they should stay with the re-interrogations for some time more. He had little hope that McConnell would find out anything more from the foreign servicemen. He said that McConnell was fit only to hand out fucking parking tickets. He told Hawkins that the one thing that worried him about local policemen was their tendency to come over all noble when the chips were well and truly down.

But they both recognized Courtney for what he was. They were used to working with informants. Capstick refers to them as '. . . vital to a detective as forceps to a dentist; but they are tricky customers'. Capstick cultivated the type of informer who was motivated by money. He said he preferred that personal friendship did not enter into it, although he admitted that there were disadvantages to this approach. He recalled a man he called Pietro, who drove for various South London criminals. For a fee, Pietro would carry Capstick in the boot of the car. One night Capstick woke up in an icy ditch. He had been overcome by fumes and Pietro had dumped him there, believing that he was dead, and that their financial relationship had ended. Hawkins said he preferred those who were motivated by jealousy or revenge. The spurned girlfriend. The criminal who turned on his companions. Hawkins liked the way they would suddenly realize what they had done. You could see the fear in their faces, the abyss they had opened in themselves. You could work with that, push them.

But they both knew that Courtney was a different kind of squeal. He had his own agendas and was keen to know theirs. Courtney was a schemer. He brought an air of dissimulation with him, of furtive wrongdoing, blackmail, crimes of tenebrous subterfuge. He had to be played right. They had come across men like him before, and knew that there was no point in trying to discover his motivation. There were motifs of self-interest, the desire to torment.

'Do you think he knows anything?' asked Hawkins.

'Could do. These homos always know something about other deviants. They knock around together. Maybe he knows somebody is likely for it.'

'What do we do? Play along with him?'

'For the time being. Meantime we try and find something on the little bastard.'

'I'll work on it.'

'Know what I want? I want to get one of them into an interview room. Itching for it, I am. Sweat it out of the bugger. Shake it loose.'

Corporal Radford thought that Gordon talked too much about the Curran murder. 'The way he went on you would have thought that she was his best friend.' Gordon said that she consulted him on matters of dress, etc. He said that she asked his advice on relationships with the opposite sex. He also went on about his close friendship with Desmond Curran, which was in fact questionable as far as Radford was concerned, seeing as Desmond was this big-time lawyer and Gordon was as small-time as they came. Also there was much talk of Judge Curran and the pleasant fatherly way he had of looking upon Gordon when he thought he wasn't being watched. Gordon told Davy that Radford was jealous now that Gordon was in the spotlight for once. He said that Radford only liked you when you were sat there listening to all his wit and wisdom with nothing of your own to contribute. Gordon told Davy that it had always been an ambition in him to contribute to life. He did not tell Davy that he had persuaded Airman Connors to lie for him and say that he had seen Gordon in the barracks that night.

Gordon discussed each new line of inquiry avidly with other servicemen. Such as the mystery man, known as the 'hayseed man', who ate breakfast in a café in Larne twenty miles away on the morning of the 13th. He had an 'odd appearance' and had hayseed in his hair. He was never traced.

For a while Gordon espoused the theory that a foreigner had done it. Then he pointed out the doubts that had been raised by a Mrs Betty Eaton. Mrs Eaton told the police that she heard a woman scream at approximately 9.15 p.m. on 12 November. Police maintained that she could not have heard Patricia scream. According to their reckoning, they said, Patricia had been killed shortly after she had got off the bus. They said that Mrs Eaton's house was over a mile from The Glen, on the other side of the railway tracks, too far for a voice to carry. Mrs Eaton insisted that she heard Patricia. She said she heard a woman's voice, a scream. The cry of a woman in agony, arch and parlous.

Mrs Eaton was forgotten about when Capstick and

Hawkins arrived. The London men possessed a newsworthy quality that the local police did not possess. Gordon talked about ringing them to tell them what he knew about the family.

After the trial, all the servicemen agreed that Gordon had talked too loudly and too excitedly about the murder. That he had drawn too much attention to himself. In the photograph of Gordon that is most commonly used, he is walking into court on the first morning of the trial. He is wearing dress uniform, his fatigue cap tilted neatly on his head. The photograph has caught his body in an unusual pose, leaning forward and at an angle, as in a half-completed feint, low-key bravura. He is looking directly into the camera lens. Like everyone else involved in the event surrounding the murder, he seems to be aware of the camera. His face is pale and his jaw is set. It is a nervy face. You can imagine the shyness, the solitary childhood, the cruel pranks inflicted on him by the other men in the barracks before he became a suspect in the murder. But there is something else there, and this is the reason that the photograph is the one that has been reproduced again and again. There is a certain defiance in the eyes, what seems like a genuine suggestion of a calculating and vice-ridden intelligence.

Photographs are untrustworthy. When John McGladdery was hanged for the murder of Pearl Gambol, people did not like the photographs that had appeared in the press. In the photographs, McGladdery looked boyish and open. People were aggrieved about this. They thought that this should have belonged to a subtle monster, a clean-shaven man with a knowing smile playing about his lips. McGladdery had, in fact, killed Pearl Gambol. They had been at a marquee dance in a field near Rathfriland. She was a good-looking girl and McGladdery was of below normal intelligence. He had asked her to dance and she had laughed at him, made fun of him in front of her friends. She had gone home alone and he had followed her. He had strangled her and hidden her body in a cistern. They found her bicycle behind a hedge and several days later they found the body. McGladdery confessed and was a sad, lonely figure in court. There was no glimpse of the murderous transcendence that had befallen him as he had followed Pearl Gambol home.

Equally the public felt let down by the images that appeared of the murdered girl. Pearl Gambol's laughing face, one eye almost covered by her fringe. It wasn't a victim's face. There was nothing ominous in it. No dark shadowed areas alluding to her fate, no ironic downturn of her mouth to suggest foreknowledge, mocking laughter from beyond the grave.

That was why people were intrigued by the photograph of Gordon entering the court. A photograph of a young soldier with what looked like defiance in his eyes, a young man with an unsavoury personal history, walking with what seemed an ill-starred jauntiness. It seemed a perversion of wartime values, the recent past in which pale-faced, determined young soldiers were photographed as they confronted the enemy. His stance seemed derisive of the public mood, demanding to be chastened.

TWENTY-TWO

Ferguson noticed that Esther was at home more often when he came home, but on the nights she went out she stayed out all night. She moved quietly around the house. His shirts were ironed and put on hangers. The bedroom was tidied. It was intended to provide a contrast to the livid disarray of her life. It was intended to highlight her pain and show it to him for what it was: a paltry, unfruitful thing. She slept a lot. On the nights when she was at home she went to bed at nine or ten, sleeping until noon. He saw that she had bought new clothes. Once or twice she arrived home in a taxi on Saturday morning and he had met her coming through the back door, her stockings laddered, her shoes in her hand and her make-up streaked. She walked past him then as if she did not see him. She looked wild-eyed, wandering, subject to visions and touched, as though she had come in off a blasted and visionary heath, and he let her climb the stairs without reaching for her or talking to her.

They never spoke of these episodes. Ferguson wasn't sure if she remembered them. He assumed that she had been with Capstick. She started to ask him questions about the case. He tried to remember the things that McConnell had told him. She wanted to know details of how Patricia was found, who had found her, what she had been wearing. She returned to the subject of what Patricia had been wearing several times.

One evening Ferguson came home and found her waiting to go out. She was wearing a tailored black knee-length coat, strapless patent shoes. She wore elbow-length gloves and a black pillbox hat with a lace veil attached. He

had a sense that she was recreating a look of pre-war decadence, projecting a hollow-cheeked and voguish ardour.
She kept glancing at her watch. She spoke to him without
looking at him.

'Did you hear what they're saying about Patricia?' she
asked.

'Something new?'

'The theory is that she met somebody and walked up
the drive. She was scared of the driveway in the dark.
They're saying she agreed to a . . . a court, a kiss. She put
her books on the ground, took off her hat and scarf. They
started to kiss.'

'Things got out of control. She is attacked.'

'That's what they're saying.' She took a cigarette from
her bag.

He lit it for her. He didn't ask where she was hearing
this for he already knew. 'Could have happened.'

'It couldn't,' she said, 'not really.'

'Why do you sat that?'

'She was wearing a Juliet cap. You know what that is?
It's like a skullcap. It sits on top of the head. You have to
fasten it on with pins, a lot of them. You don't take it off for
a kiss, Harry. You don't have to, and anyway it would be a
whole lot of trouble. You take it off in front of a mirror
when you go home.'

'What you're saying is that she wouldn't have taken it
off for a kiss so the theory doesn't hold water.'

'What I'm saying, Harry, is that the girl went home first.
She didn't stop on the drive for a kiss. What girl stops for
a kiss in the dark in the spot where she has been attacked?'

'They say she was promiscuous.'

Esther stepped closer to him. He could smell her. Cigarettes, gin, No. 5, the rankness of lost years underneath.
She exhaled the smoke from her cigarette, making an
oval of her mouth where he could see the tiny creases in
the skin surrounding her lips, moving to a smile like a

predatory and derisive hostess, an ageing club-girl.

'Promiscuous? I don't think she was old enough for promiscuity. Not old enough at all.'

'Reliable sources have informed us that the girl was, not to mince words, gentlemen, a bit of a nympho. Ready, willing and able.'

Capstick was standing at the bar with a man from the *Telegraph* and a man from the *Glasgow Evening Herald*. He knew he was drinking too much. He had a fear of diabetes. To stick a needle in your actual human flesh. And worse. To stop drinking, although he had heard that a man with diabetes could drink Pils beer from Germany. However, he knew that there could be a loss of circulation to the male member, which, he thought, would not do him any harm. However he had an uncle who had lost a leg through diabetes. They had it off in the hospital. Not that the loss of a leg bothered him. It was the idea of phantom pain. To feel pain in a place that no longer existed. Those were the words they always used. Phantom pain.

'You mean to say she was of loose morals?' the man from Glasgow said. He annoyed Capstick. He looked like a science teacher, dandruff on the collar, big glasses, bobbing forward in an earnest way. He was getting his jollies here and no mistake.

'The lax hand at home, perhaps,' Capstick said. 'Overbred. Like a horse. The blood gets heated. Not that it absolves the criminal who was responsible for her death, not in the slightest.' Capstick assumed a policeman's air of grim consequence.

'Have you dealt with many cases like this before, Chief Superintendent? Ones involving young ladies of a certain class?'

'Many, too many.' Capstick fell silent, allowing the reporter's imagination to work on the sex murders of upperclass girls: the blood-stained peignoir, the parted lips.

Earlier in the week Capstick had been called into Pim's office. As he was entering a nurse was leaving. There was a smell of medicines in the room, an air of sepsis, creeping decay. The curtains were pulled across and Pim sat by an open fire with his back to the window. He looked drawn. His leg was bandaged and rested on a low stool in front of him. He'll be carried out of this room in a box, Capstick thought.

'I'd be obliged to you if you would put some coal on the fire, Capstick,' Pim said. 'One feels the cold.'

Capstick outlined the progress they had made, the interviews, the hunt for informants in the Whiteabbey area.

'What about the hypothesis that a foreign soldier did it?'

'It's possible, sir. Only problem is, it's hard to prove. You can't bring Johnny foreigner in and sweat him, sir. It's the language. He don't understand you. And besides, there always has to be an interpreter present, usually an educated man, if you follow me, sir.'

Pim nodded slowly. He was aware of the implications of having a witness present during an interrogation.

'What about the girl's sexual history, Chief Superintendent? Is there not something there?'

'Thought it might be better not to delve too deep, sir. From what the local lads tell me, she had a bit of a rep, married men and suchlike. You wouldn't know who you would turn up, if you catch my drift.'

'Yes, I see. Probably nothing to do with the murder in any case, Chief Superintendent.'

'Yes, sir.'

'Still, it might be an idea for the public to see that she wasn't quite the innocent she seemed.'

'Right you are, sir.'

'Take the shine off her a little. Without naming names, of course. You could talk to the Curran girl's little pal again. Douglas, the Minister's daughter. I'm sure she has something to tell you. Pals always tell each other little things, don't they, Chief Superintendent?'

The man from *The Scotsman* wanted to know if there had really been an assault upon Patricia Curran's virtue.

'Usually has been in these cases,' Capstick said.

'Was there evidence of damage to her intimate garments, for instance?' Intimate garments. The reporter had a slack, wet mouth. He was given to girlish mannerisms such as tossing his hair and examining his nails.

'Her knickers were torn, if that's what you mean.' Capstick watched the reporter as he licked the tip of his pencil and started to write. He knew that the tears to Patricia's clothing were ambiguous and that they could have been caused by the body being trailed, or even when Desmond lifted her into the car, but he didn't say this. He was tired. He felt the spot where he thought his liver was. It felt enlarged. Fatty deposits. That was a phrase he had heard in autopsies. Enlarged with fatty deposits.

He had interviewed the Douglas girl on Saturday afternoon after Pim had obtained permission from her father for the interview. He watched her for a few minutes through the window in the door of the Queen Street interview room. You would know she was a minister's daughter, he thought. The white stockings. The big teeth and waved black hair. The wide-eyed churchy way she looked around her. One of the local constables had told him that she had a reputation as well. 'You know these vicars' daughters, sir,' he said. 'Little mares kicking against the traces.'

It took a long time to get anything out of the girl. In the end she told him about the married man that Patricia had gone out with after school. He tried to get the name out of her but she maintained that she didn't know.

He re-interviewed James Fisher. Fisher admitted plac-
ing his hand on her breast. He was hoarse, sweating. He
tried to explain what had happened. The heat of the gas
fire, rain against the windows, light fading, an overwhelming sense of day's-end moodiness; the girl in blue
overalls and dark circles of fatigue under her eyes, facing
him in the office seeming older than her years and exuding, for a moment, a workaday sensuality – work-worn,
fleshed-out, there for the taking.

There was a growing unease in the town regarding the
murder. You could see it in the way youths collected on
street corners in the evening. Women hurried home from
their shopping and gave in to pangs of inexplicable relief
to see their husbands watching television. They sat at their
dressing tables removing make-up and calling downstairs
in low, urgent voices to their husbands to make sure the
back door was locked, to check the downstairs toilet window. They felt that this was part of the brief that mothers
held. To give voice to irrational fear. To be attentive to
signs.

In the evening the men walked to the bars. They talked
about Patricia Curran. Rumours had reached them of her
sexual history. They said that she drank in the bars of
Amelia Street where the whores were. She was the kind of
girl that was referred to as being out of control. They
thought she might be better off as a victim of murder. It
brought a softness to her. Her hard little body. Her hard
little face. That feeling of an untimely end. They felt that it
had rescued her femininity. It brought a grandeur and a
pathos to the meanness of her life. It enabled them to feel
sympathy for her, feel for her as if she were a daughter,
full of promise, a little wayward, in need of a guiding
hand. They used words like wayward. They used words
like guiding hand.

Ferguson waited for McConnell one evening in the bar

of the White Horse. McConnell was drunk when he came in. Ferguson told him what Esther had said, how she thought that Patricia had already been to the house on the night of her murder.

'The umbrella, the squash racquet,' McConnell said.

'What's that?'

'She was carrying a squash racquet and an umbrella when she got off the bus. They were never found.'

'Did you find them in the house?'

'Judge Curran requested that the house was not to be searched. Also the fact that no one saw the portfolio and the hat, meaning they were left there after she was killed, not set down by Patricia so that she could engage in sexual misconduct with a person who was either known to her or unknown to her. In the first instance she was cheating on her boyfriend. In the second instance she was a slut.'

'Capstick seems to be going for the slut theory.'

'I know.'

McConnell told Ferguson that the letters were still coming in. Confessions, false leads. The freemasons were mentioned. World Jewry was invoked. McConnell said he never knew that people were so preoccupied with unseen forces, that they associated troubling events in their lives to sinister powers, that they felt themselves borne along by a murky cabalistic undertow.

He had noticed that many of the writers had gone to a great deal of trouble to give structure to their stories, false in every detail. They were afraid that their paranoia might go unedited and the point might be missed. They did not trust the police to draw the necessary inferences. They wanted to be sure that they were seen as powerless, fearful, intrigued against.

Earlier that day he had received a letter that had been posted in England. The typewritten letter explained that the author had been camping in a campsite close to The Glen. McConnell pointed out that there had never been a campsite in Whiteabbey. The writer had put his tent under the trees at the edge of the campsite, looking down on the Curran property. At about eleven o'clock, he said, he saw car headlights on the driveway. It had rained all day and it was still raining, the letter said. McConnell said that it was odd but you could sense how the writer felt. He went camping and it rained all day and all night. The smell of wet earth. The smell of wet tent. The writer added detail. He said there were pine trees in that part of the wood and nothing grew underneath them. He said it was a strange place for a campsite and there was no one else there. There was a tennis court, he said, overgrown and disused for years and suffused with the feeling that something else made recreation there.

The writer said he could see figures moving in the circle of light created by the headlights. Several men and a woman. He could hear the sound of car doors slamming, muffled by the rain. He could hear voices, a terse exchange soon concluded, but was unable to make out words or establish whether it was conducted in any language known to him. After that it seemed that nothing was said, though he thought that he saw a woman surrounded by the men but smaller than them so that she appeared to be kneeling. He had the impression that she was made supplicant because those surrounding him seemed to halt momentarily, as though they took pause in consideration of her petition before moving forward in a group, leaving the figure of the woman kneeling on the ground no longer visible.

McConnell thought that the writer had perhaps been a witness to another killing, somewhere else, a wartime execution, perhaps. A group of men in a forest clearing. The letter had a bare, haunted quality that was compelling. The voice was unhurried and thoughtful. The writer seemed to be of the opinion that a bare duty had been performed. That what had been asked of him was to bear witness and to keep faith over the years with the voice that he had heard, a woman's stark cry, cadenced, rising and falling.

TWENTY-THREE

12 November 1952. Patricia got off the Whiteabbey bus at the gates to The Glen. She stopped at the gate lodge to light a cigarette. The low-roofed Italianate gate lodge, semi-derelict. She didn't like walking up the driveway on her own, but there was no one else about. Sometimes she would telephone from the bus station so that Desmond or her father would drive to the gates and collect her, but she hadn't called this time. She knew that it was her father's night at the Reform Club, and that Desmond would be staying late in the law library.

She pulled the collar of her coat up around her neck. She thought about opening the umbrella but it would be impossible with all the things she was carrying, and she thought the umbrella would mean that she couldn't see the lights of the house ahead. There were lights. She could see them through the trees, but there was no welcome in them.

The setting seems to be put in place for a cautionary tale. The mournful house, the dripping, tree-lined avenue. It seems clear that there was no one in the house at this stage. Doris Curran wouldn't arrive home until six o'clock. Lance Curran would not be home until seven. You perceive The Glen itself as a malevolent presence, but the sense of brooding seems slightly overdone. The heightened menace belongs to a Victorian drama of domineering fathers and pale daughters with unnaturally bright eyes. A tale of stifling values, the suppression of desire, the madwoman in the attic.

Patricia started to walk towards the house, stepping carefully on the unpaved surface of the driveway. She heard the dye works hooter in the distance: a manmade sound which takes on a note of feral mournfulness as it is forced out and into the incomprehensible night. Patricia was wearing black patent shoes with a Cuban heel, and her stockings were wet. She could no longer hear the traffic from the main road. Just the sound of her own breathing and her feet on the unpaved driveway. You would expect noises in the undergrowth, rustling, a sense of being watched. But the drizzle dampened sound, into a dense, watery harmonic. There was no sense of lurking danger. The bare trees on either side of the drive seemed to preserve a benign, twiggy stillness.

TWENTY-FOUR

In the weeks following the arrival of Capstick, Ferguson found that the telephone would often ring just as he was going to bed. He would get into the car and drive over to The Glen. He never saw Judge Curran or Desmond. He suspected that Mrs Curran would ring him on nights when they were away on circuit or staying overnight in town. She would question him minutely on Patricia's last hours. He was asked to relate Patricia's last words, how she looked. He told her how John Steel had left her at York Street bus depot and how she had walked on to the platform, then how Steel had seen her turning to wave, already airy, insubstantial. She looked into her lap as he spoke. There were tears in her eyes. She was twisting a handkerchief in her hands. At the time he thought the movements were studied. Woman grieving for wayward daughter. He thought of her following the coffin wearing sunglasses. Knowing the forms to be observed in the mourning of a murder victim. The horror. The incomprehension. The coming to terms with unmistakable sexual overtones.

She brought Ferguson back to specific incidents. Did she say that before or after she lit the cigarette? How many cigarettes? If she warned her once about smoking. It grieved her that her daughter's last accountable hours were so fraught with evasion and untruth. The fire went down. They moved closer together so that their heads almost touched. They thought they could hear the voices of the past coming through, a subtle, evasive whispering.

Capstick told Hawkins to keep an eye on Desmond Curran

for a few days. To see where he went in the evening and who he met after he had finished at the law courts. Capstick was suspicious of Desmond's religious activities, the seeming intensity of his devotion. Capstick had experience of churches being used for clandestine meetings, liaisons. He felt that such shadowy places should not be allowed to exist in cities. He took issue with their tradition of sanctuary, their complex interiors and histories of doctrinal guile. In his experience, criminals were often religious. They were moved easily to tears at weddings and funerals. It enabled them to see their sins as richly ornamented things, rife with symbolism, historic resonance. It brought a wealth and completeness to their lives, entitled them to a place in the world.

However, Hawkins reported back that Desmond seemed to spend his time at meetings in basements and underused church premises. These meetings were well attended. There seemed to be quite a number of priests there, men of a modernist bent with intense faces, strong ascetic sensibilities and a taste for fundamentalist debate in draughty rented halls. There were only a few women at these meetings. 'Flat shoes, no make-up,' Hawkins said. 'Faces that would turn milk sour. You'd want to be desperate.'

'You think he's a bender?' Capstick asked.

'Could be. No sign of any boyfriends though. More of a religious nut. Got God on the brain. He could have done it, sir. He could be a wrong one. Sees the sister as a scrubber and faces her down.'

'Somehow I don't think Mr Pim would want to hear us talking like this.'

'Is that the way it is, sir?'

'That's the way it is, Hawkins.'

'With your permission then, sir, I'll lay off Desmond and go talking to my squeals again.'

'That would probably be for the best, Sergeant.'

'Statistically the use of informers is a murky area, sir.'

'Better that way.'

'I suppose so, sir.'

Desmond had been in the law library all evening and had arrived home after nine. The pathologist had not challenged the Currans' assertion that the murder had taken place between five and six, but he had said that it could not be tied down to those times. Capstick imagined the row, the accusing words. A disgrace to the family. Common. He saw the murderer standing over her prone form, the knife in his hand. You always think of them in the same way. The rasping breath in the silence. The slow spread of realization across the face. The knife dropping to the floor from suddenly lifeless fingers.

He wondered if Patricia Curran had been aware of her life slipping away. You imagined there would be pain and then a spacious and commanding disinterest. Capstick's wife had told him he had a morbid imagination. Too right, my love, he told her, ever since the night that that toerag Pietro had left him for dead in a ditch. After that Capstick had taken an avid interest in near-death experiences. People on operating tables suddenly leaving their bodies and hovering near the ceiling. The feeling of being summoned. The kindly voice. The kindly light.

Davy told Gordon not to go near Courtney's.

'I need my hair cut,' Gordon said.

'You need your head examined,' Davy said.

'I want to see if there's any news,' Gordon said. 'Wesley always has news.'

'You see this?' Wesley said to Gordon. He was pointing to an article in the paper. 'See what it says here? See what it says? "Runaway Husbands, Rounded Up, Made To Pay". The bastards. They got this special squad rounding up GIs that married girls here and run out on them. A likely tale that.'

Courtney pumped with his foot on the heavy chromium lever that lifted the barber's chair up to chest height. He took a steel comb from his pocket and began to cut.

'So how's the boy?' he said. 'Anything strange or startling?'

Gordon looked up to see Courtney watching him in the smeared mirror. He noticed that Courtney's features were out of proportion. The tiny eyes and full, wide mouth, the lips an unlikely red. It looked like a child's drawing of a face, a clownish abstraction.

'Did you hear anything?' Gordon asked. 'You know.'

'About the murder? It's what we were always saying. The girl was playing away from home. If she'd another pair of legs she could have set up business in Larne as well as here.'

'I thought she was nice.'

'Did you, now? You're full of surprises, so you are. I wouldn't have took you for a ladies' man. Good-looking girl, so she was, mind you. Well built. A good chassis on her.'

'I didn't mean nice like that.'

'Oho! Now he's playing another tune, so he is. He's sounding out the retreat. I never thought you had it in you.'

'All I'm saying is that people's making her out wrong.'

'And you made her out right? Would you listen to him. What would you know what she was?'

'I'm only saying.'

'The times that are in it, only saying things can get a body into trouble, so it can.'

'What do you mean?'

'The peelers have been in here. Hawkins. Capstick's man.'

'You're not telling me?'

204

'I am.'

'What was he asking about?'

'The usual stuff people like him ask about. Trying to get names out of you. Trying to trip you up.'

Courtney was describing the function of a policeman. You start to question yourself. You start to look askance at others. You develop a tendency towards penetrating looks, leave questions hanging in the air. Your life sinks into apprehension.

'What did you tell him?'

'Never you mind. Wesley Courtney plays things close to his chest.'

'What was he like?'

Courtney didn't answer. He could see that Gordon was thinking of detectives he had seen in films. Blunt men in raincoats with a capacity for gruff individualism. He could tell that Gordon had no conception of real policemen with their ability to elevate moral ambiguity to a guiding principle.

'Is he coming back?' Gordon asked.

'Back? I'd say so. I'd go so far as to say it's guaranteed.'

'I'd love to meet him. I could tell him a fair few things about the Currans.'

'You know them brave and well.'

'Maybe I could tell them something important they missed. Point out a vital clue.'

'Don't lose the run of yourself, son. Them boys know what they're at.'

Courtney could see what Gordon was doing. He knew that he would carry any information he was given back to the barracks, where he would be aloof, as if he had returned from an outing that had left him tinged with a pallid authority. He would sit to one side reading a paperback, ignoring the others with an air of foreboding. He would turn aside queries politely but firmly, intimating at membership of an inner circle, special knowledge.

Courtney could see what he was thinking and also knew what such fellowships entailed, what tariff might be levied on account of them and what form indemnity might take. He doubted that Gordon had any such knowledge.

Courtney looked at the small man in the barber's chair with cloth drawn up around his neck, all half-arsed anticipation and face-value owlish expectation, with the head on him sticking up like a soon-be-extinct bird.

'I tell you what,' Gordon said. 'Give us a shave.'

You had to laugh, Courtney thought. Gordon had a chin like a baby's bare arse. You could see where he was coming from now, the soft bastard. Looking round the barber shop like he was in a barber shop in a Western main street. Like he was waiting for somebody with a gun to walk into the shop. Like he was waiting for a mystery stranger to walk in, a man with a taut jaw line – thoughtful but flawed, a man given to high plains seriousness and the stoic toleration of hardship. He was waiting for ritual exchanges of dusty rectitude, the sound of gunshots, a sense of inescapable fate.

Courtney knew that you could talk yourself blue in the face and the like of Gordon wouldn't hear a word. He was the type to spend his life marooned in peripheral romance. He began to shave him.

'I could be a suspect,' Gordon said. 'Nobody seen me the evening she was killed.'

'I thought your man, Connors, seen you.'

'I told him to say that.'

'Am I following you here? You got this Connors to say he'd seen you when he hadn't?'

'That makes me a suspect, doesn't it?' The word 'suspect' relished, drawn out. Courtney could see the way Gordon sat upright in the chair, aware that he had acquired a status within the investigation.

'Why the fuck did you get somebody to lie for you?'

'I had no alibi.' Gordon was extending his vocabulary now, growing in self-confidence in his status as a suspect. He could see himself sitting in an office filled with the gritty hubbub of an investigation in full swing. Experienced detectives in shirtsleeves, complaining about paperwork, making remarks about the uncooperative nature of the general public and including Gordon in those remarks, letting him know that he held a valid position within the investigation. He imagined himself fitting precisely into their world, coming to grips with the subtlety of his position and the way things were done – nuanced, hierarchical. He would face Capstick across a chipped table. They would nod at each other with a sense of melancholy necessity, the procedural rapport of suspect and investigator established in a few preliminary sentences.

'I think you might be in trouble, son,' Courtney said softly.

'I'll be all right, Wesley.'

'No. I think you're in trouble.'

Judge Curran maintained his routine. Lunch in the Stormont Hotel on Friday afternoons, poker in the Reform Club on Tuesday evenings. His colleagues were impressed by his steadfastness. They greeted him with small sympathetic smiles, sorrowful shaking of the head before moving on. They were grateful to him for not permitting the nature of his daughter's death to intrude. They considered that the proper view of death was to be found in the obituary column. The well-ordered life accounted for, an appreciative murmuring. Patricia's death did not belong here. It was an act of unseemly flamboyance. It was wilful. It seemed a garish thing to them, drawn out and excessively mourned. They saw her photograph in the paper every day, her unquiet stare. But Curran did not refer to it, showed himself capable of small courtesies, deferred to his colleagues in a way that let them know that their own compassionate gestures would be received in a restrained and dignified manner. They thought it was the least he could do for them and they let their appreciation be known in small ways. There was an intimation that his restraint would not be forgotten, that they would not be found wanting.

On Sunday morning Desmond swam in the outdoor pool at Whitehead. The pool was fed by the sea and was only used by a few bathers in the winter. Rain pooled on the tarred roofs of the changing huts. The bottom of the pool was silted, and the iron grilles on the sea-water inlets were clogged with seaweed. The place was sunk in post-Victorian dereliction. Hawkins sat on the whitewashed ramparted wall that separated pool and sea and watched Desmond swim. Desmond swam the breaststroke, keeping his head high above the water. Hawkins thought there was an old-fashioned look to the way Desmond swam. You thought of athletes in the early part of the century. Cross-channel swimmers in cumbersome bathing suits.

Hawkins disliked the place. Its rust-stained tiling and air of general neglect. The fact that it was overlooked and therefore remained open on a Sunday. The presence of pale young men of a moody disposition. There was an impression of out-of-date virility.

Desmond climbed out of the pool and put a towel around his shoulders. He came over to Hawkins. Hawkins was wearing an overcoat and scarf but Desmond did not seem to be aware of the cold.

'You wanted to speak to me, Sergeant?'

'Routine really, sir. Re-interview central witnesses.'

'It would strike you as something of a last resort, Sergeant, a certain amount of casting around in the dark.'

'Depends who is doing it, sir.'

'You think you can succeed where the local men can't?'

'It's a matter of experience, Mr Curran.'

'Can I interest you in a pamphlet, Sergeant.'

'What sort of a pamphlet would that be?'

'A kind of an explanation of Moral Rearmament, what it's all about.'

'I don't think so.'

'You don't have much interest in spirituality?'

'Not in this line of work.'

'Well to answer your question, then, I haven't particularly thought of anything new since my sister's death.'

Hawkins looked relieved to be back in the policeman's sceptic world where everything is subject to the same dead-eyed audit.

'You know, sir, over seventy per cent of murderers are known to their victims. That is a statistic. Scientific research was carried out.'

'Really?'

'Of that group, thirty-three per cent were actually members of the victim's family.'

'I'm impressed by the depth of your knowledge, Sergeant.'

'It pays to keep to the forefront of international investigative technique. The police officer in today's world has to avail himself of all means necessary if he is to succeed in his primary objectives.'

'I'll certainly contact you if I think of anything, Sergeant Hawkins. It would be a relief to have somebody behind bars and to get rid of this wretched circus.'

Hawkins watched Desmond walk away, wet footprints on the tiles. Hawkins prided himself on his ability to read people, but he was puzzled by Desmond Curran. The way he didn't look at you. He reminded Hawkins of refugees he had met in London during the war, misplaced people who had come from Baltic states that he had never heard of. They had the same wintry manner, the way they never met your eye, but seemed to be surveying an alien landmass, a place that was remote, icebound, subject to the transmigration of vast and indifferent herds.

It was his opinion that such refugees did not put a high price on life, their own or others', but rather seemed to regarded life as a hermetic coinage to be tendered on demand.

He watched a man walk down the other side of the pool, an aged functionary wearing a cap and carrying a rusting metal bar. Hawkins looked at his watch. It was one o'clock.

'Pool's shut,' the man shouted across at him. He walked around the end of the pool until he stood above the sluices. He attached the bar to the threaded mechanism above the grilles and began to raise them, leaning all his weight against the bar and turning it until the water began to run out and the bottom of the pool became visible.

You expected to see a body on the bottom. You thought of frogmen in the water, sad-faced detectives talking about the resumption of searching at first light, the draining of ornamental lakes. Hawkins had seen dripping corpses removed from the Thames. Turned face-up on the dock, they all possessed the same dreamy, waterlogged look.

Ferguson continued to visit Doris Curran. She always wore the same blue nightdress and nylon housecoat. She told him that Doctor Wilson came to see her every week and gave her tablets. 'I don't take them,' she said. 'I throw them away when nobody's looking.' Giving him a sly look as she said this. 'Desmond is cross with me sometimes. So is Lance. They say the tablets will make me better but there is no tablet to bring back a daughter from the grave, is there?' She looked at Ferguson as though to ask him why things were not kinder to her in her bewilderment.

He noticed that she went to pains to put on her make-up for his visits, wearing too much, occasionally missing her mouth with the lipstick, leaving traces on the skin around her mouth, on her teeth. She wore too much blusher. Her eyebrows were shaved and drawn back in with heavy pencil. The effect was theatrical, as though she were preparing for a masque, an entertainment involving pock-marked nobles; an overbred and jaded European aristocracy with an appetite for the degenerate.

She said that she wished to contact Patricia through a seance. There was a woman living in Bangor who claimed to be a medium. But Lance would not let her do it. 'She could tell us things,' Doris said. Ferguson shivered at the thought. Something about The Glen seemed to lend itself to the idea of seance, the stirring of unquiet spirits. Doris said that she thought the woman in Bangor was trying to get in touch with her through the psychic world. She said that she was aware of a persistent pressure in her head which could only mean one thing. She said that if she was not allowed a seance, then Ferguson could get her a Ouija board. She looked forward to strange effects. The unexplained dimming of lights, heavy drapes being stirred by an unseen hand. She claimed that she felt a presence in her room at night when she turned out the light, but assured Ferguson that it meant her no harm. There always seemed to be someone in the corner of her eye, she said, but no matter how quickly she turned the figure was gone, slipping away into the occult dark.

On other nights Doris would not speak for a long time and they would sit in silence beside the fire, and if he had not known Doris's state of mind it would have seemed like a scene from a more companionable age. But then Doris would start to talk about Patricia, hesitantly at first. She seemed to feel an obligation to identify themes in her daughter's life and to draw them out. She told Ferguson that as a child Patricia always liked to dress up, to walk around the house in her mother's high-heeled shoes. That she wore her mother's hats, and sometimes her jewellery. Doris asked Ferguson what was evidenced by this? Could he extrapolate from the child's projection of herself into

211

the adult world a general proposition whereby you could countenance her dead body in the undergrowth? Ferguson said he could not, so Doris went on to address other aspects of her daughter's life, getting up to walk around the room, irritable and restless, with the dressing gown flowing out behind her as she walked and continued her disputation as though she were an ill-defined mentor to the middle-aged man who sat at her fireside, watching her with a worried expression on his face.

Sometimes Ferguson wanted to tell her to stop. He did not wish to see Patricia's childhood like this. Picked over, undone.

Doris told him about the times she had brought the children to the beach in Portstewart. She was not a person for the beach herself, she said, and Desmond would sit by her, bookish and withdrawn, even though she knew that he enjoyed a swim. That was the kind of son he was. Patricia was different, however. The minute she got to the beach she was gone, and warnings about the effect of the sun on her complexion in years to come or any other legitimate concern of a mother fell on deaf ears. Much less had she any regard for modesty. She played with children from the slums. She was familiar with donkey men, ice-cream men, deck-chair men. You saw her running along the beach with other people's dogs, disreputable curs that wandered unaccompanied onto the beach from housing estates. You saw her standing with the sun behind her so that you'd have to squint, hands on hips and her head to one side in a quizzical look, sunburned, eternal.

Ferguson wanted to protest at her querulous view of those days. He remembered his own childhood trips to the beach. They seemed to have a sense of wistful retrospection in-built: days salt-stained, sun-faded – dense textured sensations but always with that sense of light-dazzled reminiscence. That was the point of a day at the beach. To provide you with such memories. To act as a reference point for regret and wasted opportunity. It taught the value of a sentimental regard for the past.

But Doris was not to be swayed. She insisted on her version of those days. A day at the beach was hard, she said. It took on the attributes of an arduous trek, arid and monumental. The kind of journey that gave rise to simple but dignified monuments. Inner resources were, she said, strained to the very limit..

Doris told him that she had never been robust when she was young, that she had been a sensitive child. Her father had lost his job in his early forties and had never found another one. He had worked hard to instil a sense of romantic hopelessness in his daughter. He read to her constantly. Victorian children's literature with slightly unwholesome overtones. He took her for long instructive walks in the country in order to point out ruined buildings, ivy-covered follies, derelict gazebos in Graeco-Roman style. He enrolled her in art classes that specialized in flower painting – poppies, lilies, done in a heavily symbolic style with a suggestion of wilt, of decay. Doris said that her father wore a shirt and tie every day of his life. It was important that you did not let yourself go, he said. It was important to shave. He was a small man. The kind of man who was referred to as dapper. He had a sense of himself as being well made. This implied craftsmanship, a working to scale. Something that was refined, over-elaborate.

Her father had died in the year she met Lance. She wasn't sure what he had died of, something complex and lingering. An odour of camphor in his room.

Doris said that her father would have known what to do at a time like this. He would have talked to the policemen and told them that murder had no place in her world. He would have made reference to documented instances of murders within the families of the lower classes. The stifling of infants. The morbid slaying of a spouse. He would have assured them that this family was not like that. That they had nothing to do with these lurid events, that they were committed to the principles of well-ordered decline.

TWENTY-FIVE

Capstick joined the Flying Squad before the advent of official police photographers. Nevertheless, the evidential
value of photographs was recognized, and the least senior
member of the squad was expected to act as unofficial
photographer. It was not a popular job, involving as it did
technical expertise, proximity to corpses. He had attended
the scenes of fatal accidents, murders, drownings. He
developed the photographs himself with the aid of a Scotland Yard janitor who helped him set up a darkroom in
the basement of the building. Capstick was not an accom-
plished photographer. Sometimes there were false aper-
ture settings or overexposure. There were spillages of
light, afterimages, a face from one frame superimposed
upon another. Sometimes he felt that these accidents could
tell you something if you knew how to look. A suggestion
not of how the victim died, but of where their soul might
have gone when they died. Often there was an inexplicable thread of white light across the picture. The trajectory
of self.

This experience had taught him the value of the photograph. Every time he took on a case he could see the
images that would appear in the paper. The detective at
the murder scene looking thoughtful, exuding an air of
quiet mastery. Walking into a public building – the determined walk demonstrating the dynamic temperament
belying the calm exterior. Leading the main suspect into a
courtroom with an expression of quiet satisfaction tinged
with melancholy. On the nights when he was alone in the
hotel bedroom he would spread the autopsy photographs
on the bedspread. Looked at like this it was hard to

believe that such wounds were capable of killing her. They seemed to be scattered lightly on her skin, capable of being erased with the hand. In the photographs her head was turned away to show the bruising to her neck and the side of her face. The disabling blow and then the stabbing.

He knew there was an intimacy to this process that should be resisted. He told himself that he felt nothing for the girl in the photographs. But he was attracted to them and he realized that the reason he was attracted to them was that her face was turned away from the camera. He would run his fingers over the smooth, faintly chemical surface of the prints. She seemed to be turning away in a display of modesty, naked and abashed, seemingly aware of her own deathly allure.

Six months after he had joined the London Metropolitan Police as a constable he had been walking a beat on Plaistow Road in the East End. A girl came out of a tenement house and pulled at his arm. He followed her into the house. A woman was sitting by the fire, but she did not look up. The girl urged him towards the yard.

'Dad's drowning Mum's bastard,' she said. Capstick went out into the yard at the back. There was a rain barrel standing in the yard with a cast-iron spout running into it. The lid was off the barrel and a man stood beside it. He was wearing a vest and khaki trousers and there were military dog tags around his neck. He was holding a baby by the ankle over the water. The child was naked and still. It hung from his fist like a heavy white cloth of a sanctified material. The man turned the child's body in the air and regarded it as if it was not a baby at all but a kind of merchandise and he intended to redeem it to the full value of its existence. The man raised his eyes to Capstick as though to demand by what right he expected access to this matter. The girl watched them from the doorway, leaning against it with her arms folded across her chest and her eyes half-closed as though she were appointed to stand in appraisal of the cause between the two men.

Capstick's thoughts often returned to this scene. It had occurred to him that he knew what the man was thinking because he would have thought the same thing himself. But that he would never know what the women were thinking. The mother in the armchair and the daughter standing in the doorway. The daughter had struck a pose of congenital disinterest as she watched Capstick take the child from the soldier's hand and then beat him to the ground with his baton. But the mother did not move, as though she had fallen prey to an innate figuring of a woman in sorrow.

Hawkins had been watching Courtney, building up a picture of him. Courtney lived on his own above the barber's shop. To enter the back of the house you went down a small alley to one side of it and knocked on the back door. There was a steady stream of men down the alley after dark. Men with their collars turned up, hat brims turned down; it was a small-town scene and they seemed to feel it beholden upon themselves to look furtive, shabby. Hawkins also found Courtney at school entrances at going-home time, standing on the sidelines of underage football matches, sitting in the back seats of the local cinema among teenage couples, the whispery hormonal torpor.

There was a busy edge to this activity, Hawkins saw, a self-importance. Courtney expected things to run to schedule. Hawkins thought it might be a weak link. Courtney resembled a harassed small businessman, running behind schedule, subject to premature balding and minor stomach disorders. Hawkins scanned the local papers for activities that would appeal to types like Courtney. He saw under-fourteen band practice, boy scout activity, the commencement of swimming lessons at the indoor pool. There were church outings, athletics events.

Hawkins began to attend them all. At first Courtney acknowledged his presence with small ironic grins, a wry acknowledgement of the territory that they now occupied. However, as time went on he started to assume classic fugitive traits: anxious glances, erratic behaviour in bus stations and other centres of mass transit, the sudden unannounced break from a walk into a shambling run on the public street, drawing bemused glances from passers-by. Hawkins knew how to behave in this situation. He was careful to be laconic, unhurried, inexorable. He could see the outcome already. The villain turning to his pursuer with a snarl on his lips, run to ground.

At Edenmore, Airman Connors had approached Corporal Radford to tell him that he had lied on Gordon's behalf. Radford was often approached for advice by the conscripts. They respected his status as an enlisted man and Radford cultivated an approach of exasperated solicitude in the face of sullen disclosure.

'What the fuck did you think you were doing, going and telling a lot of lies for Gordon? That's bloody Capstick of the Yard out there. You think he won't up and find out what you done? And what do you think happens then? Curtains, that's what happens, my son. You'll be for the bloody chop, that's what.'

'Gordon just come out and asked me, so he did. I never thought there was no harm in it.'

'Why didn't you come and ask me. What you think I got these two stripes for? For being stupid? For letting my pals put a rope around their neck and go charging off a bloody gallows?'

'But still and all, Gordon never killed the girl.'

'That's beside the point.' Radford's voice was coming out low and hard, street vehemence being worked at here, a sibilance as of looming disaster not easily averted. 'That's beside the point. He knew the girl, don't you see?

He knew her. He'd been in the house. He blew hard enough about his big cheese pal Desmond, got up like he was lord high muck.'

'What am I going to do?' Connors's voice rising to a penitent wail. 'I can't go back to the peelers and say I wasn't straight with them. I'd be banged up before you could look at me.'

'Wait, wait, let me think now. Let me think.' The two men were sitting in the Stores office. A small fire of cheap and slaty Russian coal burned in the grate. It was January outside, weather systems coming in across the North Channel in an increasingly elaborate progression. It seemed like a scene from the periphery of any war, a scene that repeated itself in history. Soldiers with troubled faces, in a wartime predicament not of their own making.

'Should I tell the CO?' Connors asked.

'Hold your fire until you're asked. See how Gordon gets on.'

'You think he done it?'

'You never know, my son, you never know. I seen men sat right where you're sat now, butter wouldn't melt. Give them a drink or two and there you go. A right raging fury. Rape, murder, the lot. And then the MPs come for them, they start giving it the old "I don't know what come over me." He done it as like as not.'

'Will I say that to them if they come asking?'

'Say nothing of the kind. Principles of British justice, my son. Innocent until guilt is proven and then it's the old may God have mercy.'

Capstick was provided with another set of photographs. These had been taken shortly before the body was released. In these photographs Patricia was lying on her back. He studied them. The strange mobility of the dead face. Waiting for the undertakers. Their long, knowledge-able faces. Their waxes, tweezers, strange balms. Working late at night in windowless rooms. Their quiet breathing in the necrophile dark.

Capstick had a horror of being buried alive. He would not have said he was an enthusiast for interment of any description. You heard the stories. Enough to cause a shudder. The look of fear frozen on the corpse's face. The nails torn and bleeding from ripping at the lid. A story of horror written on the face. His wife said that wasn't the kind of talk for around a dinner table, thank you, but he told her that if he turned up the heels it was to be the crematorium and the ashes scattered, or burial at sea. He preferred the idea of burial at sea, although he couldn't see how it could be managed. Commit thy servant to the deep. The crew's faces composed in expressions of loss borne with quiet heroism. The priest's words being whipped away in the wind, words that were sonorous and full of arcane usages. The flapping of the ensign at half-mast.

He looked at the girl's face again. The hands folded across her breast, cold and expressive. Her lips had formed a moue, as though she had turned away from her death in disdain. As though she had in fact tasted her death and had acknowledged it as a wry and unconvincing linguistic device.

On 23 January, Capstick entered his office to find Desmond Curran sitting at his desk. His manner suggested the priest that he would later become. He sat straight-backed in the chair, refused Capstick's offer of tea. His gestures were dry, precise. He managed to convey the impression of a man who lived alone, without the company of women. You got a sense of austerity about him, of unheated rooms and lofty pietistic mumblings.

'I received a telephone call from a man called Iain Gordon, Chief Superintendent. Do you know who he is?'

'Gordon. Name rings a bell. There's definitely a bell going off there.'

'Iain Gordon befriended myself and my family a few months before my sister was murdered. He seemed to take a . . . how shall I say this, an interest in us. On one occasion he called to see Patricia when she was on her own in the house.'

'What are you saying, Mr Curran? Are you saying that this Gordon had romantic feelings towards the young lady?'

'If he did, then he did not have them on display. But he is a difficult man to read.'

You're not exactly the old open book yourself, son, Capstick thought. 'You said there was a phone call from this person?'

'Yes. Last week. He said that he wanted to meet with me. I told him that a meeting would serve no purpose but he was most insistent.'

'Did you go?'

'I did.'

Gordon arranged to meet Desmond at the Seamen's Methodist Mission in Bradbury Place. People noticed Gordon as he stood outside waiting for Desmond. He looked nervous, excitable. He kicked his heels against the frame of the door. A light snow started to fall. Gordon was wearing his uniform, with a red scarf that his mother had sent him round his neck. His face was raw with cold and he blew into his hands and rubbed them together with exaggerated vigour. He seemed to want to draw people's attention to himself. He kept giving sly glances to passersby. He wanted them to recognize that he was at the centre of events they read about every day in their newspapers. A friend of the Curran family. Someone who was waiting to give crucial emotional support to Desmond Curran in his time of need. The snow kept falling, not getting any heavier. It started to lie on windowsills and car roofs. Gordon saw Desmond cross at the bottom of Chichester

Street. He was holding the collar of his coat together with one hand and was striding into the snow with his head down, looking like a character from a middle-European espionage drama. A man with a past steeped in conspiracy. Familiar with a terminology of dead drops, expertly forged documents.

Davy said afterwards that he had told Gordon not to ring Desmond. 'I gave off to him when I heard he'd made the call. I says to him, "You're on rocky ground, Iain Gordon, since you got that Airman Connors to lie for you. Would you not be wiser keeping the head down and out of sight until the whole thing blows over? You fall into the hands of Capstick and Hawkins, you'll not know what hit you. They'd eat the likes of you, them two. They'd have you telling them you killed your own dearly beloved mother in the heel of the hunt."'

'I have to say, Chief Superintendent,' Desmond said, 'I had no idea why this man insisted on meeting me, and as a matter of fact he frightened me.'

The details of this meeting are unclear. Both Gordon and Desmond gave disputed accounts of it. It is known that they decided to go to the canteen upstairs for tea. Desmond described Gordon as being 'very pale'. As they went up the stairs Desmond said that Gordon turned to him and said, 'He'll be in heaven tonight.' It is almost impossible to know what Gordon meant by this. Desmond describes him as being in a state of 'high excitement', but nowhere else has the impression been created of a man liable to strike such notes of dark foreboding, and it is hard to accept Gordon as a man given to a pattern of unwholesome foresights. However, it appears that Davy thought that Gordon may well have said something strange, that he seemed distorted by the terrible attraction that the murder exerted on him and by his desire to be at the centre of the events surrounding that murder.

Capstick asked Desmond about the conversation that followed in the canteen.

'He didn't say anything much. He just sat there. I think whatever it was that he wanted to say to me had been said on the stairs.'

'You say he knew your sister?'

'He had been to the house on several occasions, yes.'

'He was a friend of hers.'

'She didn't like him.'

'Did she say she didn't like him?'

'After he came to lunch she said that I shouldn't ask him again. That he was peculiar. She said, "After all, Desmond, you have to think of us as well."'

Desmond has since repeated this statement several times. If Patricia did actually say the words attributed to her, it may have been that she was frightened of Gordon. Or it may have been that she simply did not enjoy the company of someone who was peculiar in his manner. Gordon maintains that Patricia made him welcome and that she was the 'most normal person in the house'.

The following night Hawkins met Courtney in the car park of the Roadhouse Lounge on the Carrickfergus road. The Roadhouse attracted customers from the small towns in the area and the country hinterland. It was the kind of place where you expected fist fights in the car park at the weekend. You could detect themes of country music, teenage pregnancy. You saw men wearing check shirts with the sleeves rolled up. Hawkins took a flask of brandy from the glove compartment and drank. It seemed the right thing to do. It was an action with appropriate overtones of grizzled lonesomeness, a man in a wide-open space at night, the worth of his endeavours suddenly cast into a true light. He liked the feeling of fortitude in the face of overwhelming odds that this gave him and took another drink from the flask in the hope of prolonging it.

The passenger door opened and Courtney got in. He was nervous.

'Give us a drink of that,' he said.

Hawkins had twisted his driver's mirror so that he could see Courtney without turning his head. He could see the whites of the man's eyes in the dark. 'What's up with you, then?'

'I got three visitors today. I got the Tax Inspector, I got the Health, and I got the police with a warrant to search the house. They took away a load of stuff, so they did.'

'What did they take away?'

'They says they were looking for stuff of a lewd or immoral nature.'

'I bet they found it,' Hawkins said. 'I bet they fucking did.'

'I don't know what this is about, Mr Hawkins. I never done nothing to nobody.'

'Don't give me that, Courtney. You know exactly what this is about. Too right you know. I want a name.'

'I don't have a name, Mr Hawkins. I don't know who killed that poor girl.'

'Less of the poor girl stuff. We both know you got information, so let's be having it, else I'll be down in White-abbey barracks tomorrow morning for a little light reading and it won't be lewd and immoral, it'll be disgusting and downright illegal.'

'Please, Mr Hawkins. Honest to God.'

Davy had forgiven Gordon for going to see Desmond. He was worried about Gordon. Gordon said that he had discussed the murder with Desmond and they had agreed that the investigation was going nowhere. Davy doubted that Desmond had talked about the case with Gordon. But it made him uneasy that Gordon had gone near him at all. Carnival life had taught Davy the virtue of low profiles.

Davy made tea for Gordon, gave him buttered scones

that he had made himself, left a neatly folded *Telegraph* at his elbow, hoping that the imposition of domestic virtue on events might bring about at least the appearance of well-earned respite in a homely setting which would bring Gordon to his senses. He gave Gordon apple tart that he had made, sandwiches of potted herring with the crusts removed. He cleaned the railway carriage from top to bottom in Gordon's presence, polishing the glass with Windolene and newspapers, scrubbing the floor on his knees. He wanted to demonstrate to Gordon how order could be put on the world, that even now the stormy intractable menace of the Curran family could be kept at bay. Afterwards he said that he knew he was on a hiding to nothing but he had to try. Gordon would not stop talking about the case. He began to discuss the other men at the barracks as possible suspects. He began to focus on those with working-class Glasgow backgrounds. He told Davy that they were handy men with knives. That the blood in their veins flowed without pity or remorse. That they haunted the murderous alleyways and gaunt tenements of Glasgow, the slums of the Gorbals with their statistics of infant mortality, incidence of polio and other diseases classifiable according to social class. The empire's ill-favoured offspring. The Gorbals men stuck to themselves, Gordon said. They gathered in corners and you could hear them talking among themselves, their caustic argot.

In the meantime Davy talked to the people he knew from the carnival world. He made contact by letter with a travelling carnival that wintered in Brighton. He knew that the time was approaching where he would find himself in need of sanctuary. It was something that all itinerant workers, gypsies, migrant workers had to attune themselves to. The fear of persecution, the need to carry blame when harvests failed and daughters of marriageable age fell prey to a sudden inexplicable restlessness. He knew the signs. Townsfolk turning fearful and dangerous, seeking safety in numbers. You became aware of an angry murmuring, a torchlit mob in the middle distance.

Capstick and Hawkins drove out of Belfast to Pim's house in Hillsborough, ten miles outside the city. Hillsborough was a place of big houses behind high walls, discreet sandstone terraces. In the morning, women dressed in tweeds walked dogs along the riverbank. There were fresh poppy wreaths at the foot of the war monument. Wall plaques in the church commemorated Verdun, Malplaquet. You got the impression of discretion, of the subtle monumentalizing of the truly wealthy, of discreet service richly rewarded. Capstick and Hawkins drove through deserted streets. Prominent local families made sure that the bars closed early and that servants lived at a distance from the town. They wished to preserve the sense of timeworn tradition that they had imposed on the town, the studied passing of the seasons. Capstick and Hawkins turned into the driveway of the Pim house. Chestnut trees stood in open parkland. They could hear the sound of well-kept gravel under the tyres. When they reached the front of the house, Hawkins saw the gleam of paintwork beside a yew hedge at one side of the house. He walked over to it.

'That's fucking Curran's car. The Judge's,' he said. The car was badly parked, its position suggesting a vehicle abandoned after a crime, suspects fleeing across open country on foot.

A housekeeper opened the door and led them to the drawing room. The room was dimly lit. Expensive objects stood on small items of furniture. A wood fire burned in a large grate, and Pim was standing at the fireplace. He was wearing an evening suit with white shirtfront and was smoking a cigar, and he gave the impression of having just retired from the dining table, having dispensed murmured apologies to his guests. Capstick held the opinion that the scene was suspect. That Pim wished to impose a kind of authority on the proceedings that were to ensue. That he wished the detective to observe certain truisms about the easy exercise of power. The starched shirtfront and pose in front of the fire suggested that things were to be subject to a pre-war formality, a return to certain authoritarian values. Capstick understood.

'A drink, Inspector?' Pim said.

Capstick refused. He felt Hawkins stiffen at his elbow. He turned. Judge Curran was sitting under the shuttered window. He was staring into the fire and gave no sign that he was aware of the presence of either Capstick or Hawkins. His expression reminded Capstick of the first time he had been given the task of informing parents about the death of a child.

The parents were a retired bank manager and his wife who lived in a comfortable part of Hampstead. They gardened. They played bridge at the bridge club. They saw themselves as tolerant and wry, amenable to concepts of public rectitude. Their grown-up son had been stabbed following an argument with a rent boy in a flat in Beak Street. Capstick had called at the door one wild December night when the wind was in the trees, force ten, and there was a direness abroad, an intimation of great tragedy, something to send women running into the streets wailing.

Capstick gave them the news, although he did not tell them the circumstances. The next time he saw the elderly couple they were walking together downhill on Hampstead Heath, their clothes dirty and unkempt, moving quickly as though still driven by the same violent wind that had been blowing on the night they received the terrible news, their arms moving in gestures that seemed freakish and bitter.

Pim was thinner than Capstick remembered. His glasses glittered in the firelight and his hair was brushed back in straight dark lines. As Capstick looked, Pim turned to him and the policeman found himself looking into the man's eyes, which were yellowish and prideful as though belonging to an exultant raptor. His look suggested a man who had embarked upon certain gambits and now saw those gambits bear fruit. Capstick noticed that the man's knuckles were white where his hand rested upon the fireplace, and realized that this grip was the only thing that stopped him from falling into the fire.

'The name,' Pim said.

Capstick waited before speaking, drawing out the moment. He was given to theatrical gestures in the grand manner.

'An airman,' he said. 'Scottish. Goes by the name of Iain Hay Gordon. We have information to the effect that he is a known associate of Wesley Courtney, a man believed to be involved in perverted homosexual practices with other men in the Whiteabbey area. He knew the Curran family and, most important of all, he has given us a false alibi for the night of the 12th of November.'

'Mr Hawkins.'

Hawkins opened his notebook and coughed before beginning to speak in rehearsed tones. He related how they had arrested Airman Connors and questioned him in Whiteabbey barracks. Connors had readily admitted that he had made a false statement regarding Gordon and that he had not in fact seen him in barracks on the night in question. Furthermore, he had stated that Gordon had approached him and solicited an alibi for the night of 12 November.

When Hawkins had finished, the room was silent. Capstick looked at the Judge. Lance Curran had not moved and Capstick wondered if he had heard anything that had been said. He sat in the darkness with his eyes fixed on the fire as though he were covenanted to sit in this way for a certain period. The fire had died down while Hawkins was speaking and the light in the room seemed dimmed so that only Pim was visible standing at the fire, bent, cadaverous, yet with a gracious smile on his face like an impresario received on stage to be granted his justified acclaim.

It was 2.00 a.m. before Capstick and Hawkins left the house. Neither man spoke until they had left Hillsborough and were driving through the outskirts of Lisburn. They made arrangements for the following day. Gordon would be brought to Whiteabbey barracks at nine o'clock. Hawkins and Capstick would conduct the interrogation without the interference of the local police.

'Its good to get these things wrapped up double quick.'

'We don't know that he done it, sir.'

'We don't know that he didn't, Hawkins. We don't know that he didn't do it.'

TWENTY-SIX

Gordon was in the canteen having breakfast when the two detectives came in accompanied by the CO. He knew straight away that they were looking for him but it surprised him that he seemed to have an innate knowledge of what was required of a suspect. He felt himself rise from his seat and look around wildly, then sink back down with resignation. He felt Hawkins take him by the arm while Capstick told him that he was being arrested on suspicion of the murder of Patricia Curran. He noticed that Hawkins had bad skin. Hawkins gave him a hard look. Gordon could see what Hawkins was striving for, the severity of the image that he was working towards. The detective as administrator of unwavering justice, pockmarked, unforgiving.

When they left he could tell that Hawkins wanted to lead him out of the building with his hands behind his back, his head bowed, a mild, reflective look on his face, expressing the criminal's intuitive knowledge of things coming to a predetermined end. But Capstick opened the door for him and stood aside, allowing him to go out first. There was a long-distance look on his face. He seemed to be looking beyond this moment, its sense of low-grade drama, reducing it to its component parts. The apprehensive soldier in his shirtsleeves. The small detective with bad skin, destined for the role of accomplice. The taller man directing things, opening the car door for the suspect with an air of ironic gallantry. By his actions Capstick seemed to be saying that these things would resurface later on, that every detail of the scene must bear scrutiny and that it was vital to stress the importance of authoritative gestures.

Capstick had brought Detective Sergeant Harrison along. He knew that the local media would appreciate seeing one of their own men on the case, exhibiting qualities that their readership could admire. Methodical with overtones of small-town rancour and envy. Harrison came from one of the neat distrustful villages a few miles to the east of the town. The fact that there were biblical texts painted on walls, tent missions in the summer, brought an air of the rural evangelist into the proceedings, gaunt-cheeked elders.

There were photographers standing outside the front gates of Edenmore. Capstick was holding Gordon by the arm. He held up the other hand, fielding questions with a shake of the head and a small, tight smile. There were shouted questions from the photographers. Gordon looked up at the cameras when he was only feet away so that his face would appear very white, drained of colour; in the subsequent exposure the impression would be gained of a man capable of depravity, a degree of calculation. Those searching for a physical sign of perverse sexual appetite would be reassured by his washed-out and pasty complexion. As Gordon was getting into the back of the police car, Harrison put a hand on his head. Gordon found that there was something reassuring about this. He was being confirmed in his status as a serious suspect. He found that he was comparing himself to protesters being herded into police wagons, petty offenders, those perceived as guilty of small antisocial offences. He found himself wondering if he would be led from court with a coat over his head, walking with small quick steps like a shuffling penitent hooded in rough garb.

The police car drove away from the main building of Edenmore and swept through the gates. The fact that it swept out lent further significance to the proceedings. It added a further layer of importance. Vehicles describing high-speed arcs carried out with an air of restrained competence by trained police drivers. Another police car joined them and sped ahead with its siren blaring. Gordon could see ahead to the convoy coming to an impressively controlled halt in front of a public building, car doors opening before vehicles had come to a complete stop, stern-faced men getting out and taking up predetermined positions.

Neither Capstick nor Hawkins spoke to him on the journey to Whiteabbey. Occasionally they spoke to each other, making small but pointed remarks about other officers, or commenting on minor procedural matters. The car smelt of leather polish and eau de Cologne. The driver turned on the radio. Gordon understood that this was an interlude, a reprieve in the face of the toil that lay ahead of them.

Many years later, Capstick was forced to defend the interrogation methods used in the Curran case. It would not be the first time that procedures employed by Capstick during interviews were questioned. In the case of the 'Friendly Footballer' at the 1951 Leeds Spring Assizes, Capstick is cross-examined at length about the methods used to acquire a confession from the accused, John Dand. The implication was that the local detective had left the interrogation room leaving Capstick and his London colleague Inspector Plater alone with the suspect. When he returned, Dand had apparently made the crucial admissions. Equally, in his interrogation of Iain Gordon, Capstick was alleged to have been in serious breach of Judge's Rules regarding confessions. In reply Capstick stated, 'I never felt sorrier for any criminal than for that unhappy, maladjusted youngster. But his mask had to be broken.'

When Ferguson came in that evening, Esther had the *Belfast Telegraph* spread out on the dining-room table. She did not look up when he came in.

'I'm surprised you're not out celebrating tonight,' he said.

'Why would I be celebrating?'

'I hear tell they picked up somebody for Patricia Curran.'

'Please, Harry.'

'Never mind. What does it say in the paper?'

She turned to the front page of the paper. It showed the photograph of Gordon being led from Edenmore.

'He's so young,' she said. It was an observation she often made, usually at a certain stage of the evening so that Ferguson could judge how much she had drunk up to that point. The youth of others was the kind of thing that attracted her when she had been drinking. It was a subject with an uncomplicated maudlin appeal. It entitled you to variations on a general theme of exaggerated sorrow.

'Do you think he did it?' she asked.

'I met McConnell tonight,' Ferguson said. 'Remember how Judge Curran went back to the house after Patricia was killed and McConnell says that he started to phone her friends, asking if they had seen her, when he knew bloody rightly that they hadn't. Do you remember that?'

'Yes, Harry. I do remember.'

'Well, McConnell goes into his office today and Pim is there. He asks McConnell for the phone company records. He puts them in this briefcase. He says to McConnell, he says, "I think I'll keep an eye on these, Inspector. No reason to produce them in court. It would only complicate matters."'

'So the phone records are gone.'

'The records are gone.'

'It says in the paper that this chap Gordon knew the family.'

'He was mixed up in some of that religious stuff of Desmond's.'

'And he invented an alibi.'

233

'Yes, I know.'
'So he might have done it.'
'He might have. But still.'

He heard a car engine. He went to the window. There was a taxi outside and when he turned Esther was on her feet, a little unsteady, holding on to the back of the sofa with one hand.

'Maybe you shouldn't, just for tonight,' he said. She gave him a small, dreamy smile and kissed him on the cheek. He watched as the taxi drove out of the gate. He wondered if things would have been different if she had been able to have children. He had said this to her once and she had shaken her head slowly and walked away without saying anything. Even to Ferguson it seemed too easy an explanation. She had never seemed the kind of woman to give in to what seemed to him like medieval despair. The woe of the childless woman. Accursed, barren.

Capstick was waiting for her at the Culloden Hotel. There was something about other men's wives. Turning their big, sad eyes on you. The way you could look at them with a face on you like life let me down, too, I know how you feel. Turn your eyes to them as if to say let us take comfort in each other, let us lie down just here with our ruined lives. Adulteress. He liked the very sound of the word. It was a word for something hollow-eyed and sinful. By their conduct shall you know them. His wife had said to him once that she was glad not to have a daughter. That you couldn't watch them. Capstick thought that she was right. He thought that a daughter knew where the shadows lay.

Ferguson watched the hotel from his car across the road. Rain was streaming down the windscreen. He had read that the two really bad types of pain were childbirth and toothache. He wondered whether there was a science of pain, and what scale made it measurable and how that scale was calibrated.

He sat in the dark and watched as the lights in the house went out one by one. He sat on because he felt a guardian to Esther and felt that no harm could come to her while he sat there, although his heart misgave him that the harm was already done. He turned his eyes away and watched the rain fall on the car windows until he fell asleep, car tyres going past in the rain, a lustful and godless whispering.

On 13 January 1953, Hawkins began the interrogation of Gordon in the Girls' Training School in Whiteabbey. The Girls' Training School was built to house delinquents from the city. There were long, echoing corridors, doors closing with resonant finality, extensive educational facilities to indicate an awareness of progressive ideas on the part of the authorities. At night, when the girls had gone to their dormitories, it took on the characteristics of a contemplative order. There was an impression of mature reflection in a humane context which was sought after by the management. The shower rooms possessed facilities for vermin control by means of carbolic soaps, which were carried out by female warders. There were three padded cells in the basement and a locked room containing a number of leg irons and canvas straitjackets. Capstick was shown these by the warden, who talked about concepts of physical restraint in a controlled environment. One wing of the building had been put at the disposal of the investigation, so that Capstick never saw any of the inmates in the school itself. However, sometimes at night when he was crossing the central courtyard he looked up to see them watching him silently from the windows of the dormitory block, two or three girls to each window, their eyes moving as he walked. It unnerved Hawkins, and he wanted to complain to the supervisor about it. But Capstick stopped him. Capstick thought that there was a feline awareness there, a watchfulness that seemed to fit the case, a sense of tainted femininity seeping across the courtyard.

The primary purpose of Hawkins's interrogation of Gordon was to give a context to the man, create an environment in which they could operate. Hawkins would tease out his relationship with his parents, his relationships with women. He would find out if he had been popular in school, or if he had been a loner, subject to practical jokes, sexual advances from older pupils or senior members of staff. The secondary purpose of Hawkins's interrogation was to allow anticipation to build around the entry of Capstick into the proceedings.

Gordon thought that the first part of the questioning was not unpleasant. The room was warm, with two cast-iron radiators. There were filing cabinets around the walls and photographs of former teachers, plain women with a reassuring look of kindly competence. He thought that Hawkins might try to trip him up, but they simply talked about his past and his upbringing. 'A trip down memory lane,' Hawkins called it. He seemed to be very interested in Gordon's mother. Gordon explained that she was a schoolteacher.

'Like these ladies,' Hawkins said, smiling and indicating the photographs of the women on the wall. Gordon explained that his mother was in fact employed in an academy for young ladies. Hawkins apologised for his mistake. Hawkins asked what his mother's approach to untruth might be. Gordon said that his mother was a woman of impeccable moral character. He then admitted to Hawkins that he had indeed asked another man to lie for him, and that he regretted it, but it was something he had done on the spur of the moment. Hawkins asked him what his mother would have thought about that and Gordon said that he would prefer it if his mother did not find out.

At lunchtime Hawkins spoke to Capstick.

'He's not much of a specimen, guvnor.'

'What did you get?'

'Not much of a one for the girls.'

'Well we know that. A bit of arse banditry is more his style.'

'He says he was at camp the whole time that the girl was killed.'

'Anything else we can use on him?'

'To tell you the truth, guvnor, I don't think he'll be too hard to work on. There's one thing, though, might make it easier. He's scared shitless the mother will find out and think that he's a homo. She's a bit of a battleaxe, the mother, by all accounts.'

Hawkins spent that afternoon taking a statement from Gordon detailing his alleged movements on the evening of 12 November. Through the window of the office Gordon could see that there was a crowd at the gates of the school.

'Who's that?' he asked.

'Gentlemen of the press. You're going to be famous, Gordon,' Hawkins told him. 'Murder in The Glen. That's what they're calling it.'

'I never touched Patricia, Mr Hawkins,' Gordon said. 'You know that.'

Gordon said afterwards that he was calm during this period. That he thought it was all a mistake and that the courts would not convict an innocent man. During the times that Hawkins left the room he said that he whistled popular songs to keep his spirits up. He said that he whistled 'Blue Tango' by Ray Martin. He said that he got the impression that he had nothing to do with proceedings, that it was all going on around him. Hawkins would walk into the room with a sheaf of papers and look at him as if he was trying to remember who he was and what he was doing there. A uniformed RUC man brought lunch from

237

the canteen and stood watching him as he ate it. He was aware of the man's interest. He thought what it would be like if this was the condemned man's last meal. He said this to the policeman, surprised at himself, at the unexpected confidence and stature that the morning's events had granted him. He wondered why it was important to people what the condemned man ate. The policemen said that the condemned man was expected to eat well. The meal had to be hearty. The condemned man occupied an important position in the public mind and was expected to observe protocols. The policeman said that prison staff watched anxiously to make sure that everything was fulfilled. The condemned man was supposed to be in good spirits. It was good if he stayed that way but was regarded as being better if he appeared to be downcast then rallied. This showed the resilience of the human spirit. Just before the end it was a well-regarded device of the condemned to offer generalized reflections on crime, to begin to express remorse then tail off into an embarrassed silence. The policeman seemed surprised that Gordon didn't know any of this. Afterwards he asked Hawkins if he was aware that Gordon did not realize the seriousness of his position and the consequent responsibilities that attached to it.

That evening, as he was leaving the office, Ferguson had a phone call from McConnell. McConnell said he had another witness. He asked Ferguson to meet him at an address in the docks at Larne. As Ferguson drove towards Larne he felt like a detective in a novel. Hard-hearted, empirical. Intent on the narrative thread. When he had first opened an office he spent most of his days at his desk reading thrillers he bought in the market. Mystery blonde. It was an era when women in blonde wigs were featured lying naked across the covers of cheap paperbacks. Now they seemed forlorn but at the time they seemed magisterial in their ability to replicate glamour, and he found himself content to accept the leery collaterals of their faked magnificence.

The radio said that a man had been arrested in connection with the murder of Patricia Curran and that police were now following a firm line of inquiry. Ferguson's affectation of worldly disillusion disappeared in the face of dark finalities conjured by a newsreader who allowed his voice to drop at the end of every sentence like a soft-voiced arbiter of human fault.

Ferguson's father had repaired cars in a quayside building on the far side of Larne and Ferguson was familiar with the docks area. He drove down the cobbled wharfside road. Coal was banked up on either side of the road held in place by wooden shutters. Wet spilled grain from the grain ships made the roadway slick and wet. The entrance to the basin was barely visible and he heard the horn sound in the lough so that the dock seemed the epitome of fogbound ports consigned to moody introspection.

He pulled up outside a deserted garage. McConnell's car was parked to one side of it. The double doors were chained. There was damp coal dust in the crevices of the wood. Water dripped from the eaves. A wooden staircase held to the side of the building and he took it, opening a door at the top with the brass key in the lock. He took a step inside and stopped. He could feel the cold, authentic silence of desertion. He felt for the light switch. It was a small room with lino on the floor, painted walls. There was a single bed and a cooker. The air was icy and seemed charged with unheard testimony. He called out McConnell's name and heard an answering call.

Ferguson went through to another small room, with wooden double doors opening onto the quay that were intended for transferring cargo from boats. McConnell was standing at one of these doors smoking, and a youth was sitting beside him on the floor.

'This is Davy Hyland,' McConnell said. 'He's a friend of that unfortunate that Capstick has incarcerated up yonder.'

The young man stood up, his eyes fixed on Ferguson. He had a look of wary vagrancy, a neat patch on the knee of his trousers, the dirt on his hands worked in.

'Davy says that Gordon is innocent.'

'He never done it,' Davy said. 'I know he never done it.'

'Have you got any reason for saying that?'

'He's just not the type.' From anyone else it would have seemed an empty declaration of support for a friend, but Ferguson believed him. Believed that he had learned early to take nothing in the world at face value. Davy knew how things worked and seemed to know the position of definitive friendlessness that Gordon now occupied.

He watched as McConnell paced the wooden platform in front of the doors as if the empty building required a watchman, or some other form of stern invigilation to prevent it from being swamped with the uneasy sense of corruption and trespass that seemed poised to envelope the whole affair.

'There's another thing, Harry,' McConnell said. 'Capstick maintains that our friend Gordon is a homosexual. So it would be pretty bloody unlikely that he would make an attempt on a young lady's virtue.'

'What are we going to do?'

'What I am going to do is make yet another report to Pim saying that I don't believe that Gordon did it and that we should take a closer look at the Curran family themselves. If Gordon didn't kill the girl then she was killed in the house. The report will make no difference whatsoever, apart from ending my career. I suspect our young friend here will leave the country. And to be honest, Harry, I don't think that there is much you can really do at all.'

'There is one thing.'

*

Hawkins left the interrogation room at five o'clock. A different policeman brought tea for Gordon and stood outside the open door while he ate it. The tray was removed and Gordon was left alone apart from the policeman outside the door. It was seven o'clock before he heard voices approaching along the corridor. He recognized Capstick's voice from the radio. The reassuring bass notes and underneath the wide-boy tonalities of a Plaistow accent not quite erased, although Capstick in fact came from Essex and his family has spoken the bargeman's argot of Thames mud flats, starkly lit tidal reaches; a shifty treacherous dialect of river itinerants.

Capstick stood in the corridor for several minutes talking. Gordon recognized this as part of the process. Then the policeman at the door stepped quickly to one side and Capstick entered. He was everything that Gordon thought he would be. The hair was silvery, authoritative, swept back with Brylcreem. The detective was smoking a pipe. He was wearing a charcoal double-breasted suit with a pink carnation in the buttonhole. He faced Gordon straight away, standing across from him with his hands resting on the table, his eyes scanning Gordon's face in a manner that he knew to be searching.

Looking back on moments like this, Gordon would have said that he felt dread, but also elation at having drawn down such renown on himself.

Capstick was smiling. He shook his head. 'What are we going to do with you, son? What are we going to do with you at all?'

Capstick turned on his heel and walked out of the room. As he passed the policeman Gordon heard the words 'nine o'clock sharp'. Ten minutes later the CO was leading him out into the car park of the school, into the cold February air. The photographers and reporters behind the wire fence of the school were quiet. He knew that they were taking his measure. He could see their breath hanging in the air. They were regarding him with something like longing, a small man surrounded by larger men in uniforms. He was hunched over and cold-looking, stumbling across the yard with an awkward gait, yet he could feel them attentive to his forlorn charisma.

Ferguson knew that there was a late assizes in Coleraine that night and that both Lance Curran and Desmond Curran would be attending. He drove to The Glen. The sky was overcast, threatening rain. He felt a sense of mission settling on him. This was what he needed. Noble sentiment in the face of adversity. He parked at the front of the house. There was a light on in the drawing-room windows and the curtains had not been drawn. He went to the window and looked in. Doris was sitting on the floor. She had a small case on the ground beside her that had been covered with stickers. The names of foreign capitals, the coats of arms of historic English towns. Bath. York. The case was open and Doris had spread its contents on the floor, dozens of memorial cards, photographs of the dead edged in black with short verses of remembrance on the reverse side. In most cases they were in formal dress, the faces having been cut from larger photographs of weddings, anniversaries, christenings. They wore what seemed to be troubled smiles as though aware that the camera had conferred a type of life past death, and they were uncertain as to the meaning of this stern bounty.

He rang the doorbell. After a few moments Doris opened the door. She looked like one of the normal middle-class women of Whiteabbey. She greeted him, ushered him into the front room, making small sounds of apology, of regret that things had come to this, that she had breached her obligation to maintain an orderly life, that she had allowed delinquency to be at large in her life.

'People send them to you,' she said, 'all the time.'

There could be a kind of companionship in them, Ferguson saw, a baleful kinship.

'I suppose I should make one of Patricia,' she said. 'Lance says I should. He says it would be the normal thing to do. But I don't have any photographs of her left.'

'No photographs?' Ferguson looked around the room. There was a tapestry picture of two girls on a swing in one corner, but there were no photographs. Even the wedding photograph of Judge Curran and Doris had gone. He looked on top of the piano, on the bookcase. He thought to himself that they must have it in another room, the photograph of a beloved daughter, the gap-toothed smile, awkward, not yet beautiful. Her mother would keep it in the kitchen, or on a bedside table where she could refer to it, going back to the day it was taken, the sense of definitive moment.

'There are none of her things left. We burned them.'

Afterwards Ferguson wondered who she meant when she said, 'We burned them'. Her husband. Her son?

'Show me,' Ferguson said.

They went upstairs. It was the first time Ferguson had been upstairs in the house. The walls were covered with muted floral wallpaper. The stair carpets were battened down with brass rods. The girl's room was empty, the door of the wardrobe open, the steel-framed bed stripped down to the mattress. The curtains were tied back in neat loops as though steely restraint was required even in minor household matters relating to Patricia. Ferguson felt as if he had been conducted to the bare room of an historic figure, a place of exile and reflection.

'We done our best by her,' Doris said. 'We burned her things the day and hour she walked out the door never to return.' Ferguson noticed that Doris's Whiteabbey accent was disappearing to be replaced by a harsh rural dialect; putting together some of the things she had told him about her childhood he began to see her as the daughter of

243

a minor provincial figure, unfulfilled, prone to displays of low-key bitterness.

'Such a child gets the rearing she deserves,' Doris said. 'Many's the skelp she got off me but you might as well be hitting that wall there with the brazen head and the foul mouth on her.'

Ferguson turned his head to look at Doris. Her eyes were brimful of a dark artfulness that made him draw breath.

TWENTY-SEVEN

Four years after the murder, the Curran family sold The
Glen and moved to Cultra. Three years after that, the family who had bought the house contacted the police. They
said that they had lifted an old carpet in one of the
upstairs bedrooms and had discovered underneath it
what they believed to be a massive bloodstain on the
floorboards. After several further telephone calls two
plain-clothes detectives arrived from the city. They made a
cursory examination of the bloodstain. They said that
there was no way of telling if the stain was blood or something else. The qualities of the stain had to be pointed out
to them. The brownish colour, the way it congealed
between the floorboards. The smell of old blood in the
room. The detectives said that there was no way of prov-
ing who the blood belonged to. That in any case there was
nothing they could do about. That it would be better to
leave it alone.

The Glen burned to the ground in 1964 and the blood-
stained floor was consumed along with the rest of the
house.

Ferguson told McConnell about the encounter with Doris.
In her original statement Doris said that she had gone
shopping in Robinson Cleaver's the day of the murder.
The following day McConnell showed a photograph of
Doris to staff in Robinson Cleaver's. None of them recognized her. He looked in the household department to see if
he could find a knife that fitted that pathologist's description of the blade that killed Patricia. However, the blades
he saw seemed to mandate a finesse in the matter of flesh,

whereas he was looking for a knife that was short on lustre but possessed perhaps of a crude but reliable killing ability. He went to the army surplus store in the markets but the owner had never seen the woman in the photograph. He looked at bowie knives. He looked at bayonets. There were commando knives with thick plastic handles and serrated edges. Butchering knives with curved blades. Slender throwing knives. The closest item was a cheap secondhand blade with a wood-effect handle. He bought the knife and showed it to Ferguson but said that he still did not believe a mother capable of stabbing her own daughter thirty-seven times. Ferguson said that McConnell hadn't seen the look in her eyes. He said he could imagine her picking out the knife. He could see her wanting to give the impression of being a frightened amateur, a thin adolescent with awkward bones. Someone to stand over the body, looking pale and motiveless.

Gordon was brought back to the Girls' Training School at eight o'clock the following morning. The atmosphere had changed. As the car carrying Gordon went through the gates, photographers pressed closely round the car. Several of them fell against the bodywork, forcing the driver to brake sharply. The careful control that had been maintained around the investigation, the air of mild but cheerful connivance that existed between the press and the suspect, had gone. A small crowd of bystanders was held back by a police line. Several journalists described the mood as ugly. There was talk of a torch-lit procession to the town centre that evening where participants would be addressed by speakers on issues related to law and order.

Capstick was on good form. He disliked the new police stations in London and preferred the older stations in the provinces when it came to interrogation. This school was not a police station but it shared some of its attributes and he intended to make use of them. He always felt buoyed up by the environment you encountered. The sleepless cells, the dull gloss varnish charged with consequence. In the old buildings a suspect felt the need to be believed. To convince someone that the dramatic lurked at every corner of his life. He disliked the new style of things – strip lighting, civilian secretaries. The introduction of a twentieth-century lyric gloom.

Gordon sat at one side of the table as before. Capstick and Hawkins stood at the other side.

'When did you start being a homo?' Hawkins asked.

'I think he means when did you decide you preferred boys?' Capstick said.

'You see we know your horrible little secret,' Hawkins said.

'Your chum Courtney told all,' Capstick said. 'Very revealing. Who'd have thought?'

'Your bum chum,' Hawkins said.

'The White Horse Hotel. Very refined I must say.'

'Don't try to deny it, son. We been round the houses with you lot before.'

'What I can't understand is why kill the girl?'

'Gets off on it, sir. He's a fucking pervert.'

'You did kill her, didn't you?'

'Course he did. Wrote all over him, plain as day. He'll get the rope for sure, sir.'

'Just a moment, Sergeant. Let the boy speak.'

Gordon tried to explain how he had known Patricia as a friend. How he had sat in the same room as her as she dried her hair at the fire. Her dark mendicant head bowed.

'A judge's daughter,' Hawkins said. 'Plain old judy ain't good enough for chummy here.'

'Where'd you get the knife, son?'

'Fucking perverts. If I was one I'd top myself.'

'That's enough now, Sergeant. We're in the business of upholding the law, here. Now, son. Your mother's on the way here. Just to let you know. I phoned her last night. I'm sure she'll have a thing or two to say to you. Better to get all this unpleasant business over with before she gets here.'

'Where is she?' Gordon asked.

'She's taking the Larne-Stranraer ferry. So tell us where you were on the evening of the 12th of November last, Iain. You met Patricia coming off the bus, didn't you?'

Gordon denied that he had met Patricia. He said that he had posted letters in Whiteabbey and had then gone back to the barracks for his tea.

'But nobody bloody saw you, did they?' Hawkins said.

Gordon agreed that nobody saw him. He was asked about his relationship with Desmond.

'Were the pair of you at it? That's what I want to know. Was that what you were, Desmond's bit of rough?' Hawkins said.

'Well, Iain, were you and Desmond pals, were you at the old give the dog a bone?'

'Jealous of the sister maybe, her living in the same house as him?'

'What did you stab her with, Iain? Your service knife? What did you do with it?'

'Must have been blood on your clothes, old son. What did you do with them?'

Throughout the morning and afternoon of 14 January, Gordon continued to deny any involvement. Sometimes Hawkins and Capstick interviewed him together. Sometimes it was Capstick on his own. When Hawkins wasn't there, Capstick spoke gently to him, reminisced about his long career in the Met. He told him about the Ghost Squad, regretted his inability to give up the pipe, expressed his astonishment that he and Gordon should find themselves in this place, men who would be friends in another situation now driven apart by an uncaring, often brutal system. Gordon thought that Capstick was a person he could relate to, someone who could appreciate how it felt to actually know people who were involved in a murder, who had lost a loved one. He felt that underneath it all there were currents of empathy in Capstick. A man who knew what it felt like to be a parent. To be a husband.

That night in the barracks Gordon was given his own room adjacent to the officers' quarters. People were gentle with him. He was accorded respect commensurate with his position. Even the officers were solicitous, seeming to recognize in him a rank that supplanted all preceding hierarchies, military or otherwise. However, when the light was turned out he began to think of his mother embarked in lonely passage across the North Channel and the grievous disappointment that awaited her when she got to the other side. He knew that sexual relations between men were a crime in the military, and that he might be given a dishonourable discharge. He lay awake all that night thinking about it. He thought about the times that he had let his mother down in the academic sphere. He did not think for a moment that he would be charged with murder.

The following morning he was faced by Capstick on his own. Gordon gave his account of what had transpired in court. He said that Capstick kept saying that he was sick, that he needed help. He said that if his 'dear mother' found out he was a homosexual it would kill her. He kept repeating that, Gordon said. How it would kill his mother. Capstick said that if he confessed they would get a doctor to cure him of his homosexuality. There were such doctors, learned men with well-tried techniques in dealing with the unsavoury, the irrational.

Capstick's notes on the morning session, which were read out in court during the trial, were blunt.

'I questioned him at length re masturbation, gross indecency, sodomy.'

The afternoon session consisted of the writing of Gordon's confession. In this Capstick adopted a novel technique in which each alleged event in the chain of events was put to Gordon as a hypothesis. He would ask Gordon that, if he had met Patricia on her way home, would he have offered to walk her home? And if he had walked her home, would he have taken her hand? As Gordon answered a hesitant 'yes' to each question, Capstick wrote it down as if the action described had in fact taken place. When they had finished Gordon signed it.

TWENTY-EIGHT

Extracts from Statement of Iain Hay Gordon,
15 January 1953

I walked back alone to Whiteabbey and met Patricia Curran between the Glen and Whiteabbey Post Office. She said 'Hello Iain' or something like that, and I said 'Hello Patricia'. I forget what we talked about but she asked me to escort her to her home up the Glen. I agreed to do so because it was fairly dark and there was none of the family at the gate to the Glen.

We both walked up the Glen together. After we had walked a few yards I either held her left hand or arm as we walked along. She did not object and was quite cheerful. We carried on walking up the Glen until we came to the spot where the street lamp's light does not reach. It was quite dark there and I said to Patricia, 'Do you mind if I kiss you?'

We stopped walking and stood on the grass verge on the left-hand side of the drive. She laid her things on the grass and I think she laid her hat there as well. Before she did this she was not keen on me giving her a kiss, but consented in the end. I kissed her once or twice to begin with and she did not object. She then asked me to continue escorting her up the drive. I did not do so as I found I could not stop kissing her. As I was kissing her I let my hand slip down my body between her coat and her clothes. She struggled and said 'Don't, don't, you beast' or something like that.

I struggled with her, and she said to me, 'Let me go or I will tell my father.' I then lost control of myself, and Patricia fell down on the grass, sobbing. She appeared to have fainted because she went limp. I am a bit hazy about what happened next, but I probably pulled the body of Patricia through the bushes to hide it. Even before this happened I do not think I was capable of knowing what I was doing. I was confused at the time, and I believe I stabbed her once or twice with my service knife. I had been carrying this in my trousers pocket. I am not quite sure what kind of knife it was.

It is all very hazy to me, but I think I was disturbed by either seeing a light or hearing footsteps in the drive. I must have remained hidden and later walked out of the Glen at the gate lodge on the main road. As far as I know, I crossed the main road and threw the knife into the sea.

I am very sorry for having killed Patricia Curran. I had no intention whatsoever of killing the girl. It was solely due to a blackout.

I have felt run down for some time and the black-out may have been the result of over-studying and worry generally.

TWENTY-NINE

On Monday 16 January 1953, Iain Gordon appeared before Whiteabbey Magistrates' Court charged with the murder of Patricia Curran. That afternoon Ferguson met McConnell in the White Horse. McConnell seemed quiet and preoccupied.

'He didn't do it, McConnell.'

'Earlier this morning a paper knife missing from the office of Wing Commander Jackson from Edenmore was handed in at Carrickfergus barracks. The harbour master reckons that a knife thrown into the sea at Whiteabbey on November the 12th would fetch up at Kilroot. That was where it was found.'

'What happened to your report?'

'Pim. He said it was interesting. He gave me this look. You know the kind of look them boys have. Tells you you're fucked. He wants to see you.'

'Why?'

'I don't know. The Stormont Hotel, tonight at eight. I'll see you there.'

Ferguson drove to Whiteabbey. He stopped again at the gates to The Glen but this time he did not get out of the car. It looked like the scene of a terrible wartime episode you read about now that the war was over. You imagined hunters coming across human remains buried just under the surface, just under the leaf mould. He felt as though he should do something to stop the proceedings that had been set in train. He felt as if someone had put all the elements in place and now awaited him. The forest gloom. The lonely avenue. Nightfall and a tale of violent death.

He got out of the car and walked along the beach towards the mouth of the Whiteabbey river. The town had been built on salt marshland, reclaimed over centuries. Its early history described it in terms of ill health, a place subject to ague and fever. The reclamation had disturbed the tidal currents so that silt collected at the end of the river and a dredger worked all year round to keep the port channel clear.

Ferguson thought about the layered silts, the infected stratum. He reckoned that it must work its way up to the surface somehow. Contagions, bacteria, pathogens seeping into the air.

Ferguson thought to himself that no man would want to have his mortal remains interred in such ground. A breeding ground for germs of all descriptions, no odds if you were dead or not. Even the deceased have rights, he thought, to take ease in clean, well-drained soil. No matter if acids preserved him for all time. He turned away and walked back towards the town, pulling the collar of his overcoat up against the seeping marsh damp, the birds seeming to chant now, like the voices of the dead generations, dictating the path back with cold, atonal cries.

The foyer of the Stormont Hotel was empty. The night porter directed him to the Carson Suite upstairs. He opened the door. Pim was standing in front of the fire talking to Capstick. Judge Curran sat silently to one side of the fireplace. McConnell was pouring a whiskey and soda at a side table. Capstick said something and Pim threw his head back and laughed. A fire burned in the fireplace. There was a chandelier over their head. Ferguson thought that they looked like a gathering of a European mercantile class, an affluent and corrupted bourgeoisie. They watched as Ferguson crossed the floor towards them. Pim stepped forward with his hand outstretched.

'Mr Ferguson. I'm sorry to call you here at such short notice. Have you met Chief Superintendent Capstick?'

Ferguson shook Capstick's hand. He thought that he saw a small gleam of triumph in Capstick's eyes but found he was in no mood for the antagonisms of petty erotic duellists. Besides, Capstick was not the first man he had met who had been caught up in Esther's insistent, depleting trysts. He looked past Capstick to the Judge, who gazed up at him with the eyes of a man who has at last franchised all that remained of conviction in his own life in favour of future temporal largesse.

Ferguson noticed that McConnell was keeping his eyes down.

'You wanted to talk to me?'

'I think we have something to discuss,' Pim said, 'in relation to the Patricia Curran case and the ongoing investigations. I believe you have expressed some doubts as to the guilt of the man we're holding in custody.'

'I think that you should be looking closer to home. I think your case doesn't stand up.'

'And what course of action do you propose to take?'

Before Ferguson could answer McConnell spoke.

'He knows, Harry.'

'Knows what?'

'Details of interview with adult male, aged forty-eight, resident of the Whiteabbey area. Interviewee admits that he had sexual relations with the deceased, Patricia Curran, at the Whiteabbey athletic grounds on an unspecified date in January 1951,' Capstick said.

'It was you, Harry,' said Pim. 'You were the middle-aged man. Inspector McConnell here tried to keep things under wraps for you from an admirable sense of loyalty, but Chief Superintendent Capstick spoke to Miss Hillary Douglas last night. After some, I have to say, rather rough questioning, she identified you. Honestly, Harry. You're as bad as the rest of us.'

'All right,' Ferguson said, 'all right.'

'They're not going to hang him, Harry,' McConnell said. 'Isn't that right, Sir Richard?'

'The defence will press for a verdict of not guilty by reason of insanity. The prosecution won't contest it. The judge will also direct the jury towards the same verdict. After a few years in a nice clean hospital Mr Gordon will be released. No harm done.'

Ferguson wasn't listening. He remembered how cold it had been that night. How he had told her it was a cold front from Siberia and that she had laughed.

McConnell was standing at his shoulder.

'He has you, Harry,' he said. 'Esther could never take it if it got into the papers. You know that. He has both of us.'

Ferguson and McConnell left the Stormont Hotel and went drinking. They had started off in the airy saloons of the town centre. The Victorian bars with high ceilings and strict decorative regimes that suggested the existence of stern boundaries. They were seen in the Kilmorey. They were seen in Henry T's. Later that night they took a taxi to Larne. Looking for the lost bars, the bars that dealt in the peripheral emotions. Bars to let yourself down in. In each bar they said the same thing. That they were going to get Pim. That they were going to mark his card. The other drinkers listened and said nothing. This was nothing new to them. They were serious drinkers. They were men who had divested themselves of family and friends in order to gain a surly expertise in the area of empty promises and they were willing to grant the two men the same kind of tolerant distance that they felt would be required when it came their time to fall to prey to idle boasting.

The following morning all the newspapers carried the formal photograph of Patricia in the cowl-neck dress. For the first time Ferguson saw that she carried the lineaments of mourning about with her. It was in the bone structure, the extravagant dark under the eyes, the intimation of pleasure dearly bought. Her mouth was the token of an adept in mourning: over-refined, imperious, forbidding.

That afternoon Capstick and Hawkins flew back to London. At a press conference at North Queen Street RUC station, Capstick recognized that he would have to return for the trial but said, 'My job here is done.' Harry Ferguson searched the bars of Whiteabbey for his wife in vain. He found her at Nutt's Corner airport. Capstick's flight had just left. There was something about large echoing public buildings that soothed her. The calling of far-off destinations, the tinnily articulated recital of place.

As he was leading her out of the airport building he saw Pim sitting on a bench beside the departure gates. Pim was wearing a white linen suit. He exuded a sickly vitality. Ferguson found himself thinking about the stories that had begun to surface regarding Nazis who had fled to South America. Men in panama hats sitting on verandas overlooking the jungle, an awareness of historic evil in their faces. Richard Pim was to die of liver cancer in February 1953, two weeks before the beginning of Gordon's trial.

Gordon had been remanded to the custody of the Commanding Officer of Edenmore to appear at Belfast Assize Court. He remembered little about the weeks that he spent on remand at Edenmore. There were showery spring days. His mother came to see him twice a week. She was staying in a bed and breakfast in Carrickfergus. She said that the owner of the guesthouse was a common woman. Gordon's father had met his MP in Scotland. They were hopeful of developments. They had spoken to the authorities.

Gordon went on trial on 1 March 1953. He was represented by Mr H. A. McVeigh QC. The first two days were taken up with legal argument in the absence of the jury as to the admissibility of the confession that Gordon had made to Capstick. Capstick maintained, 'I took the only course open to me.' The judge ruled that police procedure had been 'entirely proper'.

Wesley Courtney was in the public gallery. Gordon looked for Davy but he had gone to England. The book-maker Hughes was there. Gordon noticed small things. The wood on the inside of the dock was scratched and scarred. The brass bar that ran round the top of the dock with spikes on it was attached by small screws, which had loosened so that you could lift it off it you wanted to. He found the proceedings lacking in gravitas. You expected awe, stern-jawed men driven by an awareness that life hung in the balance. The floor of the courtroom was dirty. There was a smell of drains.

Desmond Curran related the events that took place on the night of 12 November. He did not look at Gordon at any point. He mentioned that Patricia had remarked upon Gordon's odd demeanour, the fact that she had apparent-ly asked Desmond not to bring Gordon back to the house. The strange remark that she had made. 'After all, Desmond, you have to think of us as well.' Mrs Crangle was called. Constable Rutherford was called. Gordon felt tired. He wondered what it would be like in the death cell of Crumlin Road prison. He saw himself walking unaided towards the gallows in the pre-dawn cold, his thoughtful gait, a smile playing about his lips. The last witness called was the paperboy George Chambers. His evidence was delivered with narrative flair and the court acknowledged his right to embellish his tale with lurid atmospherics. The testimony introduced a steadying note to the final part of the proceedings. This was a character familiar to the jury, the plucky urchin.

On Saturday 6 March, after two hours of deliberation, they brought in a verdict of Not Guilty by Reason of

Insanity. Iain Gordon was sentenced to be detained in a secure mental institution during the Pleasure of Her Majesty.

THIRTY

Two years after the trial, Desmond Curran abandoned his career at the bar and began a noviciate to become a Roman Catholic priest. He was ordained in Rome and the ordination was attended by Sir Lancelot Curran, by then a Lord Chief Justice of Appeal. Desmond Curran went to South Africa as a missionary priest. He maintains that he believes the case against Gordon to be substantially true. As a man in his late sixties, Desmond agreed to be filmed by a camera crew in his church in South Africa. It is a small tin-roofed church with a dusty board floor. You can imagine the township surrounding it, the preternatural glare of the sun from galvanized roofing, the blazing veldt. Every pew is full. The men are all wearing suits and are obviously aware of the presence of the camera. A strange incident takes place as the service is being filmed. Desmond Curran begins a homily on the subject of forgiveness. He tells his parishioners that they must all learn forgiveness, that the sins of the past must be left in the past. Then he brings up the subject of Patricia.

'Many years ago,' he says, 'a man murdered my sister. I have had to forgive that man, and we must all learn to forgive.'

As he says this he turns his head and looks directly at the camera, just for a moment. The moment stands out in a man who habitually does not meet your eye when he is talking. You still the moment, go back to it. It seems a self-conscious thing to do, addressing the camera, something that he has decided to do before the service. It seems a defiant look, saying that this is the truth about Patricia, a truth that has gathered the authority of the years. It is an actor's look, weighted, deliberated over.

Harry Ferguson continued to visit Doris Curran. She told him how her father had died of a wasting disease. She told him that he had kept a careful account of each loss of function in the hope that this might slow the course of the disease or at least introduce a salutary frugality. She wore wing-tipped glasses. Diamanté sparkled on the frames. She wore a tailored tweed suit and poured tea for him in bone china cups. She took the phone off the hook. She placed two armchairs facing each other. There was an air of strange interrogation. Each detail was noted. He thought she was a woman who was given to the making of records. But memory was unreliable. It puzzled her. She said that Patricia's last day should not have been so full of shadowy incident. It seemed to Ferguson that she began to withdraw from the world. He thought that she had been engaged in gathering material so that this withdrawal might take place. She died in 1975.

Ferguson lived long enough to see The Glen burn down in 1965. The following morning's *Belfast Telegraph* contained two photographs. The first showed The Glen as it burned that night. In the monochrome image the flames in each window appeared white, so that it looked as if the negative of the photograph had been printed and that the actual photograph was still awaiting print, the real image filled with sirens, the roar of flame, the creak of collapsing timber and masonry, people shouting at the fire, giving voice to their awe. It was what he had remembered. Not this stark composition, the firemen in the foreground profiled, bent forward into the incendiary night.

The other photograph showed the scene the following day. Firemen on the ground floor hosing down piles of smoking rubble, their faces pale and smoke-marked, giving them a melancholy look. He remembered the air of exhaustion, the smell of wet, burnt timber. He remembered that all morning he had been approached by people with anecdotes of tremendous heat. They were eager that he hear them. They used words like 'furnace'. They talked about how the fire had melted brass fittings, that windows a hundred yards away had cracked with the heat. When they ran out of anecdotes they stood before him resentfully. They felt that their wonder was going unmarked. They pointed to the building. They felt oppressed in a cold and indifferent world.

When he went back to the building the following morning the firemen were still there. They allowed him onto the ground floor and showed him the drawing room. One wall seemed almost untouched by the flames. The firemen shrugged. These things happen in fires, they said. Often there is a strange sense of hiatus, the flames die down, and they are aware of a sentience in the fire, an appetite obedient to its own precept, though none of them were willing to speculate as to what form that ordinance might take. There are blowbacks, incendiary phenomena. The fire draws back to reveal strange scenes. Flame creeps through wall cavities. The interior fills with charnel smells.

The smell of damp charcoal, broken water pipes dripping through the frame of the building, the motifs of flame on the interior walls seeming inked-in and baked to a kind of shellac, pristine and diagrammatic as though a precise construction of the events that had occurred in The Glen were rendered in an unknowable tongue.

Harry Ferguson died later that year following a car accident. Esther Ferguson outlived her husband for many years, although her health was poor from decades of alcohol abuse. She died of pneumonia in a rest home in Bangor. John Capstick retired from Scotland Yard on full pension and his autobiography sold widely. He was a popular after-dinner speaker and was often invited to functions hosted by local Conservative branches and police associations. He died of a massive coronary thrombosis in the garden of his home in Braintree, Essex. The giant hand.

Iain Hay Gordon spent seven years in Holywell Mental Hospital. The superintendent of the hospital was satisfied that he did not suffer from a mental illness and he received no treatment of any kind when he was there. The superintendent was asked if he felt he was justified in detaining a man who he believed did not suffer from any mental illness. The superintendent replied, 'I have examined my conscience in this matter.' It is thought that if he had made an issue of Gordon's mental health then he would have been returned to Crumlin Road jail. Iain Gordon was released after seven years in Holywell on the intervention of the Minister for Home Affairs, Brian Faulkner. He was given a job for life in Glasgow on the basis that he changed his name and did not tell his work mates of the events that occurred in the winter of 1952. Iain Gordon has retired. He has been active in seeking to have his conviction overturned. On 20 December 2000, in the Appeal Court, Lord Chief Justice Carswell held that Gordon's confession to Capstick should be ruled out. He went on to say that 'the remainder of the evidence against the appellant consists of a certain amount of circumstantial evidence and some suspicious behaviour on his part . . . we therefore conclude that the jury's verdict cannot stand. There can be no question of ordering a retrial after this length of time and we therefore allow the appeal and quash the finding of guilt.'

In April 1973, McConnell, who had retired, was walking past Whiteabbey Presbyterian Church. He saw the bookmaker Hughes on the other side of the road. He crossed it to meet him. Hughes was an old man now, moving painfully on a stick. In the manner of old men he had not shaved properly and there were tufts of white hair on his face. Hughes acknowledged McConnell and they sat on the low sea wall facing the church. To their left they could see the remains of the gate lodge belonging to The Glen.

The gate lodge was scheduled for demolition. A develop-
er had bought the grounds of The Glen. They talked about
Gordon for a while.

'I suppose he was the real victim in all of this,'
McConnell said.

'Do you not think Patricia was? After all, he never did
manage to find anybody who could say where he was that
night.'

'I could never work out what your interest was in Patricia, apart from your financial involvement with the Judge.
Ferguson told me.'

'To tell you the truth, Mr McConnell, my interest was
this. I never cared that much who killed her. I cared about
who she was, what they done to her, dragging her through
the muck.'

Hughes told McConnell that in 1950 Hillary Douglas
had persuaded Patricia to help her in works for the poor
that her father was involved in. Hughes's mother lived in
a terraced house in the Irishtown area of Carrickfergus.
Patricia had come to the house and looked after his mother. She came every Saturday morning. Neighbours spoke
of her among themselves as a quiet girl. Hughes's father
was a drunk who had broken every piece of crockery in
the house before he died. Patricia went to the market with
no make-up, her hair tied back. She bought cheap delft
from the stalls, carnival ware, willow pattern plates, and
laughed at her own helplessness in the face of the venality
of the traders. The house was small, with a kitchen and a
living-room downstairs and two bedrooms upstairs. It
was a house where a large family had been raised on a
meagre income and Patricia was true to the spirit of it. She
sat in the kitchen drinking tea and talking to his mother
and gave every impression of belonging to the women of
the street, their easy sentiment, their legendary thrift.

'That was where I met her and as far as I was concerned
that was the kind of girl she was,' Hughes said.

McConnell remembered the photograph of Hillary and Patricia, looking at the camera, their adolescent heads tilted to one side. He supposed that the photograph would be faded now, the girls barely visible, still looking at the camera. That Vogue look. The peerless limbs and clairvoyant skin. The cool, phantom stare. It was spring and a warm breeze stirred the dark trees of the avenue to The Glen, and the sun lit the hill in front of them and the wind blew upon its faded grasses and then stopped and they were left in the stillness of The Glen for a moment, a share of its silence bestowed upon them, its memorial calm.